THE
THIRD TRIBE

THE
THIRD TRIBE

ROB CHIDLEY

CanaanPress

CanaanPress

Copyright © 2009 – Rob Chidley

First published in Great Britain by Canaan Press in 2009

Canaan Press
PO Box 3070
Littlehampton
West Sussex
BN17 6WX
office@canaanpress.co.uk
www.canaanpress.co.uk

The book imprint of
Matt's Canaan Trust
www.mattscanaantrust.com

British Library Cataloguing in Publication Data
A record of this book is available from the British Library

ISBN: 978-0-9551816-7-2

Designed by Andy Ashdown
www.andyashdowndesign.co.uk

Cover illustration by Liz O'Donnell
www.lizodonnell.co.uk

Manufactured in Malta by Gutenberg Press Limited

To my Tribe:
Mum and Dad,
sister Jenny,
and my dear wife,
Amy.

CHAPTER ONE

RUTH LAY STILL AND LISTENED. The Herders and their animals were nearby. She could hear the goats bleating as they moved between grass tussocks. The sound carried on the sandy wind up the dunes to where Ruth was hidden in a smear of brittle grass.

She anticipated the movement of the herd well: she was out of sight on the edge of the narrow valley through which the herdsmen would drive their flock. They had spent the recent months following the grasses that sprang up in short seasonal waves across the edge of the desert. Now they were returning to the inner fields where they hoped for better grazing. Even in her short life Ruth had noticed that there was less with every passing year. The tired grass was wearing out, but that didn't bear thinking about.

Ruth kept every part of her small body low to the dust. It would be difficult to lure one of the skinny goats away without being seen, but a good hiding place was a strong start. Even without looking through the frail, grey grasses that lined the hilltop, she knew how close the herd was. She could smell the thick stench of the goats and almost feel the heat of their yellow eyes. The skittish fall of cloven hoofs seemed loud to her even on the soft going of the crumbling dunes. Each goat was a plentiful supply of hair, horn and milk and, at the right time, meat, blood and skin; each one was a small miracle of life in the dying lands. The goats seized life from the rough grasses that survived in the sandy ash soil and, despite the danger, Ruth would take one if she could.

A typical herd was made up of about 15 beasts. Yesterday, when she first spotted this one, she had seen around that number. Fifteen beasts meant two or three Herders, but Ruth did not know for sure.

It wouldn't be easy: Herders were fierce fighters who guarded their precious flocks jealously. If they saw her, they would kill her. But that did not put her off the task. There was a small part of her that would relish the chance to fight a herdsman, however strong, because there was within her an absolute focus of hatred that overwhelmed fear of her own death. The tribesmen of the Herders were brutal and cruel, and folk even said they were cannibals. Ruth's father had taught her to hate them, and she had been a willing pupil. But at the age of 12 she was still a child and could not yet take bloody revenge. Her father had made it painfully clear to her that she must never put herself in the power of the Herders. He had filled her dreams with stories and twisted them into nightmares so that she would only ever flee from them.

But it had not quite worked. She wanted to fight.

In a year she would come into womanhood, and then, Ruth had decided, she could fight. It was more likely that she would be given to a man of her tribe, a Miller, so that she might become a mother. Children were rare. Most died in birthing or infancy but she had survived and was now on the cusp of adulthood. She was a Miller, one of the last children in a dwindling tribe and, when circumstances demanded, she was a hunter.

Ruth pushed aside the grass stalks and looked to where the nearest goats were grazing. Further down the valley there were more Herders and more goats, more than she had seen the day before. She guessed there might be five dangerous enemies. This couldn't be a single herd; two must have met before the dawn as they returned from the same grass migration. She lifted her head and, shading her eyes with her hand, counted 21 goats. They seemed to be in two rough groups, one larger than the other.

Suddenly, a bony hand grabbed her hair and thrust her face down into the dust.

'Stay down, girl,' growled her father softly. 'If they see you, we're both dead.'

'Sorry, Father,' she answered, spitting, her mouth fouled with ash dust.

Dan, her father, was old, older than anyone she had ever known. He never said how old he was, but she thought he must be at least 36. He was thin and wrinkled with matted grey hair and weak in one arm. His frail limb fell from a swollen purple shoulder and ended in black nails hooked on a claw-hand. He cringed as he shifted his body into a less painful position on the dune.

'Do you have enough bread?' he whispered.

'Just enough.'

'You'd better take some more. If we're going to do this we need to make sure it's worth our while.'

He pulled at the hair cords that secured the mouth of his skin bag and from the opened flap produced two flat bread-cakes. Ruth took them and felt their rough texture between finger and thumb. They were made of gritty flour ground from the seed of the grasses that the Herders followed. Ruth and Dan were Millers and the Herders were their natural rivals. A single goat could quickly destroy a large crop of grass, and Dan and Ruth never needed further justification for their poaching beyond their loss.

Dan spoke. 'You go. I'll be ready with the millstones.'

Ruth nodded and put her own skin bag by her father's. As he retreated down the slope away from the herd, Ruth crawled forward over the brow of the dune to the next dry clump of grasses. She paused and broke up the hard cakes. There were a number of goats feeding nearby on the patches of grass dotted along the slope. With a swift flick of her wrist, Ruth sent a piece of bread spinning through the dry air to land a few paces in front of the nearest animal. The goat leapt forward, ate up the bread quickly and looked around for more. Ruth sent another piece towards it. It hopped closer, bleating loudly.

Hearing the cry, a goat further down the slope looked up and skipped a few paces forwards. Ruth held up a third piece of bread and the first goat came towards her, staring expectantly. The second bleated again from where it stood. Dan hissed a warning from further up the dune.

'Stop! Herders!'

Two Herders at the bottom of the valley had turned from their discussion and were looking up at the goats Ruth was luring away. Ruth froze, but her target goat didn't. It trotted forward, ears pricked and alert. A heartbeat passed. The second goat resumed feeding on the wispy clumps of vegetation and the two herdsmen turned back to their noisy discussion. The animosity between the herds seemed to be intensifying.

Relieved, Ruth flicked another scrap in the direction of the goat. It came forward again, and Ruth crawled backwards up the dune to the summit. Still the greedy creature came on. Ruth disappeared over the hilltop and lay close to Dan, the last of the bread held out in her hands. Dan grasped one of the millstones in the fist of his good arm, tense and ready. The goat came forward over the brow of the dune, its yellow eyes fixed on the bread.

With tremendous force, Dan swung the stone and let it fly. The goat's head snapped sideways and the creature slumped forward into the dust, making mud of it with the hot blood that shot fitfully from the wound. Dan stowed the millstone in his bag and pulled the goat's body down the dune away from the summit. Ruth turned to follow, but suddenly the second goat leapt to the top of the slope, bleating loudly.

'Shut that up!' hissed Dan.

Ruth grabbed her bag and swung it up under the goat's jaw. The blow struck hard and sent the animal spinning down the slope into the valley. Two herdsmen turned at the noise of the crying beast in time to witness the rising clouds of dust that marked its rapid descent. They started forward, but at that moment the Herders' argument boiled over and they turned back, drawing their horn knives.

'Run!' cried Dan, and Ruth scrambled down the slope and followed her father. 'Come on,' he called.

They were heading away from the grass pastures into the dust plains. The Herders could not follow without leaving their herds undefended on the pastures. Life did not last out on the desert plains for long, but Dan and Ruth had some bread and a fresh kill so their chances were reasonable. While the two herds clashed they would make good their escape.

When they were sure that they were not being followed, they slowed to a walk. Dan adjusted the weight of the prone goat on his good shoulder, grimaced, and smiled. It made his face look strange, Ruth thought, almost like another person. She had only ever seen him smile after striking back at the Herders.

'A good job, Ruth, don't you think? Though, perhaps you could've killed that second goat. Well, we got one, didn't we?' he added, smiling again. 'It would have been a different story if they hadn't been fighting, especially as that second one raised such a terrible racket. Still, their weakness is our strength.'

He gave her a sideways glance as she plodded along beside him. 'Remember that, won't you? Their weakness is our strength.'

They walked for an hour away from the pastures and out across the plain with its rippling of low dunes. When it seemed as if they weren't going to stop, Ruth spoke up.

'Father, how much further are we going?'

She glanced over her shoulder towards the higher dunes of the inner fields and then checked the position of the climbing sun. Dan saw her looks and understood their meaning.

'We'll camp soon,' he replied, 'and we'll dig our shelters before the sun gets too high. I've not forgotten. I'm just keen to get as far out into the desert as I can to stop anyone following us.'

After another hour of walking, Dan finally stopped.

'You've done well today,' he said, almost smiling again. 'Get your breath back, and then we'll deal with this goat.'

Ruth dropped her bag, collapsed onto the sand and let herself slip into her tiredness. Her eyes closed, and before long, they flickered under their heavy lids.

The sky was dark and bloated, as if a blister had formed in the atmosphere, swollen and ready to burst. One of the wiry hairs that stuck to Ruth's cheek rose as the muggy air moved. The claustrophobia of her life lifted for an instant and under the blackening, bruising sky the dry valley looked almost pleasant. Faintly, she heard her name whispered on the voice of the small wind.

Ruth!

Something thudded into the dead ground 20 metres ahead. The sound was quiet but quickening, and Ruth felt as though it meant something.

Thud came another. *Thud. Thud, thud. Thud, thud, thud. Thud.*

More and more things were hitting the ground. She looked up in fear at the dark shapes flying high in the air. They were bursting, breaking up and falling on her. *Thud, thud, thud thud thud.* One of the pieces hit her on the top of her head and splashed down her hair and onto her shoulders. The encrusted dirt of a little over a decade darkened and ran. More pieces, droplets, fell and covered her whole body and the ground about her as far as she could see.

In a few heartbeats, the dust on her clothes was darkened with moisture. The sand around her breathed forth a scent of damp like a sigh. In a few more heartbeats the never-ending desert was drenched. The droplets came in a storm of enlivening, revitalising liquid, thudding into the ground like a heart throbbing again after years of silence.

Ruth! the voice cried again, louder.

Ruth felt the cool moisture wash over her. It collected in pools in her hair and ran down her neck in dark streams, carrying the first layers of dust away. Her face and arms began to change in the flood; she felt clean and fresh in a way that did not adequately compare to anything she had experienced in her conscious life. The voice called on, *Ruth, Ruth!* She felt as though she knew who it was. She shouted into the deluge.

'Father! Where are you?'

In a final heartbeat, the vision dispersed and suddenly all was bright and dry and dusty.

'Here, you silly girl. Get your gourd. Mine has split, we must catch this blood.'

Ruth blinked in the bright sunshine. The drops in the sky had gone, and all she could see other than the endless desert was her father with the goat on his shoulder, holding it by the throat, and blood running over his hands. At his feet lay the gourd, a stitched drinking-skin with a gory tear running across its width.

'Move it, girl. Get your gourd!' Dan urged.

Ruth cursed under her breath, fists clenched. Weeks ago, the last time this vision came to her, she had also been disturbed by her father and had not seen it all the way through. She reached for her bag and pulled out the flaccid skin container that held their precious liquids. It had been days since it had had any water or blood in it. She unrolled it and opened the mouth just below her father's bloody hands.

'I had that dream again,' she murmured, quietly.

'Hold it steady, we'll lose some,' said her father.

She tried again. 'I felt clean, as if the desert wasn't all there was.'

'Dreams mean nothing,' Dan grunted. 'Blood and water and grass are what matters. We must save it all or we'll suffer.'

'Father …' said Ruth, weakly.

'Ruth, can your dreams get us more grass? Or kill the Herder scum? Or even stop the dust storms from tearing flesh and bone apart?'

'No …'

'Then I'm not interested,' he said firmly. 'Water from the sky … ridiculous,' and he continued to drain the goat of blood.

Ruth set about her work, but her eyes were fixed inwards on the vision and any meaning it might have.

Evening came, and the blue shadows crumbled down the dunes and across the plains. The heat dulled and faded into cool, still air as the land turned from a feverish invalid into a sickly corpse, chill and numb. Cold stars emerged from the depths of the heavens, indifferent and distant.

Dan looked upwards with tired eyes and searched the sky. Ruth lay in her refuge, under the blanket that in the daytime was her dress. Survival in this unforgiving land meant Ruth's people had learnt to dig trenches, lay their skirts or cloths in the bottom, stretch their robes over the top and weigh them down with millstones. Into this small cavity they crawled, half-naked and cold, to wait until their body heat filled the space. They slept away the nights in this warm shelter, the dust storms passing over and the cold unable to find them.

It was into such a grave-like hideout that Ruth slithered, but she turned and poked her head out far enough to see her father sitting on the sand under the moonlight. He was navigating.

'We must travel north tomorrow, and then north-west the day after,' said Dan when he noticed her. 'That should keep us ahead of the herds. We'll be further up the pastures than they are and might not see them for the rest of the season.'

Good, thought Ruth sleepily. She looked past her father to where the dunes turned over and over into the distance. She wondered if there was anything beyond them, any other pastures or a place where there were no Herders. No desert. As the sweet relief of sleep soaked into her mind, Dan rolled himself into his own trench a few paces away and prepared his bed for the night.

They woke early, before sunrise and crept up out of their dens. Ruth stretched in the cold air, woke her stiffened limbs, and dressed. Her father did the same and when he had finished he began his arm exercises, rubbing and shaking the painful limb. Ruth tried to ignore his exertions and obvious discomfort; she had grown up with it and she hated it. She forced herself to pretend that he wasn't there and everything was all right. At least she wouldn't have to deal with watching him hurt.

But it wasn't enough just to think pain away. She couldn't make her father better or vanish the Herders or make the grasses grow taller by thinking. Life wasn't governed or changed by thoughts because life was too cruel for that. She sat on the ground and looked up at the blue-grey sky as it began to turn yellow-grey in the morning. She watched the stars slowly withdraw one by one, then flopped backwards onto the ashen sand and fixed her eyes on the last star in the sky. It seemed to her brighter than the others had been, stronger and whiter. As she stared, her eyes refocused and the star flickered and swelled. It filled her vision with its brightness and she wondered at it.

What are stars? she thought aloud. Someone had told her once that they were oceans of frozen water, whatever oceans were. She wondered if the oceans would ever come down to the ground. Someone else had told her the stars were the eyes of demons, but she knew what demons were. Whatever stars really were, at that moment they did not seem as cold or as distant as usual. To Ruth they were a fixed point in an ever-changing world. The dunes moved with the winds, and the moon grew and shrank, but the stars stayed the same. They were as constant as the cruel sun, but more gentle.

Suddenly Ruth was aware she was alone. She sat up and twisted around to see Dan's empty trench. She jumped up and scanned the surrounding sands until she saw his footprints leading away from their camp across to a spur between two huge dunes. She found him on his hands and knees, with his face bent low to the ground.

'Ruth!' he said, in a state of excitement. 'I've found one! I've not seen one in years, but here it is!'

'What is it, Father?' his daughter asked, crouching down beside him.

'Look,' he said, pointing to a thin tube that poked up a few fingers' width above the ground. 'It's a Jacobswell plant. On the other end of that stalk is a reservoir of water. You can draw it up into your mouth. This little plant grows up out of the sand to get the sunlight, but underneath it sucks up all the water from the ground into a sort of hard bag. You can pull off the head of the stalk and drink, and satisfy your thirst.'

Ruth leaned forward to drink but Dan kept his hand firmly over the end of the tube.

'Don't have it all, now. We must share,' he warned.

'Yes, Father,' she replied, cowed.

He removed his hand from the crumpled straw and she leant forward tentatively to drink. Her cracked lips closed over the end and her mouth was filled with water, warm and salty, but water nevertheless. How long had it been since the last drink of such volume? She drew it out of the ground with manic fervour, her small body gripped by the violent zeal of the desperate. The survivor. More and more she drank, but too soon there came no more and she was left thirsting. Her father pushed her angrily to one side and tried to drink for himself.

'You've finished it all!' he snarled, venomously. 'What am I to drink now? Dust?'

He stood up quickly, loomed large and dangerous, but then he turned away. As if wrestling with himself, he swung back towards her, a threatening mask of anger covering his face. He didn't look much like her father, but the instant passed and he shrank back to his familiar size and stomped away towards the camp leaving her alone.

Ruth turned back to the object of her guilt, and looked down at the stalk with the severed head of the leaves lying to one side. A few metres in front of her was another Jacobswell stalk and next to it a second crumpled head of leaves. She crawled over and put her lips to it, trying to draw up the moisture as she had before, but there was none in the reservoir. She sat back on her heels, her knees forward, thinking, Father must have already tried that one and found it empty. That's why he was so upset when I drank too much from the second one.

But she did not feel satisfied. The familiar, painful thirst was still there. She was not quite yet an adult, and must have drunk nearly a whole plant dry, but her craving was still great.

When Ruth returned to the camp, Dan had already packed up his belongings and put hers in a pile next to his. He had kicked the sand back into the dugouts and was scouring the site for any dropped belongings. She helped him in his task and when they had finished she packed up her possessions, shouldered her skin bag and gourd, and followed her father up the northern dune. The gourd felt very heavy with blood, and her bag was weighed down with her stones and the supply of grass seed. On one shoulder Dan carried both his bag and the drained goat corpse that would feed them later in the day. Their situation meant a long march if they were to reach the pastures by nightfall. Because of the sun's intensity they had only about three hours now before being forced to make camp anyway. They marched in silence, Dan in front, Ruth behind. They spoke only to express a need to pause in order to adjust their packs or to rest.

The early morning wore on and as the sun climbed higher, the need to prepare food and make shelters from the burning sun grew.

After scooping out their beds, Dan set about preparing the goat for cooking and Ruth made the bread. As a Miller, this was the only life she had ever known. She opened her skin bag and removed the two millstones and the grass seed. The larger, flatter stone she placed on the floor in front of her and piled up some seeds in the middle. The smaller stone she gripped with both hands, and pushed in oval motions across the seeds. They broke up and exploded under the pressure of her coarse stone, and the flour appeared. Ruth added more and more seeds, and before long her hard work had produced a large quantity of white-grey flour, dotted frequently with the dark chaff. To this mixture she added the thick and coagulating blood that they had taken from the goat yesterday. She worked it over and over in her hands until they reeked and were almost black with the dark, heavily scented mixture. She shaped the bloody dough into squares, beating it with her fists and fingers until the thin loaves covered the entire stone.

Later, as she lay in the den under the shelter of her robe, the sun baked the bread.

CHAPTER TWO

RUTH POKED HER HEAD OUT from under her shelter and looked towards her father's. She called him, and after a moment his head appeared above the sand. He glanced at her and she smiled back, and they dismantled their shelters and dressed.

Ruth saw that her father had been busy while she had been preparing the dough. Stretched out on his larger millstone were strips of goat meat that he'd pulled off the thin bones. He'd worked very quickly. Lying next to the bloodstained platter was the skinned and stripped corpse of the goat. Very little of the animal was left, only what was of no use at all. Some of the larger bones had been taken, the sinews had been harvested, the ligaments, and even the some of the gut. These materials would repair torn clothes, keep the water skins from splitting, and provide them with weapons.

'Want some dinner?' asked Dan. 'Catch.'

He threw a small portion of goat towards Ruth, which she caught easily and examined. It was an eye, baked by the heat of the midday sun. Without flinching, she popped it into her mouth and bit down on the rubbery flesh. The jelly spurted out of the split sides of the eye and scorched the inside of her mouth. She threw back her head, opened her mouth and blew the heat into the dry air. Her father laughed as she hopped up and down, flapping her hand in front of her lips in an effort to cool the burning.

'When will you learn, girl?' he said, with a smile.

'Thanks for the warning, Father,' she spat, annoyed. 'I assumed you'd taken it into the shelter to cool for a bit before giving it to me.'

He turned away, still smiling, and began to wrap the cooked meat up in the new skin.

'This skin will be good for us,' he said. 'That goat was quite healthy. It's good timing what with my water skin tearing. I could have done with a new robe, though.'

'Is your old skin any good?' Ruth asked.

'The split was pretty wide, but I think I can use some of it for patches and a belt. My old woven straw belt is getting very tatty. Even old skin is better than grass straw.'

They stowed their belongings in their bags, put the remains of the goat into one of the shelter holes and filled them both in. It was more out of habit that they took these precautions, as they were sure that nobody was following them out into this dead land. The Herders wouldn't dare leave their flocks, and they hadn't seen any other Millers for a long time. Dan and Ruth had no quarrels with their own kind, and it was unlikely the Herders they'd robbed would follow. Nevertheless, he was not someone to take unnecessary risks.

Dan didn't believe the fireside tales of wild cannibals who preyed on Miller and Herder alike, but Ruth was not so sure. In the cold of the night, she sometimes shivered at the thought of monstrous men creeping out of the darkness into her shelter and eating her.

They walked on and long into the evening before the night once more spread its cold fingers over the land. Ruth was glad that they were so close to the pastures. Tomorrow they would reach them before the midday heat, and in the afternoon they could harvest some grass to restock their vanished supplies and bake some new bread. Under her shelter, she heard her father breathing slowly as he slept, and before long her mind, too, sank into the gentle lull of sleep.

Ruth opened her eyes; it was still dark and very cold. In her sleepiness she heard the faint sound of footsteps crunching over the frozen sand. The last drops of slumber fell from her mind and she sat bolt upright, nervous and afraid.

Were the footsteps coming towards the camp or away from it?

She listened again, but heard nothing. The wind was dead and the dust storms were far away. She had to know but feared to find out who or what it was that was walking about in the darkest hours.

Carefully, she lifted the edge of her shelter and scanned the cold, rigid dust for the source of the sound. There were footprints leading from her father's dugout into the frosty sandscape. They led back along the route they had taken yesterday. Shivering, she dressed and moved quickly along the trail.

Ruth found her father at the top of a low dune that lay 200 or so paces away from the camp. He crouched on the floor with his weak arm flung out to one side to avoid lying on it. He was staring intently out into the moonlit night, scouring the ashen sand – for what Ruth didn't know. Sensibly, she ducked to the ground and crawled up next to him. She was by his side before he acknowledged her.

'Trouble, girl. Something doesn't seem right. We're in danger,' he said quietly.

Ruth shuddered. There were many kinds of danger in these dying lands, but there was only one that would make you leave your shelter in the dead of night.

'Where are they?' she whispered.

'Out there, among the dunes. I had a hunch so came to watch earlier. I saw some shapes moving on the edge of the pastures. They came down about half an hour ago. Their herd must be over the ridge.'

He pointed to where the dusty plains crumpled violently on the shoulders of the large dunes that bordered the pasturelands. They were not far from where the last vegetation on earth sprang up out of dust and ash, but with the terrible Herders in front and the unending desert behind them, they were cut off and in grave danger.

'Look there! There! Down to the left of the oval dune.'

Dan pointed his bony fingers towards where the shadows of the pastures ended and the moonshine lit up the land. Grey-blue shapes were moving in the darkness. They flitted along the lowest points between the hills, but even in the black-blue of night Ruth could see them picking their zigzagging way unmistakably towards her and her father. She felt the coldness of the sand creep into her body and bury itself deep down. Her immediate impulse was to hide her face in her hands to pretend they weren't coming, but they were. She wanted to run as fast as she could out into the desert, but that was suicide.

'What shall we do, Father?' she whimpered.

'Run,' he replied.

They both crawled backwards down the dune until completely out of sight and then hurried towards their camp. Being already dressed, they only had to push their supplies, spare cloth, tools and millstones into the bags and then cover up all traces of their ever having been there. Ruth packed quickly and had already begun to fill in her trench while Dan had only managed to stow half his possessions. She jumped up and ran to him to help, but he snarled at her.

'I can do it. Get back to your own, girl.'

'No, Father, we must hurry together,' she pleaded, and his face softened.

They packed up and hid all traces of their camp. The Herders might be coming to get them, but there was no point giving them a definite marker to start their search from. Ruth shouldered her bag, and Dan his, but he took care to trap his weak arm underneath the bag strap that crossed his chest as if he was wearing a primitive sling. Then the withered limb would not bounce painfully about as he ran.

'We've not got long before the Herders arrive. That isn't a good start, but we must make the most of it!' said Dan, and he headed off towards the unending, unforgiving desert.

'Are we going to die, Father?' Ruth begged, fear crunching her guts like a fist of flint.

'Yes, Ruth, but we are not going to give them the pleasure of our deaths. I won't let them drink our blood,' he said, grimly.

The reality of these hard words struck her to her heart and she wept tearlessly as she ran. Her soft agony carried in the still air across the plains and into the darkness. Her distress made Dan uncomfortable, and he tried to comfort her:

'Ruth, we are going out into the desert and when we get far enough we will dig our trenches. We will go to sleep but we will never wake up; the sand will be our resting place where we will sleep until the time comes to see your mother again.'

Ruth did not know why he was saying these things. He had never said them before and she looked hard into his face to see if the belief of reunion with her mother was there, but she couldn't see it. Life with her father had always been hard and dry and occasionally bloody, but it was real.

'What?' she asked, disbelieving his words, but he didn't answer. He ran ahead of her away from the dunes that bordered the pasturelands and out into the desert. She was glad the storms were not raging here tonight. If they were, the flaying sands that roar and whistle on the open plains would have torn the skin from both Dan and Ruth. They would have to be careful though, because at the first whisper of such a windstorm stirring they would need to drop down to the floor and dig for their lives.

Not daring to look back, Ruth ran after her father for as long as she could. When they stopped, the pasture borders looked very small and remote in the enormous moonlit space of the desert. Everything was still. The land seemed like a corpse after the twitching and bleeding have stopped. Dan collapsed onto the sand and Ruth let herself fall beside him, tired from running and exhausted by fear. After a time, they roused themselves and dug the shallow holes that they would sleep and perhaps die in. Before Dan disappeared into the ground, Ruth came over to him and sat on the edge of his pit. She dangled her legs in and stared at her tired feet.

'I'm frightened, Father.'

'I know. I'm sorry I got us into this,' he replied. 'I shouldn't have crossed the desert. I shouldn't have taken you with me.'

Dan turned his back to her and stared up at the lightening sky. Dawn was less than two hours away and, though they were doomed, the survival instincts were still strong. They would try to run again, out into the burning sands and let the heat consume them.

'Please sing for me, Father,' came Ruth's plaintive cry.

Dan turned and sat beside her. He put his good arm over her shoulder and in his dry voice sang softly to her.

'All the world's a dusty field,
Stalk and ear the ground doth yield;
Seed and blood together sown,
Until we add our own …'

Ruth's father sang on, his voice lulling her into peaceful tiredness that would allow some sleep. When the song finished, she settled in under her robe, shut her eyes and forgot it all.

Ruth woke; she was still alive, but her throat felt as though it was on fire. She choked on her own breath, the dry air scourging the tender flesh. She shook her limbs and rose, although she didn't know why. What was the point of getting up? They wouldn't last out here. They were without any liquid supplies and the shade of the pasturelands was on the other side of a deadly enemy. They would have to get to a source of water before the sun rose tomorrow or they would be finished.

In the grey hour between starlight and dawn she crept out of her trench, dressed, and made her way back along the path they had taken the night before. She couldn't help feeling that there must be another way to safety, and even if there wasn't she wouldn't just lie down and die. Perhaps the Herders would have lost interest and moved on, or presumed them already dead. The way they had hunted the two of them with such relentless aggression was unheard of as far as she knew. Maybe the dust devils and furies had come out of the sand and possessed them. Ruth smiled bitterly at her own silly childishness; such things were only fairytales.

She could see better now in the flinty half light because the sun wasn't warping the hot air into dizzy blurs as it had done yesterday. After a short while she stopped, sat down in the dust and waited. It was not long before her eyes accustomed themselves to the range and she looked to the distant dunes. Her gaze followed down and along the path she had taken with her father the night before, and at a couple of miles' distance she noticed something moving.

She blinked in disbelief. Then she looked again.

To her horror, she saw the shapes she had seen before. The Herders were moving about in a loose line across the route Ruth and her father had taken last night. Occasionally one would drop to the floor and the others would move over to him, as if they had found something important or interesting to their wicked intentions. They must have left their herds on the pastures to come and get her and her father. There was no other explanation for their being that far out from the grass.

They were tracking Dan and Ruth.

Being so close to the enemy and, as yet, unseen produced in Ruth a kind of uneasy fascination. She had seen them before, but they had always been minding their herds while she crept around and separated a goat to kill. They had never hunted anyone in her memory. She imagined what it would be like to see one close up, to be fixed by its terrible gaze, and fight it blood, stone and flesh. With a shudder, she let the moment pass, then leapt up and ran back to warn her father.

When she got back to camp, Dan had risen, dressed and was dividing up the baked goat flesh. He had retrieved the bread cakes from her bag and portioned them out into two piles. She went over to him, and sat on the sand by the bread.

'They're coming again, Father. What shall we do?' she asked.

'The Herders are still coming? Have they caught the madness? They've left their herds to come and get us.'

'What are we going to do?' she asked again.

'Why would they leave, what, 20 goats for two of us?' he went on, ignoring her. 'They must be demons or dust devils or something. Relentless, they are, relentless.'

'Father, tell me what we are going to do!' Ruth was growing more and more agitated at her father's inaction. Why was he sitting there thinking instead of doing something? 'Father! We must go. Now!'

'What?' Dan said, surprised by her outburst. 'Go ... Why? Where? Further out into the desert? No one has even been this far in my memory. We're just lucky the weather hasn't come down on us yet. You haven't seen a real dust storm.'

'Well, right now the dust storms aren't coming but the Herders are. Father, get your bag and we must go,' she pleaded.

'If we run again before noon, we'll be two days out of the pastures with less than one day's water supplies. We are going to die, either slowly or brutally.'

'I'm leaving, and you're coming too.' Ruth answered him with an authority she didn't feel. 'Get your pack.'

Marching over to her pack, she piled in the bread and meat, and then slung it across her back. She strode back to her father and gave a hard slap to his good shoulder. At the sudden pain, his eyes refocused on her in a fit of anger, but instead of hitting back he grabbed his bag and sprang to his feet. Without giving him the chance to speak, she turned and strode off over the dunes away from the pastures, her father and the enemy.

As she gained the top of the small slope, she felt the wind move, and looked to her father as he came up the dune. When he reached her, he sensed the breeze and frowned.

'We'll keep an eye on that, girl,' he said, grimly. 'I don't trust the wind out here. The storm is bound to find us eventually.'

They trotted down the other side of the ridge and then wound their way around the dunes as their hunters did. There was little point in hoping that the Herders would not find them, even if they hid their tracks as best they could. The slightest sign of life would point to them simply because the land was desolate except for the phantom winds that moaned softly in the opaque vastness of the desert.

They travelled on until the sun was dangerously high and they were forced to hide in hastily dug trenches. Before they retired they listened to the wind. It had dropped to a deep hush, as if the whole desert was waiting for the first roar and lift of the air. The anticipation was maddening, but Ruth's exhaustion overruled it. She fell into a fitful, feverish sleep.

Some hours later she awoke. The noise of the wind had greatly increased. She dared to look out of her hole towards her father's but in the instant that she lifted the edge of the robe, her shelter was filled with slashing, blinding dust.

The wind was rising. The storm had found them.

CHAPTER THREE

THE AIR SCREAMED, tortured by the swirling violence of the sandstorm. The empty sky was a deadly battleground where the calm of yesterday was routed before a monstrous foe. Like an ancient terror, the dust storm arose from the sand and threw its corps into the defenceless atmosphere. A thousand tiny blades of sand flew in every breath; each mite tore its passage through the open air, screeching in agonised delight.

Under the turmoil and death throes of the world, Ruth lay shivering in her trench. The booms and crashes of the strange war echoed through her body and down into the sandy depths. She felt as though the world was ending. She was desperately afraid, more so than when she had contemplated her own death, because this horror overwhelmed her. The structure of the desert was collapsing under the storm that rampaged above her, and through the walls of her shelter Ruth could feel the dunes moan in their overthrow. When would the sand around her collapse and drag her small body into the pits of dust? Her voice shrieked in the close air of her shelter, but the act was mute and meant nothing under the tumult. The light of day disappeared in the flight of the sand and an enormous, corporeal blackness pressed down on the insignificant shelter. The darkness drowned her and the world became empty and without shape.

Then, out of the nothingness, appeared another vision. Like the brightest of stars suddenly shining out of the night, it came, and with it the familiar voice, still, small and calm, calling her name -

Ruth!

Ruth was no longer in her trench. Instead she was hanging high above the ground in the air. Her senses were numbed except for her sight, which was sensitive beyond her imagining, and she could see everything. As she looked over the sand and desert, she felt peace in a way she had never experienced, and she smiled. She gazed far beneath and saw the brown rage of the dust storm whirling shapelessly over some of the dunes. How small it looked from here, how insignificant. She looked east, out into the wilderness of the desert and saw something truly miraculous. She became aware that she was not alone – but the meaning of all this was beyond her understanding. Then her vision faded, and she sank down into the darkness of the storm.

Ruth was once again hidden in her shelter. She opened her eyes and through the filter of the cloth covering saw that the darkness was dividing and light appearing. The storm was not quite over, but through the dying gale early evening was emerging. The noise of the wind changed and the roaring dropped. The swish of the slicing dust tailed off and all felt still

Ruth dared to reach up and lift the edge of her shelter. Sand that had settled on the hem poured in on top of her and she struggled against it. There wasn't much to overcome and, spluttering and blinking, she stood in what had been her refuge. She clothed herself, climbed up and stared amazed at the wreck of the landscape.

As far as she could see, the dunes had changed. The shapes of yesterday had been gouged and blasted by the storm. The proud heights of the rolling dust hills had been brought low, thrown into the air and re-formed in a new pattern. This part of the desert had been transformed forever by the waning power of a dying world, but she was in awe of the scale of the destruction.

However, to her amazement, the low dunes that immediately surrounded their camp were untouched. Those mounds in the small, protective circle had remained firm and kept Ruth and her father from drowning under the massive churning of sand beyond. Through the freak chances of nature's fickleness, this low tower of sand, no stronger than the least of the dunes that had been torn to nothing, had survived, and kept the two of them protected.

As Ruth's astonishment faded, her thirst once more burned into her. She felt drunk on pain, and reeled under the weight of dehydration. She staggered, groaned and fell next to her father's shelter.

'Father,' she croaked into the dry air above Dan's trench.

Dan cursed and laughed in a cracked voice. The sound was not like the voice of her father, but like one of the shrivelled dust ghouls from the campfire stories. Back on the pastures they had had camps and fires and water. Now they had thirst and madness and soon, death. Ruth wanted to cry, to scream, to do anything except crave water, so she rolled onto her front and tugged her father's shelter-cloth off. The cover came away and collapsed onto the half-buried form of Dan. He slowly raised his head, eyes closed against the sudden brightness of the sun.

'I should be dead,' he wheezed. 'Why aren't you dead?'

'Do you want to die?' Ruth whispered. 'I don't. I'm going. Are you coming?'

Her father laughed his demonic laugh again.

'Going? Going where?' he jeered. 'Going to starve? Going to bake? Going to drink dust?' He broke off in a dry cough.

'I'm going east and I'm going to live,' she replied curtly, and she turned her body on the sand and crawled away from the camp.

Dan heaved himself up on his good arm and called in a rasping voice, 'You're dreaming, girl. We're dead. We're dust!'

Ruth's throat was so dry she could hardly reply. She hissed one word that drew an angry coughing fit from Dan: 'Vision.'

Dan dragged himself up out of the trench and staggered towards his daughter. After a few paces he fell over and crawled painfully after her, snarling, 'Ruth! You think water will fall from the sky? Ruth!'

Ruth turned her head to see her father trailing his dull arm in the dust and hauling his body across the sand towards her. She crawled up the eastern side of the small ring of dunes around their trenches and half-rolled, half-scrambled down the other side. To reach the object of her vision, she knew she must cross two small dunes, go down a short valley between two larger ones and finally climb another small one. Three days ago she could have run the distance in a moment or two, but parched and half starved the space might as well have been miles. Even at this desperate moment she could allow herself to sink into the dust and disappear. But with the menace of her father behind her, and the promise of the vision in front, she pulled her small body over the low dunes and through the shadowy valley of the higher slopes.

The last, low dune rose above her, its convex shape hiding the summit. Dan was not far behind now, still moaning and shouting, although his spite had lost its coherence and he just cried and roared wordlessly. Ruth began her ascent but the sand of the newly shaped dune shifted under her waning strength. She flailed for a moment, fear of her father's intoxicated rage rising to overwhelm her calm, but then her hands reached firm sand and she climbed quickly. In the heat and pain and terror, the passage of time lost all meaning and Ruth did not know how long she was scrambling up the western slope. Some desperate moments later she reached the sandy crest. She looked down into the tiny valley on the other side and gaped.

Before her lay the miraculous. Dotted along the sides of the valley were clumps of grasses so thick that she could hardly see the colour of sand in its depths. She gazed north and south and saw that, as in her vision, the line of vegetation extended as far as she could see. The vein of growth followed as straight a line as the contours of the dunes would allow and Ruth remembered that, from her position high in the air, the line had looked like a path. In the early evening light, the plants to the south appeared shades of brown and black, and those to the north seemed brighter than the colour of the youngest grass shoots she had seen in the grassy pastures. Further east, beyond the mysterious trench, lay nothing but swirling sand and empty dunes.

A shout of anger snapped her out of her wonderment, and Dan's hand grabbed her trailing foot. He had recovered his words and he screamed them at her hoarsely.

'Visions, child, visions, visions don't mean much! Visions don't feed you …'

He broke off, unbalanced by Ruth jerking her leg away from him. His weak arm swung out and throbbed painfully. He fell forwards, still snatching at her, and they tumbled down the slope the other side of the dune and into the strange vegetation. Dan rolled over his daughter and his momentum threw her into the air, but he didn't let go. She landed in the soft clumps of leaves, Dan rolling over her again. Once more Ruth was thrown into the air but, instead of landing on the vegetation, she landed on her father, knocking the wind out of him. As Dan lay groaning in the grasses, Ruth pulled herself away from him and looked around.

Up and down the sides of this miniature valley grew strange plants that Ruth did not recognise. She only knew of the thin, spindly grasses and shorter, broader blades that fed the Millers and the Herders' goats. These plants had many different leaves; some short and as broad as her arm; some thin as her fingers; some long; and some were even covered in tiny hairs! Still others had stalks with much smaller leaves on top that at first reminded Ruth of the

Jacobswell plants with their life-saving reservoirs. The leaves on top of these stalks were brightly coloured and the softest things she had ever touched. Some were bluer than the afternoon sky and others were nearly as red as freshly spilled blood.

Ruth crawled forward, her agonising thirst momentarily suppressed by wonder. A few metres away from the prone form of her father, she found what she would have been looking for if she had not been so dazed by dehydration. It was a Jacobswell plant. She tore the head off, clamped her lips over the decapitated stalk, and drank. The water flowed over the dried slime inside her desiccated mouth and onto her parched throat. It ran deep down into her and seemed to fill her from the toes upwards, but too quickly it was finished and she was left desperate for more.

Even through the all-consuming desire, she felt pangs of guilt; she had not saved any for her father. She looked up to search for more and to her joy there were at least 12 stalks within two arms' length. She drank again and again. Each time she drew water from the stalks her limbs felt stronger and her head clearer. She stood and breathed deeply. The little valley smelt sweet, the aroma seeming to come most strongly from those brightly coloured but delicate leaves on stalks.

The evening sun was now low enough not to dazzle or burn and it cast a warm, yellowy light onto the sand along the top edges of the slopes. She smiled, and her face felt as if it wasn't broad enough to contain such a smile. Opening her mouth, she breathed loudly, and it seemed as though the smile had escaped on the wind and was fluttering about the valley. She supposed it was a laugh, but it wasn't mocking or hurtful like laughter always was. It was different, not like her father's.

Her father! Ruth had forgotten him again. She turned back to him. He lay on his side with his eyes closed. She could not see if he was breathing. She flopped down beside his face and listened closely. Hoarse breath still fought its way in and out of his nose and mouth.

She spoke his name into his ear, but there was no response. She tried again, louder, but again there was nothing.

'Water,' she murmured to herself, 'he must have water.' But from where? Her gourd was with her abandoned belongings far and away over the dunes, and Dan needed the water now.

She ran over to the Jacobswell plants, ripped off another head, and filled her mouth with the liquid. Then she rushed back to her father, leaned over him and spat it into his face. The liquid covered his hair, eyes and nose and the encrusted dust darkened and ran. She called again.

'Father! Wake up! Come and drink!'

Still he lay silent and motionless. She ran back to the Jacobswells to see the water overflowing from the stalks and shooting into the air with some force. She filled her mouth, but swallowed the revitalising liquid. There were so many plants around her and she filled her mouth again from another. Returning to her father, she bent over him once more, opened his lips with her fingers and carefully directed a water jet through the air into his mouth. Much of the water was lost when Dan awoke suddenly and coughed. He stared up at Ruth as if dazed and then softly spoke.

'My daughter, my daughter …'

'Father,' she replied.

She tried to help him to his feet but he was too weak, so she hooked her hands under his arms and dragged him slowly towards the Jacobswells. She felt as though she should be weak, too, after her ordeal, but perhaps the water had strengthened her. Perhaps her father was lighter from the starvation. Whatever it was, she found she could bodily drag him when weeks before she could not have hoped to be so strong. Her father drank deeply from the plants, and there were so many he did not go without. Ruth drank, too, but before long the evening dissolved into night and it was all they could do to make camp before exhaustion closed their eyes.

When morning came, Ruth and Dan were unsure whether they were dreaming or awake. Their savage darkness of dehydration had lifted, and they felt stronger and more alive than ever before – but what they saw when they stepped out of their shallow trenches was incredible. It was just as they remembered: plants covered the valley floor, and up and down the sides there were more, all of different kinds. To the south the plants were black and brown and to the north they were yellow and green. Dan told Ruth the scented leaves were called 'flowers', and in the gentle morning sun they smelled as sweet as they had last night, although Ruth noticed that their heads seemed heavy on the stalks.

They breakfasted on stems and stalks of the unknown plants, and drank from yet more Jacobswells that they discovered not far from the campsite. The earth seemed firmer and browner where the plants grew, and Ruth found that when she placed her feet on the dark ground it did not shift beneath her weight. It was easier to walk and run on it without getting tired, and she and her father explored a short way up and down the valley. The different colours of the plants north and south of their camp could be explained by how dry they were.

The further south Dan and Ruth travelled, the drier and more skeletal the plants became. Initially they wilted and drooped, rotting quietly under the heat of sun, but as the two of them walked on they saw that the plants had dried out and they crunched underfoot. Near to the north, it was very different. The bubbling, sliming rot had not yet taken hold of these plants and, although they drooped slightly, they were edible and delightful to walk among.

Further north the vegetation was greener still, and obviously fresher. Whatever had caused these plants to spring up in this endless plain of death seemed to be moving northwards. The only shoots that remained turgid and green were the Jacobswells, but Dan pointed out that that was because they sucked in the water from the surrounding earth, accelerating the death of the other vegetation.

As the day passed, it became increasingly apparent that if Dan and Ruth did not move north quickly, they would be left in the desert in the midst of drying, dying and dead flora.

'Well, let's go, then,' urged Ruth.

'No, Ruth, we can't go now. We've haven't got our stones, bags and supplies. We must fetch them.'

Her father was right, of course, but Ruth had forgotten the baggage in the day's excitement. In all her short life she had never seen such growth, and in a few brief hours the astounding nature of her situation had whispered to her that she would never want for anything again.

Stay on the path! Ruth remembered the night outside the grass pastures where the Herders had slithered through the darkness to capture them. That night she had longed to find new pasturelands where the grass was not grey and coarse, but green and soft like new shoots. She heard her father's practical words, but felt that her heart was already running along the valley to catch up with whatever was causing this miraculous growth. Reluctantly, she walked with him to their camp, and then they turned due west to look for the campsite of two nights ago. They climbed the valley side, and in the moment when she stepped off the straight path cut by the delightful vale, she felt a sadness that told her she was slipping away from something or someone wonderful.

I saw this in the vision, she thought to herself. I should not be leaving now. We must go further on.

She wanted to tell her father about the vision in the storm, but his responses had changed from aggressive incredulity to disgust to anger. She knew he had been maddened by starvation and thirst, but the memory of the last time she had mentioned the word 'vision' was all too clear. She shuddered to think what he would have done to her if she had not escaped.

Ruth and her father hurried watchfully to their previous camp and quickly retrieved their belongings. They had to look hard to find them because the sand had shifted again since their departure. It seemed to Ruth that the dust had not finished moving and she feared that the unstable ground might collapse beneath them and drag them under at any second. It was not a moment too soon for her when they rejoined the fragrant valley and began their northward journey.

As the light improved with the climbing sun, Dan and Ruth could plainly see that even since last night the plants were ailing and rotting at an accelerated rate. What lay around them was no longer fit for food, and in the heat of the day the green leaves had developed blackening, bubbling sores. They were wilting fast. An urgency overcame father and daughter and they picked up their feet in a fearful effort to catch up with the receding source of life.

It was not long before they found they were walking through yellow leaves like the vegetation they had first discovered, so their pace slowed. They ate the leaves that were not quite sour yet and drank from the warming Jacobswell plants, and smiled together. The sallow foliage seemed delicious compared to dusty cakes and blood, and they gave little thought to the green plants ahead. Ruth began to feel as though she wasn't as close to adulthood as she had been a few days ago, and Dan found he was not disturbed by his arm as much as he usually was.

The days passed. All the time, they were under calm weather, and for a while congratulated themselves on their escape – but death followed swiftly behind. In the evenings, when the sun's rays fell low over the dunes, Ruth could see the column of blackened, withered plants marching up from the south. She would look north, taking comfort from the yellowing greenery that lay ahead. She did not know how long they travelled on the path among the vegetation; for the first time in her short life she did not awake in fear of whether or not she would survive the day. Ruth felt her surroundings belonged to someone else's life, and she and Dan moved in a delirious haze.

As two dreamers mutely accepting their miraculous circumstances, father and daughter travelled on until their path opened onto a vast and deep valley bowl. Ruth gaped. Even after the last weeks, the sight before them was astounding.

The valley was large – to Dan's eyes it looked nearly half a day's walk from end to end – and the sides were steep, as if a gigantic subterranean rift had dropped this part of the desert deep into the earth. The floor was entirely flat. There were no dunes, hillocks or bumps on the surface of the basin. There were no hills, except one. The fragrant path of plants ran as straight as ever directly into the valley and towards a small mound that crouched in the centre of the basin. Atop the hill was a spike, like a splinter of bone or horn but perfectly conical and straight, then suddenly wider at the base. It looked as if some unseen giant had thrust a monstrous dagger up from the bowels of the earth to puncture the sky. The sides of the hillock were bare but around its base, like the patched mass of matted hair around Dan's bald crown, ran a wide ring of earthen structures.

Dan gave Ruth the word before she asked. These were 'houses', most made of sun-baked sandy blocks but others of large, cracked stones. Where the stones had come from in such large quantities, he did not know. Ruth's eyes followed Dan's arm as he pointed out the next wide ring that encircled the settlement, and she saw 'tents' of cloth material that lay in the second ring. She gazed out even further to a third ring that was devoid of tents or houses, but here and there she could see the shapes of goats and men moving about on fields of short-cropped, murky-looking grass. There were at least 30 men and over 100 animals. She shivered at the sight of so many Herders.

Beyond them out into the plain itself, irregularly dotted like dark stains on the sand, was vegetation. Tall grasses grew up in circular blots, uneaten by the goats. In the patches of scrubland, and moving quickly between them, were Millers. Ruth stared, open mouthed and disbelieving. When she looked at her father, she saw that he, too, was gazing awestruck down into the valley.

'I'd never have believed it if I hadn't seen it myself, Ruth,' he murmured. 'This is the City.'

CHAPTER FOUR

'CITY? WHAT'S A CITY?' Ruth looked at her father questioningly.

'City means this place, and it isn't *a* city, it's *the* City. There's only this one. It's where we began, where we came up out of the earth. It's the one thing that hasn't been swept away or covered by the dust.' Dan paused, suddenly thoughtful.

'Why haven't you told me about it before?' she asked, frowning.

'I half thought it was made up – a place of legend – but here we are!' he smiled. He was almost dancing. 'Come!'

Dan started down the hill.

'But, Father,' Ruth cried, 'there are Herders here! Look!' She thrust out her arm towards the third ring of earth where small shapes of men moved around large numbers of tiny brown goats. 'They'll kill us!'

'Ruth, they say that in the City, Herders and Millers live together. Look at those dark patches. Those patches are grasses. I bet that when we pass by you'll see people milling. I heard that this grass is nothing like the thin, grey stuff we're used to. It's thicker and browner and people eat the stalk as well as burning it for fuel.'

Ruth's fears could not overcome Dan's excitement, so father and daughter descended into the wide valley along the miraculous path that ran towards the centre. Around them the yellow plants were beginning to turn brown, and behind them the plants of yesterday were already rotting. In front of them, as ever, the vegetation were greener and fresher, as if whatever caused it to spring up had moved along some days before.

Ruth and Dan passed nearby one of the brown grass plantations where, to Dan's immense satisfaction, figures of Millers were going to and fro collecting grass seeds. On the field's edge there were pieces of stone large enough for two or three Millers to grind the seed at once. The workers squinted at the newcomers suspiciously, and shapes of children ran through the shimmering heat towards the grey spike at the City's centre. Ruth observed this uneasily but Dan soberly assured her the folk were only taking sensible precautions.

'You can't let strangers wander about your camp without being challenged,' he said. 'I know it isn't a normal camp, but the same sort of rules must apply. They'll realise we aren't a threat to them.'

By now Ruth and her father had reached the third ring where the Herders and their goats lived. The grass here was greyer and more familiar to Dan's and Ruth's eyes. They stared straight ahead, fixing their gaze on the central hill around which the City was arranged and did their best to ignore the Herders.

'They can't possibly know we took a goat from one of their clans, can they, Father?' Ruth asked quietly.

'No. Unless they search your bag.'

Out of the corner of her eye, Ruth could not help but notice the Herders turning to face them. It couldn't be her imagination, she thought. There was something predatory and threatening about these people. There seemed to be a hidden stream of malice that flowed silently underneath the shabby cloth and flesh of their outward appearance. To look them in the face was enough to incite their violence. She walked on.

Before long they reached the second ring, the one made up of tents. Each one consisted of a low series of upright stakes made from

bone or thick plant material that Dan claimed was 'wood', over which
were draped large sheets made of hair and skin. Ruth had never seen
so much material. No wonder her father hadn't believed the stories
about this City. It was rich indeed.

The word of new arrivals had reached the tent ring, and the
people crawled out from underneath the material to see them. As
they did so, Ruth saw that inside the tents, the floor was dug some
feet down into the ground, so that the inhabitants could stand
upright under cover without stooping.

In the innermost ring of the City, the structures looked simply
astounding. There were squat houses about the length of a man in
breadth and width, and not quite his length in height. Dan could
only give Ruth half the words for the things she saw. Blocks of
hardened sand lay on top of one another to create walls. Some walls
had rectangular holes in them with material hanging over the gap.
Ruth supposed that people used them for going in and coming out.
On top of the walls, protruding from the sand blocks, was more
wood, although these pieces were larger and they stretched across the
huts. More cloth material kept the inhabitants covered from the sky
and, like the tents, the insides were sunk some way into the ground.

The pathway ran straight through all of this, through gaps in the
buildings, following the line of an established road. Dan and Ruth
were walking along the main thoroughfare in and out of the
settlement. The people of the City who were not out in the fields
and pastures crowded around them, but did not obstruct them. They
stared at the ground immediately behind where Ruth and Dan were
walking, as if the newcomers were moving too quickly for their eyes
to keep up. Their expressions were both sad and fearful, though they
looked well-fed, even healthy. They formed a corridor-like escort that
steered the pair towards the grey spike on the hill. Ruth looked wildly
round for a gap in the bodies, but found she could only move
forwards. Impatient hands pushed her on and she had to skip ahead

to avoid them. Wherever she tried to go, there were hands, arms and bodies in the way. Every way except towards the low hill.

'Go back into the desert! You're not welcome here!' one of the braver onlookers yelled, emotion quavering in his voice.

Dan, sensing the other man's uncertainty, turned on him with a fierce stare. The onlooker shot an appealing look at the crowd and, seeing he got no support, backed away. He mumbled something and stepped into the anonymous mob. Dan turned towards the grey structure again and walked on. The silent intent of the crowd was tangible, and Ruth felt the mute violence would scream for bloody murder soon. She fell into step with her father and he spoke quietly, under his breath.

'I hoped just to walk in, find the Miller Chief and get a place here, *quietly*. I didn't expect this, so we must make the best of it, I suppose. We'll find the Chief, show him we're not robbers and then get ourselves a tent. Or even a house!'

'Father,' Ruth replied, 'what about the green path? What about those plants?'

'Ruth!' Dan responded. 'The path led here. Did you see those fields or are you now blind? Those plants had something to do with this place. I am sure the Chief will tell us. We've reached the end. No more roaming! We can stay in the City.'

Closer now, Ruth could see that the conical point of the grey building rose up out of a ring of tent material that obscured the base. Her attention was drawn back to her immediate surroundings when a brawny man of Dan's height stepped out in front of them. He was dressed in a dark robe unlike those in the crowd around him, and his face was sunburned and pockmarked. He wore a smile which revealed a violence that fed on the anger of the crowd. As he raised his hand, the pushing from the surrounding mob lessened, and a tiny arena appeared around himself and Dan.

'I like your daughter,' the man said. 'Give her to me.'

Dan bowed in a show of supplication. 'First tell me your name,' he said.

'I am Haman,' the man answered, inclining his head, pleased with Dan's show of respect.

Dan straightened up and thrust out his good hand. The millstone flew from his open palm and struck Haman in the forehead, whipping his head backwards. Dan stepped his left foot forward onto Haman's and brought his right knee up into the man's stomach. Haman crumpled into Dan's rising fist, and the blow threw him backwards. His trapped leg straightened and twisted awkwardly as he fell, his foot pinned to the ground under Dan's. With a loud crack, Dan stamped down on the stricken man's knee, stepped up onto his stomach and chest, then over his head towards the tented spike and mound.

Calmly, Dan picked up his millstone and replaced it in his bag, leaving the man in the dust. The shocked crowd gaped, and it was Ruth who moved first. She skipped sideways past the fallen man and ran after Dan. The people did not press so closely in on them now, she noticed.

In a few moments, they'd reached the foot of the mound. The crowd spread out around them and along the hillock's base, but not a single one placed his foot upon it. Dan and Ruth climbed up, the plants from the Wonderful Path still around them, seemingly guiding them to the strange edifice.

As she approached, Ruth looked above the tented section and saw that the spike was not made of the crumbling bricks of hardened sand that she had seen in the town, but of larger, smoother rock, like gigantic millstones fused together by some strange material. The stones seemed to be connected by a lighter substance that reminded her of the exposed ribs on a skinned body. She let her eyes run up and down the height of the rocky peak and swore to herself there were patterns in the arrangement of the slabs, but how could something so large be created by people? She had witnessed the power of nature in destruction and chaos, but never in patterned *construction*.

Her eyes fell on the tent, which was much finer than the patchwork efforts in the City below. The pieces of material were large and stitched together, and any tears or rips had been repaired. They seemed to be stretched over some sort of rigid frame and secured to the ground by stakes attached to thin ropes of hair. The unseen frame allowed the tent to stand at over the height of a man, giving headroom without the need to excavate the floor. Compared to the City's tents, this was magnificent. In front of her was a loose-hanging section of material that flapped gently in the tides of the breeze.

Her thoughts were interrupted by noise from within the tent. She and Dan froze, ready for anything. The curtain of material twitched and was drawn sideways; something was behind it in the gloom.

A small, ancient man emerged, blinking against the sunlight. He raised his hand to shade his eyes and carefully regarded Dan and Ruth.

'My friend!' he cried, suddenly full of energy. 'Friend, you have come at last although you have fallen behind your brothers.'

He capered across the sand towards Dan and took his withered arm. Dan winced and the tiny fellow was all simpering apologies. He led Dan towards the opening in the tent.

'My name is Esar,' he announced, 'and welcome to the Sanctuary. Shall we go inside? I wish to speak to you about all that has happened.'

'Sir,' Dan began, 'you are too kind, but my daughter and I ...'

Esar cut him off. 'Oh, your daughter,' he frowned. 'Yes, I had forgotten. Very well, let us not go inside, but walk and talk together.'

Esar smiled weakly and motioned to Dan to walk along the top of the mound away from the crowds. As he turned away from Ruth, Dan gestured to her to follow. He introduced first himself and then his daughter before complimenting Esar on the state and size of the City.

'Are you the Chief, sir?' he asked.

Esar paused in his stride, smiled and looked up at the taller man. 'I am a chief of sorts. Those who live in the City would know who you meant if you called me Chief or Sir, but I am the right hand rather than the head. The word we use is 'Minister' because I *administer* the running of the City. Don't worry, you'll soon get used to our ways. Perhaps you should think of me as the Chief of chiefs.'

'The *Chief* of chiefs?' Dan repeated, impressed.

Esar did not reply, seeming not to hear him, but turned to look out over the large plain. Dan followed his gaze as it swept across the far dunes, over the pastures and grasses, over the tents and huts, and finally over the people below.

'All that you see is under my stewardship, Dan,' Esar explained. 'I must be a good steward. I must make things grow. The people must be fed and in turn they must feed us. We must look after them and they must look after us. If they withhold, then we withhold from them until they give again. If they give to us, then we will consider giving back to them in return. Do you see, Dan, how we work in partnership?'

Dan nodded dumbly while Ruth listened from a few paces behind. To her, Esar was too earnest to be honest, and very well practised.

Esar went on. 'You must find your place in this. If you please me I can help you, and you could become a man of position, Dan. When my brothers told me there was another traveller on that road from the desert, I thought, yes!' He underlined the exclamation by punching the air with his little fists. 'Here is a man who could be an equal!'

He turned briefly to see if Ruth was still there and walked Dan in a short circuit around the spike so that they were back at the entrance. He stepped towards the doorway and, looking at Dan, said, 'Come in, please.'

Dan stepped into the shade of the tent and Ruth followed, but at the curtain Esar put his hand out to stop her.

'Wait here please, little one,' he said.

Slightly indignant, Ruth regained her voice.

'Can't I come in? Is there not enough room inside?'

Esar smirked, looked from her to Dan, rolled his eyes, then glanced again at Ruth.

'There is more than enough room, my dear,' he smiled, 'but the tent of the Sanctuary is not a place for the many, but for the few. It is our palace.'

He looked at Dan. 'I will see to it that your daughter is well cared for while we talk.'

Dan turned to Ruth to quell her rising temper. From the moment she and her father had met Esar she had felt uneasy and, as the two men talked, the feeling swelled up and now fear flooded her body. Dan stepped back over the threshold towards her and bent to speak at her level, face to face.

'Now, Ruth, I won't be long. I'm just going to speak with the Minister about what we can do in the City. Wait.'

Belittled, Ruth turned on her heel and tramped down the side of the mound, not stopping to think whether the predatory crowd might hurt her or not. Dan followed for a few steps, half-heartedly inclined to encourage her, but instead he sighed and walked back to Esar. The two men paused at the entrance to the tent, and as Esar drew back the curtain to go in, another man came out bowing low. Esar spoke briefly to him and he stepped respectfully past and trotted to where Ruth sulked at the foot of the hillock. Without a word, he put his long, bony fingers around her upper arm and marched her away from the mound and in between the huts and tents. Twisting around, she saw Dan disappear from the sunlight into the dark interior of the tent.

He was gone. Ruth was alone in the City.

She turned back to her assailant and kicked him sharply in the shin, but received a powerful slap across her ear that made her cry out.

'For that display of disrespectful aggression you will not be allowed to wait on your father again. You will be put to work,' the man said to Ruth.

The sour knot of fear twisted in her stomach. Those three weeks of marvellous road had been a carefree time of plenty. She had felt free and clean, as in the best of her dreams. Now the memory of her visions of falling water swept over her and she wanted to weep.

A small voice not unlike her own spoke quietly to her: 'Get back to the road, just get back.'

But the immediate brutality of the City and its people overwhelmed her.

The man continued, 'The Minister was merciful. You have set foot on the holy mound. That is a crime only punishable by death. It was only because of your brothers that you have been spared,' he said. 'For now.'

'We didn't know!' Ruth gestured wildly at the people around them. 'We don't know the law. We're outsiders. We're strangers!'

The man paused. 'We shall be merciful, as we are taught. You shall be delivered to your new mother.'

The crowd was quickly dispersing, and the man led Ruth further into the City. Shocked and unresisting, she let herself be led away from the path where the plants grew, and in between the slums, tents and low shacks. The man's grip on her arm lessened and as they walked, he told her about the miracle of the City and Esar's blessing on it. Ruth hardly listened. She had begun to believe herself an adult, but now she did not feel strong enough. She felt tiny, like a grain of grass under the millstone. Why had Dan left her alone? Why had he not stayed with her or invited her inside the spike?

They stopped outside a crumbling hut of bricks and cloth. It looked as though it had once been entirely made of bricks, but now it was a near ruin, merely a pit surrounded by broken walls and patched with tent material. A woman of perhaps 20 stepped from it towards the man, and he smiled and put out his hand. She touched it and performed a low curtsey. Her movements were graceful and her body modestly covered with ragged cloths carefully wrapped together. She kept her eyes on the floor, not daring to look the man in the face.

'Child, this is your new mother,' the man said. 'Woman, this is your child. Look after her until she is wed.'

Some time later, Ruth lay on her back and looked up into the darkening sky. She had not spoken a word to the woman she'd been left with nor eaten any of the food that she had been offered. Through the gaps in the cloth that served as a roof, she could see the day dying and the night growing. Starlight slipped through the net of evening and before long more and more pinpricks of white light opened up holes in the heavens. Beneath her, the heat in the earth seeped away leaving behind a chill that spread to the air and touched her lips and nostrils so that she breathed a delicate mist.

The woman came towards her with a bundle of cloth in her arms. Ruth ignored her as she spread it out and gently draped it over the girl, leaving only her head exposed. The cloth was far too big and the woman folded it back over Ruth again so that she was covered by a double layer. She straightened up and smiled, but turned away when there was no response. Then she lay down at the other end of the room and pulled her rags about her. Ruth turned onto her side, her back to the woman, and listened to the sounds of the City.

Outside the cloths, the chill deepened and now Ruth could hear the sand crunching underfoot as men moved about in the darkness. A wailing cry rose and fell in unearthly rhythm over the City, and Ruth heard the woman whisper, 'Curfew,' in explanation. From nearby houses came the coughs, snorts and snores of the inhabitants. Ruth heard voices but, muffled by the obstacles of brick and cloth houses, she couldn't tell what they were saying.

The rise and fall of voices reminded her of times with her father and the other Millers of her tribe. She remembered when they had sat around the harvest fire, telling stories of the rich seasons and conflicts and the betrayals committed by the Herder peoples. There were things that were hard to recall, too, and finally sleep began to settle on Ruth. In the moments before complete unconsciousness, she saw forgotten faces float out of distant memories into her forming dreams. Bright days and warm nights felt familiar somehow, as if it hadn't always been a time of burning heat and sharp cold.

All of a sudden, the sounds of the City intruded on her senses and the noise of bleating set her heart and mind racing. She sat bolt upright, ready to run, but there was only darkness and the woman breathing softly in the gloom. Ruth strained her ears, but the bleating had died away. She lay down again and adjusted the cloth around her.

Sleep returned and she fell limply into its gentle arms. The world turned around her and the stars wheeled overhead, but the noises of the City never quite faded away. A few times she awoke in the night, fearful and suddenly alert, but each time it was nothing and again she slept, the soft, rhythmic snores of the woman nearby soothing her back to sleep.

She dreamt of her father and Esar standing on a flat plain, the sun high overhead. Her father was talking with him but did not notice when Esar began to change. Slowly at first, like a shadow falling across his face, he began to transform into a monster. He became a creature of insubstantial darkness, as if he'd stepped into unseen shadows and away from the light. And all the while Ruth's father noticed nothing. In the fear and confusion of her dream it was daylight, but even in the brightness of the morning sun, Esar seemed to disappear into a corporeal gloom.

Ruth saw that Dan's eyes stayed fixed on where Esar had been, and his mouth kept moving as if the Minister was still there to hear him. But the shape in the darkness was not listening to Dan; it stalked around him, ever hidden by the blackened veil of intent that hung in the air, a blackness that Ruth's eyes could not penetrate but her mind could feel. Ruth wanted to cry out to save her father from Esar, but she couldn't. As the darkness moved it swelled, until it became taller and wider than Dan. Dan spoke on, quite calm in his illusory conversation, eyes not seeing the danger.

Very quietly, almost too faint to hear, there came a sound of suction. In two heartbeats it grew louder and louder until there was no mistaking what it was. Ruth's heart leapt with terror.

It was the sound of a quick-pit – a pit of sucking, choking, pulling sand that dragged you from this world down into the crushing depths of the dust.

Another heartbeat passed and Dan was chest deep in the sand and sinking fast. Ruth found her voice and screamed as his head and arms disappeared. The thing of darkness turned, searching, hunting the source of her voice. Dan's hands vanished and Ruth collapsed on the ground, sobbing.

All was suddenly dark. Ruth felt arms around her and all she could hear was the lullaby cooing of the woman.

'It's all right, you're safe, you're safe, you're safe.'

The inhabitants of the City woke later than Ruth expected and the sun was already above the dunes before they began the day's tasks. Ruth stayed under the cloth, despondent and unresponsive. The woman tried to rouse her, but could not. She held out some bread, a sliver of cured meat and a crumb of soft goats' milk cheese.

'We're not supposed to eat before the morning gift, but no one will know. You must be starving. When did you last eat?'

Hunger writhed within her, but Ruth ignored the older woman, who held the food out for some time before giving up and putting it on the floor of the house.

'You can have it when you're ready, then,' the woman said.

Ruth stared at the wall. The woman prepared herself for the day, and after a short while she was ready to leave. Ruth still lay prone under her cloths.

'It would be best if you don't leave the house until I get back,' the woman said softly. 'I would hate it if you got lost. I won't be too long.'

Then she said goodbye and was gone out into the City.

Ruth heard her footsteps fade into the low bustle of activity outside the house. She glared at the wall, consumed with the effort of turning her fear into rage. Where was her father? And why had he abandoned her in this strange place? She felt friendless somewhere she didn't understand. The world here was different: there were 'buildings' and the people stayed in one place all of the time. The stories of the City had not come down to her generation; they had stopped at her father's. Ruth did not know how to fit into this world. Where was she? In an unknown part of the desert with an unknown people. Would her own stories make sense here? She had seen what looked like Miller people in the fields, but they might be strange or unfriendly.

She rolled over onto her other side and saw the food laid out for her on a scrap of cloth. Caught as she was between hunger and sulking, Ruth struggled but could not resist. The food looked wonderful. There was a rough kind of bread, a few strips of dried meat and a crumb of cheese. Ruth sat up and attacked the meat and bread together, gulping the rough fare too quickly and in too large chunks. She left the cheese till last. She had only eaten it once or twice in her life, in times of truce between her people and the Herders. It was a symbol of the good times, of peace and of water, not plentiful but enough. She wanted to savour it. It was only a tiny morsel, but when the other foods were finished, she took the precious speck and squashed it between her tongue and the roof of her mouth. She worked it over and over, to get every portion of taste from it, before finally, reluctantly, swallowing it. Then she folded the scrap of cloth on which the food had been served, and tucked it into her robe.

Lying down on her back, she stared up at the roof of the house. It was formed of a patchwork of ragged cloths stretched over a makeshift framework of ancient bits of bone and wood, lashed together by twine made of grass straw or hair. The cloth was thin and grey, blasted by sandstorms and bleached by the sun. The weathered structure represented great wealth, but it felt ruinous, as if the ancient crafts that had made it had been forgotten and it had been ill-repaired by the Cityfolk. The sun rose higher, and relentless sky sieved bold blue through the grey material canopy above her.

Before long, the woman returned, bringing with her a skin bag slung over her shoulder. A swirl of dust followed her heels as she stepped down into the low house. Ruth had already turned towards the wall and continued to stare in silent outrage. The woman noted with a smile that she had eaten. She placed the bag down in the corner and dug out from her belongings a small bundle which she took to Ruth's side. Kneeling by the girl, she spoke softly to her.

'I have something for you.'

Ruth did not immediately respond. The woman tried again, and when Ruth turned defiantly to face her, she saw that the other was holding out the bundle towards her.

'What is it?' she mumbled dully.

The woman frowned and unwrapped the cloth from around the object. As the fabric dropped away, Ruth saw she was holding a little clay cup. She sat up quickly and took it from the woman. She turned it over in her hands, feeling the patterned striations that ran around the side of the hard baked vessel. Dots and cross-hatching encircled it just below the rim, dividing it from the smoother breadth of its side. It was in itself a tribute to a rare craft, one requiring deep excavation and a water supply that could be spared. But also it was symbolic of peaceful living. Such delicate items were unsuited to the nomadic life Ruth and her father had lived. This was a rich object indeed.

'Is it for me?' she asked, suspicion hidden in her words.

The woman nodded.

'What do you want for it?' Ruth continued.

'Nothing! It's a gift!' the woman answered, puzzled and unsure if she should be offended by Ruth's attitude.

Ruth dropped her eyes back to the cup to study it again.

'Thank you,' she said at last, so quietly that the woman could hardly hear.

'You are most welcome,' the woman replied, delighted, 'but

please be gentle with it.'

With that, she went back to the skin bag she'd brought back with her. 'Would you like some water to drink?'

Ruth's eyes widened. This woman was giving her so much and for what in return? Seemingly nothing so far, but the food was generous enough. The cup was like nothing she'd ever been given, and now water, too?

'This is the best I could afford, I'm sorry to say. Hold up your cup … That's it.'

The woman poured a dark liquid from the new skin bag, enough to fill half of the cup. Ruth raised it to drink and she sensed the coolness hovering on the surface of the water. It smelled old, as if it had come from the deep and forgotten places of the world. She sipped it, and winced at the bitter edge that coloured the liquid with the sensation of rot. Hiding her distaste inside the cup's rim, she composed herself to smile when she lowered the vessel from her mouth.

'I'm sorry it isn't the finest water,' the woman apologised, anxious to excuse her poor supply, 'but water is expensive these days. It's the best I could afford.'

Ruth restricted her response to a wan smile because she could not trust herself to say the right thing. Then she braced herself and drank again. Satisfied, the woman turned away and prepared for the day.

'I've got to go out to the fields now and work, but I'll be back for midday. Please stay here. If you go out before the burning hours and get caught under the sun, you'll get hurt. The other Cityfolk won't let you into their shelters. The only safe place for you is here.'

She turned to leave but as she did so, Ruth blurted out her overdue introduction.

'I'm Ruth,' she said, the name tumbling out over her defensive reserve.

The woman smiled again. 'I'm Naomi,' was her reply.

Then she was gone.

CHAPTER FIVE

THE HOURS PASSED and the sun rose ever higher. As the heat increased, Ruth was glad she could enjoy the filtered shade of the low house's roof. She fought with herself about obeying Naomi's request to stay safe in the house or go to seek her father, and, at last, her feet decided for her. Stepping up through the ragged curtain that hung over the doorway, she went out onto the City pathways.

It was mid-morning. The burning hours were approaching. She looked around her and saw the strange spike rising up to the north-west. She remembered that the spike was in the City's centre, and the settlement itself was round, so she must be in the south-eastern quarter. She looked about her, trying to find distinctive landmarks that would remind her which of the low, weathered structures was Naomi's. Seeing no discernible difference about Naomi's house, she decided to trust her memory and judgment.

Ruth went west and found the straight path that she and her father had been forcibly marched along only the day before. There was no one about; the City seemed deserted. She looked south, out into the fields, and under the high sun she saw many Herders and Millers at their work. They moved in separate groups, so perhaps the harmony Dan had described was not as real as the rest of the legend.

She looked north towards the centre and her gaze naturally fixed on the otherworldly structure that rose up like a splinter of bone into the brilliant blue sky. It was a symbol of endurance; a mysterious construction that could not be natural. Yet surely no one of these days could have made it, so it could only be from another time. In her mind's eye Ruth could almost see the wind of desert years blowing past it, leaving it discoloured but unchanged. It drew her to itself, and her footsteps followed.

She went along the path towards what the Minister had called the 'holy mound' and, as she walked, she noticed freshly dug holes, gently filling with dust, at irregular intervals along the way. She heard voices ahead and saw figures in black robes digging into the sand. They were Esar's men. Her heart quickened; perhaps her father was with them. She drew closer and saw they were tearing up foliage, the same small plants that Ruth and her father had followed along the Wonderful Path to the City. The men were removing all trace of them. One of the workers saw her, and he immediately marched towards her, his hand raised in a gesture to stop.

'This isn't your business. You have no reason to be here. Go.'

'But I …' Ruth began.

The man in black ignored her words and raised his voice. 'Go back to your work. You'll be punished for this. Go. Now.' There was a hint of aggression in his tone.

'I don't …' Ruth tried again, confused and afraid, but the man would not let her speak. Instead he drew back his hand and punched her hard in the shoulder. She fell backwards onto the sand in surprise and pain and, before she could get up, the man grabbed her hair and pulled her along the ground. Ruth screamed.

'No one questions the Order!' he declared, as she writhed and shrieked on the end of his arm.

After he had dragged her some way he dropped her and looked closely at her, as if seeing her for the first time. She scrambled backwards away from him.

'I know you,' the man said. 'You came yesterday. You're one of *them*, aren't you?'

Ruth dared not attempt an answer.

The man smiled cruelly. 'If I were you I wouldn't try anything here. This is Esar's City. No one else's. Esar's. Now get back to your work.'

In a state of shock, Ruth scrambled away and ran to Naomi's house. She tumbled inside, terrified, and hid there until the woman returned from the fields.

By the time Naomi returned, Ruth had composed herself somewhat, although the older woman could tell that something had upset her. She suspected it was not simply the fear of a girl separated from her father, but Ruth was not forthcoming and Naomi was not sure what to do or say. Instead she gave Ruth some more water and a scrap of bread, and then sat quietly to wait out the burning hours. Ruth stared for some time at the murky pool in the bowl of her cup, trying to form her fears into useful questions, but the task seemed too great.

'Naomi, what is the Order?' she asked at last.

Before Naomi could reply, the air was torn by screams. In the west, a woman was shrieking and crying. Ruth tensed and stared in wide-eyed alarm at Naomi, who was sitting with her eyes closed and mouthing silent words.

In the next instant, a man could be heard bellowing with rage. His voice was countered by others, who argued back at him, and in moments an almighty disturbance began. A fight was under way. The screams of the woman changed in a way that suggested she was moving, perhaps being forcibly dragged away. Then the man bellowed again, but in pain more than rage, and the sounds of the fight died. Still the woman screamed as she was taken away, the noise fading enough for Ruth to guess she had gone from the City and out into the fields.

'What's happening?' Ruth hissed, her fear full in her face.

Naomi opened her eyes and Ruth saw they were brimming with tears.

'Naomi, what's going on?' Ruth insisted.

Naomi closed her eyes again, as if the horror and injustice of what was happening was lessened by doing so.

'Out in the fields they came to us. The Order – Esar's men – who rule the City. They said,' Naomi began, hardly holding back the sobs, 'that this woman sinned. That she took what was not hers. That she ate from the plants that had newly grown in the paths of the City.'

Ruth gasped and Naomi looked at her hard.

'What do you know, Ruth?' she asked with an urgency born from fear rather than condemnation.

Still the distant woman screamed.

'I saw men in black. They were pulling up some plants,' Ruth blurted out. 'Then I came back here! That is all!'

Naomi seemed immediately relieved.

'Were those plants always forbidden?' Ruth asked.

'No!' Naomi cried, the sobs breaking through her hard-fought reserve. 'They were not known in the City until three days ago. Then they appeared. They flowered immediately and berries came quickly. We … she didn't know they were sinful!'

'What is going to happen? What *is* happening?' Ruth whispered, fearing the answer she knew was coming.

'A burning,' Naomi said, her voice shaking.

'No!' Ruth cried, as memories long-defeated found new strength to rise up against her from within the depths of her being.

Far off, the woman still cried loudly; her shrieks rang out over the broad valley and echoed across the fields. Ruth felt dizzy and sick. The low house reeled as if suffering sun-sickness, and Ruth fainted into the gap between memory, screaming and the darkest of dreams …

Ruth was small, at least much smaller than she usually was, and she seemed to be slung on the hip of an adult woman. A man was nearby. He was smiling, although his arm hurt him. Sand appeared to blow in Ruth's face and the dream changed.

Now the man was with her, holding her tightly. They were hiding. Somebody was looking for them. Herders? Then they noticed someone else, a little way away. It was that woman. She struggled and she screamed. She fought but it was no good; there were too many of them.

Ruth and the man still hid. They were safe; they were in the shade.

The sun climbed higher and the woman cried. Sand blew in Ruth's face again and her dreams grew darker. The face of the man was close to hers.

'Herders!' he said softly. 'They killed her. They burned her. We hate them!'

Ruth writhed in a swell of nausea and loathing and her dreams dissolved.

The room was bright and Naomi was crouched over Ruth, looking terrified. The far-away woman was still screaming. Ruth blinked and sat up. Then she lurched to one side and her whole body convulsed in a gagging choke. She was suddenly sick; a brief surge of black foulness.

The screaming did not last much longer, but neither Ruth nor Naomi was able to speak. They both fought to keep out the horror of the midday burning.

The burning hours passed in an exhausting spasm of fear and tension. Naomi pulled herself to her feet and stretched her aching limbs. She pulled back the curtain over the doorway and looked out into the pathways of the City. Folk were stirring. The sun had moved over and it was safe to emerge from the shelter of the shade. She turned back to Ruth, crouched by the sitting girl and gripped her by the shoulders.

'Ruth, please, *please* stay here,' she begged. 'I don't want anything to happen to you. Please do not leave this house. I have to go out to work, but I will find out what your place is in the City as soon as I can. When we know your position here, then you will be safe to go out.'

Ruth sensed from the older woman's tired and frightened eyes that there were words left unspoken. It was as if the City, this place of grass fields and apparent plenty, was somehow more savage and relentlessly brutal than the desert itself.

'There's a little water in this skin if you need it,' Naomi said, gesturing to the folded skin bag that lay to one side of her carefully bundled possessions. 'I'll be back around sundown.'

She stepped out into the afternoon light and was gone. Ruth heard the sound of feet upon sand and the murmur of conversation as the Cityfolk went out to their work. A man was shouting orders in a loud voice.

'This way!' he barked. 'Go out this way! See the fruits of disobedience!'

Ruth poked her head out of the doorway to see if she could watch what was going on, but the low walls of the nearby houses obscured her view. She went quickly and lightly across the sand towards the main path, ducking sideways as the last of the Cityfolk strode by on their way to the fields.

'This way!' the man called again.

Ruth peered around the corner of the last house leading to the path. The folk going out to the fields were being taken past a knot of men in black robes standing a little way out into the plain. To one side of them was the prone form of a woman with limbs and head outstretched, making the figure of a five-pointed star. Ruth squinted in the afternoon heat and saw that the woman had been tied down with woven grass ropes, plaited together for greater strength. The ropes were fixed to four stakes, one for each wrist and ankle. There she had lain, under the full strength of the sun, for hours.

The last field workers passed by, and the black-clad Ordermen stooped and with great effort pulled up the stakes that held the woman. They began dragging her body back up the path towards Ruth, who panicked and ducked into a house, the door of which looked out onto the pathway. It was empty; the inhabitants were out in the fields. Once inside Ruth scrambled sideways and lay still. The tramp of feet and hiss of sand moving around the dragged body grew louder and louder. As the men passed by, Ruth could not help but look out at them. She immediately wished she hadn't.

The woman was unrecognisable. Her exposed skin was the red, black and vile orange of overwhelming burns. Her dead face was a mask of cracked, charred skin over a silenced scream of agony. Her wrists and ankles were torn and bloody as she'd strained at the ropes that held her under the merciless sun.

This was the justice of the City. This was the punishment for eating from the plants that had saved Ruth and her father from death.

Where *was* her father? Would this happen to him? Would this happen to *her*? Ruth did not know, but feared the worst. She wished she had stayed inside. She wished she could unsee this grisly spectacle.

The men continued into the City. Ruth dared not move until they were surely gone. When her chance came, she left her hiding place and went back to Naomi's house to wait for her.

Naomi returned as the sun slipped down over the far dunes. Ruth was already under the bedcloths and Naomi did not disturb her, except for laying out a small amount of food. Ruth waited until Naomi was asleep, or at least pretending to doze, before she ate. Then she returned to her curled up position under the cloths to await the night's forgetfulness.

When Ruth awoke Naomi was already up and moving about.

'Good morning,' the woman said, as cheerfully as she could.

'Time to get up. We must go and receive Esar's Gift. Bring your cup.'

Naomi picked up another of the small bundles and unwrapped it to reveal her own cup. Ruth dressed quickly. When Naomi stepped up out of the low house, Ruth was right behind her. As they picked their way between the buildings, they passed many men going in the other direction, towards the edge of the City and the fields beyond. All the women were walking with them towards the City centre.

Ruth pointed this out to Naomi, who replied, 'There is a certain way of receiving the Gift from Esar, an order to be observed. The men take it before the women. Women are not allowed to receive when the men are still taking the Gift, so we wait until they go out to the fields. The Gift-giving can take a very long time. Once we have received our gift, then we follow out to work. When the ritual begins,' she added, 'do not say anything at all, but just copy the other women. Do as the others do.'

Ruth followed Naomi onto the main pathway along which the burnt woman had been dragged. All the women of the City were processing down the road and, hopping sideways momentarily, Ruth saw past those immediately in front of her. They were part of a long line that snaked towards the base of the mound surrounding the stone spike. More women were joining the line behind Ruth and Naomi.

'Is the Gift water?' Ruth asked.

Naomi glanced about her before answering. When she did, her voice carried an edge of guardedness.

'Yes, of a kind. We'll talk about that later.'

'And will my father be there?' Ruth continued, more earnestly.

The question seemed to trouble Naomi more than the previous one.

'Let's talk about it all later. You'll be working with me today so we'll have plenty of time *later*,' she replied, hoping to finish the matter for now.

It was some while before they reached the start of the queue, and Naomi spent the intervening time talking with the women around her about names Ruth didn't know and areas of the City she had not been to. Every time Ruth asked a question about where her father was, or who Esar was, Naomi would answer shortly, 'Not now, Ruth, please', or, 'Ruth, *later*'. So Ruth gave up.

They reached the foot of the mound and the queue spread out. The women hurried to find their place in the single file that encircled the holy embankment, and Naomi whispered her apology to Ruth.

'I'm sorry we couldn't speak. You never know who might be listening. We'll talk in my house and when we're at work. As for now, just do as the others do.'

Ruth followed Naomi around the mound until they came to the end of the line. Each recipient of the gift stood ten paces apart from the next with head bowed and hands folded together. It was some time before Esar and his followers appeared on Ruth's side of the mound, so she had time to look more closely at the women. She could see that some were whispering to themselves with their eyes closed, their mouths moving quickly. As the moments passed, their murmuring became louder but their words remained indistinct.

Gradually, the sounds of Esar's Gift ceremony grew in volume as Esar moved around the mound. Occasionally there would be a harsh rattling, followed by the drone of Esar's voice drawn out into a monotone. Finally, a sweet, light ringing sound made the air seem crisp. Then a few moments later, the pattern of sounds would repeat.

Esar appeared around the end of the sand bank, followed by three men in dark robes. They processed to the next receiver, who knelt as they approached, and a curious ritual ensued.

One of Esar's attendants raised a short bone or stick above his head – Ruth couldn't quite make it out – and shook it. This was the harsh rattling sound she had heard. The assistant lowered his arms and Esar approached the woman, inclining his head in a peculiar way. When he reached her, he put his hand on her head and spoke in the droning tone; once again, Ruth could not make out what he was saying.

A second attendant then passed Esar a large object that he took in both hands and tipped towards the outstretched palms of the kneeling woman. When Esar passed the object back to the second man, a third attendant raised his hands and struck them together violently, creating the unusual ringing sound that seemed to signal the end of the ritual.

Ruth looked on as the next person received her Gift, but Naomi whispered hoarsely, 'Ruth, don't look! Keep your eyes on the ground in front of you!'

Ruth obeyed, but it meant that she could only listen to what was happening. Then at last it was her turn.

She remembered to kneel as Esar approached. When the first attendant raised his rattling stick, Ruth looked up and saw that it was not made of bone, but of dark wood. It was long and thin and straight, but at some point it had been much longer, for the lower end of the shaft was splintered and broken. At the other end, the highest point, there was set into the top a beautiful shape made of a bright material that seemed to shine like the starlight. Indeed it looked like the four-pointed stars that glimmer in the heavens. As the staff moved in the man's hands, the light from the symbol flashed and shimmered across its polished surface. Hung below the glowing object was a gourd that Ruth guessed was full of pebbles or grains of grass to make the rattling sound.

Esar placed his hand on Ruth's head, took in a long breath and chanted, 'Beloved daughter, submit thyself to our holy protection, blessing us and remembering our merciful Love in all thy thoughts and deeds.'

He turned to the second attendant and took from him a large jug. He held it as high as he could against his chest, and continued his mantra: 'By this Gift, seal in thy heart the mystery of our blessing, and confess that it was by our Love that thou wast raised from the dust and sustained for such time as now. Therefore receive the generous outpouring of our Charity in agreement with your obedience.'

Ruth stared up bewildered, unsure what to do. Esar leant forward, hesitated, and glared angrily down at the confused girl. The moment was broken; the aesthetic beauty of the ritual ruined.

Ruth shot an anxious glance at Naomi, who was frantically gesturing for Ruth to raise her cup to Esar. Ruth did so. Esar sighed and then repeated the last phrase: 'Therefore receive the generous outpouring of our Charity in agreement with your obedience.'

Once again, Esar leant forward and touched the spout of the jug against the rim of the mug. A heartbeat passed as he made tiny lifting movements. Suddenly, several large beads of liquid dashed over the edge of the jug and fell into the cup. With an intake of breath, Esar quickly pulled back the jug. The third attendant looked expectantly at Ruth and smiled as she lifted the cup to her lips. He did not see that she didn't drink. Then he raised his hands and Ruth saw that he had what looked like a small upturned bowl in one of them and a rod in the other, both made of the same shining material that topped the rattling staff. He struck the bowl with the rod and it made a ringing sound that was both delicate and sharp. The ritual was complete and Esar and his attendants moved on.

Ruth lowered her cup and looked down into its well. The 'Gift' was a murky puddle of cloudy water, foul smelling and dark, but it filled nearly a third of the cup – and water was water.

She tipped the vessel up, took some of the liquid into her mouth and nearly choked. It was cold, bitter and felt thick across her tongue, as if it was somehow rotten. She forced herself to swallow and stared into the cup, revolted. The water Naomi had given her was not quite as bad as this. Even the water from the Jacobswells had been unpleasantly warm, but at least it had come from living plants. It had felt alive. The Gift water felt like death. Ruth was not sure if she could finish the rest. She turned to look at Naomi, whose ritual was just beginning.

When it was over, Naomi returned with Ruth to her house. She did not talk with the girl on the way about what happened, but once they were within the walls, she listened to Ruth's questions and answered them as best she could as she went about her preparations for the day. Ruth squatted down with her back to a wall, trying to keep out of the way.

'What's going to happen today?' she asked.

'We must go to work. You will come with me into the fields. We'll be able to talk as we work because we'll be quite close together. When the sun gets high we will come back here to rest and work on the cloth. Then in the afternoon we will return to the fields and work into the evening before the cold comes down.'

'Where is my father?'

Naomi paused, seemingly still unsure how to answer. 'I promised that we'd talk, Ruth, but we must get out to the fields before long. We need get to work or someone will take notice. Here, eat this.'

She unwrapped a bundle of cloth to reveal a small loaf that she tore in two, giving half to Ruth. Then she reached into a small excavation that had been made in the brickwork, and from this small enclave she produced another of the precious cups. This one was full of shrivelled berries and she gave some to Ruth. They were a dark crimson colour, almost black, and when Ruth handled them they gave off a rich fragrance. The smell evoked memories within her that she couldn't quite grasp from a time long ago, before the ruining of things. But somehow they did not feel as though they belonged to her.

She crushed a berry between her thumb and finger and it stained her skin with the remainder of the moisture that the dry air had not stolen.

Naomi fixed her with a grave stare. 'Do not tell a soul about these,' she said.

'What do you call them?' Ruth asked, wondering at the bitter-sweet taste that filled her mouth.

'No one has quite decided on a name yet. They've only grown here of late …'

Naomi's voice fell to a mumble before she began again.

'These are the same kind of berries that the poor woman had picked. But we all picked them. At first Esar, the Minister, said they were a new blessing from the Order and we should be extra thankful to him. They were a reward for our faithfulness. But they grew everywhere, and Esar could not control them. Of course, you would know what they really are.'

Naomi looked at Ruth with an uncertain, wavering glance. Ruth stared back, puzzled, and Naomi could not meet her gaze for more than a few instants.

'So, where is my father?' Ruth asked again, determinedly.

This time, Naomi could not ignore her so she stopped her preparations and came over to sit by the young girl.

'How old are you, Ruth? Ten? Eleven?'

'*Twelve*,' Ruth stressed.

Naomi continued, 'Well, that means you are nearly an adult and so I'll be honest with you. Sometimes things happen because of bad timing, or because of an accident or because we don't know what we've done wrong. You and your father came over the dunes and set foot on the holy mound. You didn't know what you were doing, but *you* are here, alive, because you are a still a child. You are a girl on the edge of womanhood but still a child. How could you know what you were doing was wrong?

'Your father is not so fortunate. He's been taken into the Minister's holy tent and I can't tell you when he will come out again.'

She raised her hand quickly to quieten Ruth's response. 'Look, my dear, by stepping on the holy mound in front of nearly half the folk in the City, you forced the Minister to act. And you did it so soon after the uproar caused by the others like you who came out of the dunes. Things were bad for your father because he violated the holy mound. But now he has been *inside* the tent he is faced with joining the Order and serving Esar – or facing Esar's displeasure. We must pray that Esar is merciful.'

Naomi rose and put out her hand to Ruth. 'Come, we must go to the fields.'

By now the sun had risen far above the dunes that made up the valley's eastern border, and the temperature was rising. The light and heat fell unrelentingly on the township of crumbling sand bricks as Ruth and Naomi emerged into the open air.

The idea of life in a permanent settlement remained strange to Ruth; there seemed to be too many people in too small a space; too many souls and too much hardship focused in one place. To her, the City was like a camp on a massive scale, but a camp that had died and rotted into the ground. It looked very large, but as Ruth walked through its pathways at Naomi's side, she felt that it was indeed very small. It would never move to fresh ground; it would only continue to crumble and decay, always in the shadow of the strange holy mound, the tent and its unearthly spike. The world of the City was limited to the block-like, broken houses, the tents, the fields round about and the distant wall of dunes. In the life of a nomadic Miller, she might never find an end to the desert in all of her days, but if she never broke camp and moved on from the City, it was a certainty that she would never find the richer pastures that the small voice in her dreams whispered of.

Finally, they left the tented area and walked through the herding ground. Ruth shuddered; there were Herders all around her, tending their animals. She kept that little bit closer to Naomi and fixed her eyes on the Miller fields in the near distance. Unconsciously, Ruth took hold of Naomi's hand, an act that made the older woman smile.

While still some distance from the Millers, Naomi turned aside and walked in the direction of the nearest Herder.

Mortified, Ruth hissed after her, 'Naomi! What are you doing?'

Naomi looked round, surprised, and frowned, 'Going to work! Come along, I'll introduce you.'

She turned back towards the Herder and walked on. Not wanting to be left alone, Ruth hurried after her.

Naomi approached the Herder and gave a short bob in courtesy. Ruth stood one pace behind her, slightly hidden, fighting a lifetime of hatred. The Herder was tall and broad, and wrapped from head to foot in a patchwork of animal skin and the same dirty hair-cloth that was the tent material of the city. He had a coarse beard that tumbled over his chin and stood on the brink of his folded robe. He wore a broad belt of goat hide loosely wrapped around his middle. It bulged in places, indicating hidden items. On his head was a turban of a different kind of material that Ruth could not identify. It was pale, patchy in places, and in the folds there were suggestions of a darker, more vivid shade that had been the original colour. A small, four-pointed star made of shiny material was pinned to the turban above the man's forehead – the same star shape she had seen in the ritual – and Ruth guessed it was a mark of Esar's authority.

The Herder's left hand rested on a short wooden rod that was tucked into his belt. It was very similar to the dark staff that Esar's attendant had held during the ritual, but this one was not as smooth or even. It was heavily notched along its length, as if it had been struck many times against something much harder than itself, or cut in that way for some unknown purpose. Whatever the history or reasoning behind the marks, the Herder Chief's staff and star served to reflect the authority of Esar and his Order, who skulked in the tent below the strange spike in the centre of the City.

Naomi turned around to face Ruth, and the girl took two involuntary steps backwards. Naomi smiled and put out her open hand towards her, but it was to no avail. Ruth was looking past Naomi at the dark, unreadable face of the Herder Chief.

'Ruth,' Naomi said, taking a step forward. She could see the colour draining from the girl's face.

Ruth stepped back again, her heart racing, eyes twitching as she struggled to focus on the embodiment of her nightmares. Her next backward step faltered. The world became suddenly quiet and she fought to hang on to her senses. She closed her eyes and let the surroundings spin. A heartbeat slipped by in what seemed like an age, and when the darkness passed, she found herself still standing upright on unsteady feet with Naomi beckoning to her.

In another moment, her hearing returned and Naomi's voice seemed loud and painful to her ears.

'Ruth, don't be afraid.'

But Ruth was afraid, very afraid.

She turned towards the southern fields where she could see the shapes of Millers stooping as they worked, and ran. She ran as fast as she could without stumbling on the longer grasses that had not yet been clipped by the teeth of goats.

When she was among the Millers, she threw herself on the ground. Naomi came after her, more slowly, and found her between the grass clumps sobbing. She knelt by her side, lifted Ruth's small body into her arms and wept with her.

Later, when the sun rose too high to walk outside and they were back in the shade of Naomi's house, Ruth told a little of her story. Naomi sat quietly and listened and, when Ruth had finished, they ate together, then slept.

Chapter Six

Ruth awoke when Naomi lifted the doorway curtain, bringing dust and heat with her as she stepped down into the shade of the house. Naomi removed and neatly folded her headscarf, and set it down on top of her bedding.

'I went to see the Herder Chief to beg your case and to ask that you be allowed to work with the Miller folk,' she said. 'I implored him at great length, and finally he agreed to speak to the Miller Chief, but I don't know when that will be.'

'How long could it take?' Ruth responded, hotly. 'I don't want to stay here for the rest of the day; I want to go and see my father!'

'Oh, Ruth, I'm afraid you can't go and see your father this afternoon or any afternoon. You have been assigned to work as a Herder and …'

'What?' Ruth exclaimed, but Naomi hardened her tone and ignored the outburst.

'And until the Chiefs agree and get Esar's approval, you will work as a Herder. There is no alternative: if you don't work, I am not allowed to feed you. Please, Ruth,' and Naomi's voice softened, 'for your own sake, please don't upset Esar or the Chiefs. Be a good girl and come back to work with me in the fields. I will ask if we can work on the edge of the pastureland, away from most of the others. Let's change the subject, eh? Have some more water.'

Naomi produced a water skin and handed it to Ruth. 'It's all right, Ruth. You can drink it. We're not going to run out but if we do I can get more. Although perhaps don't drink all of it! It is difficult to get hold of – more water means less food.'

Naomi made another attempt at changing the conversation. 'We've got a little while before we have to return to work, so why don't you ask me some of those questions that you have.'

Ruth thought for a while and finally asked, 'If I can't go to see my father and – ' but Naomi cut across her.

'I've told you all I know about what is happening to your father. Please ask something else.'

Ruth thought again. 'What is the holy mound? Why is it holy?'

'The holy mound is sacred to Esar and his Ordermen,' came the reply. 'Without the holy mound, the City wouldn't survive because the mound is a place of life. They guard it against anyone who might come and disrupt the work they do there.'

'What work?' Ruth asked.

'Esar works miracles inside his tent that summon water back into the desert: it is said that he can draw the water out of the sand and channel it into our fields and pastures. When we go out into the fields, see if you can see the places where Esar has sent his water. There are patches of land that he has chosen to bless to make it possible for the grasses to grow. The Gift is another instance of Esar's blessing for us all – it's the same water that he sends to the grasslands around us. Out in the far desert I hear that the seasonal grasses are fading and people are starving. Here in the City there are no seasons like there are where you come from – Esar has stopped the seasons and the grass grows all year round.'

'All year round?' asked Ruth, incredulously.

'Yes, all year round!' Naomi replied, half smiling. 'The City wouldn't survive if it relied on the seasons. It's all because of the holy mound; through it Esar feeds everyone, Miller and Herder alike. You see …' she began.

Ruth interrupted. 'So Herders and Millers are at peace here?'

'Mostly they are – although we aren't without differences, but it's much better than it used to be. There was a time when the Order had to take some very strict action because of the problems, but we haven't seen that level of trouble for a long time. At least not between Herders and Millers.'

'What did the Order do that was so strict? Did they hurt the troublemakers?' Ruth asked, touching her tender scalp in remembrance of the Orderman's rough assault.

For a moment it seemed that Naomi didn't quite know how to answer, but then she spoke.

'Oh … the Order … they don't have to hurt anyone to get what they want; they … just stop giving the Gift of water until the offending people promise to behave,' Naomi said, rather too lightly for Ruth's liking. 'I can't recall what finally happened to those troublemakers, but they soon stopped when they realised that the whole City would starve and thirst if they continued to fight. A few carried on causing problems, but I think some of their own men killed them.'

Naomi suddenly turned grave and spoke more earnestly. 'Please, Ruth, don't upset the Minister. It may be difficult for you, but you must try to do what is asked of you – and that includes working as a Herder this afternoon.'

Ruth sighed and then nodded compliantly. Naomi looked pleased.

'Let's go back to the fields,' she said. 'You can work close to me.'

'Naomi, are you a Herder?' Ruth asked, not really wanting to hear the answer to this inevitable question.

'I don't know, Ruth. I don't know which of the tribes I belong to any more. I thought I belonged to your tribe, but now I am not so sure. I suppose I belong to the City and to the Minister. I have been told to work as a Herder so that is what I do. Does that make me an enemy?' Naomi smiled. 'Are we supposed to fight each other?'

Ruth smiled back. 'No. I won't fight you.'

Ruth worked in the Herders' fields for the rest of the day, helping Naomi with a small flock. She was pleased to see that they were nowhere near the other Herders because each of the flocks moved across the pastures in waves with a good distance between them. Ruth was glad that there was little chance of meeting them, but she was frustrated in her attempts to talk more with Naomi. She had to keep a careful eye on the goats, and she and Naomi herded them in such a way that kept the animals between them. It was difficult work, as the goats seemed intent on going in all directions at once, but, with encouragement and instructions from Naomi, she managed.

As she worked, Ruth couldn't help noticing the quality of the grasses around her. But the Miller in her instantly saw the lack of grass seeds on the heads of the stalks: it didn't look like poor growth, but instead as if the seeds had already been harvested, only without the stalks. As she looked closer, she could see that perhaps only one clump in many had grass seeds, while the others were gone. This was strange to her. She did not like the thought of the Miller folk leaving good grazing behind for the Herders. The goats would only be interested in consuming as many stalks as possible. They wouldn't care for the seeds. But the City's Herders did not let the goats strip a patch of grass to nothing; they moved them on in a method quite different from their nomadic cousins.

The day wore on, and Ruth became more familiar with the work of herding, and allowed her mind to wander gently. She felt a rhythm in the movements of the herds as they orbited the City in broad sweeps, and when she planted her feet, she felt the steps of the Millers who had trodden this ground before.

It dawned on her unconscious mind that the ebbing life was being reinforced and bolstered here by careful management. It would not be good for the goats to strip a patch of pasture completely bare, so they were kept moving. If water was in abundance here, moderately cropped grass could recover quickly enough to feed another herd. And the seed heads that were left alone would be allowed to grow into new shoots of grass. The Millers must have already moved over this patch to harvest the precious seed heads for their bread. Perhaps the Millers and Herders swapped pastures and successfully avoided destroying each other's food source. Half dreaming, Ruth saw herself and the whole City as a ring of life revolving endlessly in a dead place. The arc of growing up and dying away had been replaced by a circle.

Ruth cast her eyes out into the faraway desert where she and her father had worked out their meagre lives. There the grasses were dying. The patches of grey-green life that sprang up over the dunes were becoming fewer and farther between. There the Herders let their ravenous livestock destroy swathes of good grassland, leaving it unable to recover.

Not in the City, though. Perhaps there was hope for the people here, although it seemed to lie with Esar and his dark brotherhood under the tent and spike. If Esar could hold the obedience of the tribal Chiefs, then perhaps peace between Miller and Herder was possible.

The day dwindled, and the light took on a golden tinge on the eastern dunes. Gentle shadows soothed the burnt faces of the western hills as the sun moved over and beyond into the edges of the flawless blue sky.

Two men walked out of the City towards Ruth and Naomi. They were black-clad Ordermen, and they walked purposefully. Naomi was the first to spot them, and Ruth noticed her nervousness before she saw the men.

Something was out of the ordinary.

The two men reached them and the taller one spoke loudly, but it was clear he was addressing only Naomi.

'We come from Esar with his orders to instruct the child. Bring her here.'

Naomi hesitated, and then sprang into anxious activity. She took Ruth by the arm and led her to the waiting Ordermen.

'Kneel,' the same man commanded.

Naomi's hand moved quickly and pushed firmly on Ruth's shoulder. Ruth knelt, strongly sensing that any delay could cause trouble.

'Step back, woman,' the man said to Naomi.

He looked round and nodded to his companion. The second man stepped forward and held out three scraps of ancient cloth, each two or three hands' breadth across. They had pictures on them.

'Now see the holy tapestries,' the taller man began, speaking not to Ruth but following some internal mantra.

He held the first in front of Ruth's face. She had not seen anything like it before in her life. The cloth was woven from thick threads of different colours, twisted together and combined to show images of men. They had strong outlines and had perhaps been brightly coloured once, but now the threads were dull and dirt-encrusted. Age and rottenness had combined to ruin the tapestry's brightness, but it was still an item of wonder.

This first tapestry was a bleak picture of sand and sky and little else but two lonely figures. Each seemed to represent the tribes: one man with a scraggy goat, and another with millstones and an empty bag of grass seed. It was clear from their open mouths and tortured expressions that they were in misery.

The Orderman spoke again. 'The first. Here you see the desolation of disobedience. The desert and the suffering. The people were lost in a place of death.'

He turned, reverently passed the tapestry back to his companion and received the next.

'The second. Here you see the coming of Esar, and wonder entering the world.'

The image was of a tall man with a grim face and powerful arms – not like Esar at all – and he was dressed in what had once been a bright robe but, like the whole of the picture, it was ruined and threadbare. The entire tapestry was fraying in decay. Yet the image of the man was compelling. He held a staff in his hand and he walked among green grasses. Next to him, by his feet, flowed what seemed to be living blue sky. There were strange animals there around him, goat-like but hairier and plumper, and they were dipping their faces into the curious blue ground. Ruth's eyes widened. What were they drinking?

Before she could take it all in, the Orderman turned and exchanged the tapestry for another.

'The third. There is food for everyone. The people are happy, and they give thanks to Esar. They are saved.'

The last tapestry was of the man with the staff, but this time he was seated on some kind of frame that Ruth did not have any words for. Strange creatures and people dressed in wonderful clothes surrounded him, and the man looked very powerful – even less like Esar. Again, before Ruth had finished drinking in the images, the man took them away. As he returned this last picture to his companion, Ruth noticed a nodding inflexion and a slight bob; the man was bowing to the tapestries.

'Now you have seen the holy tapestries,' he said, 'you know that the Minister is to be obeyed. To disobey leads to death. Now, go back to work.'

Without so much as looking at her, he turned on his heel and marched away with his companion, back to the City.

Ruth did not rise immediately; her mind was still full of the strange pictures she had seen. It was not until Naomi's hand touched her shoulder that she came back to her surroundings. By now the sun had reached the western dunes.

'Ruth,' Naomi whispered, 'we're all going to take the herds back to their pens now. You don't have to come – why don't you go back to the house? I'll see you there as soon as I have finished.'

Ruth turned north towards the City, and was struck with a very similar view of the settlement as when she and her father had arrived the day before. So much had happened in the short space of two days; she could barely take it all in.

Others among the Herders were making their way back to the City whilst those left in charge of the herds were heading towards the west side. Ruth waited for a moment to allow the Herders to get ahead of her so that she could keep them in view and avoid meeting them. Seeing them here in the fading light, spread out among the grassy blotches, reminded her of their feral brothers stalking through the dunes all those weeks ago. She shivered and moved more quickly towards the safety of Naomi's low house.

Before she had gone any distance, she heard the sandy crunch of approaching footsteps. Without turning, she quickened her pace and fixed her eyes on the first row of tents before her. The soft thump of feet increased in speed to match her own and, as she was about to run, the person following her called out a furtive, 'Hey!' She broke into a sprint, leaving whoever it was behind.

Reaching the line of tents, she ran off the main path, weaving her way through the sand-bleached material until she found herself passing by the first of the solid houses. Ruth did not know where she was until she saw the strange spike and the holy mound towering above the low buildings. It looked softer and more yellow than grey in the fading light. She made towards it, hoping to find her way back to the main path from which she could navigate. More people were returning from the fields as she reached the centre of the City. An Orderman appeared at the top of the mound, having climbed up the north side, and he disappeared into the dark mouth of the hilltop tent. Ruth stared at the door flap, willing her father to open it and come out to meet her, but it didn't move except for the tiniest flicker of the corner lifting in the slight breeze.

Once she had recovered her bearings, she realised she was too far in, so she turned south and walked back down the main path towards where she thought she'd find Naomi's house. As she approached the correct turning off the path, one of the field workers coming in the other direction stopped and addressed her.

'Hello. Are you Ruth?'

The young man did not yet have a beard, which made him perhaps 15 or 16, and he was tall and gangly, clearly well-fed in a place of scarcity. He wore a waist-length, hairspun robe over goatskin trews and carried a small skin bag in which, Ruth guessed, he kept millstones and flour.

'Yes, I am Ruth,' she answered diffidently. 'What do you want?'

'Only to talk to you,' he replied. 'Why did you run away just now?'

'Why do you think? Somebody I didn't know was chasing me,' she said accusingly. 'Who are you, and what do you want?'

'What I want,' he answered undeterred, 'is to talk. As to who I am, I'm called Boaz.' He smiled, trying to draw out a less guarded response from her.

'What do you want to talk about?' Ruth asked frostily.

'You're not how I imagined you, that's for certain,' Boaz said quietly, mostly to himself. He still wore a smile. When Ruth didn't return it, it flickered on his face and he became more serious.

'Look, I want to talk to you about your tribe. Can we go somewhere private?'

'You must think I'm a fool. I don't know you.'

'We can't talk here. I can't risk openly asking about *them*,' he responded, his enforced patience suppressing a rising sense of urgency. 'I want to learn more from you and your people, more about your way of life and,' he dropped his voice, 'what makes you so different from the rest of us.'

'My people? You're a Miller, aren't you?' Ruth replied, gesturing at his bag. 'What do you need to learn from me?'

To her surprise, her words seemed to confuse the young man.

'Yes, I am a Miller,' Boaz said, working the matter over as if he had missed something, 'but that's why I want to hear about *your* people. Look, I overheard from the woman, Naomi, that you have a problem with us – especially the Herder people. We get on in the City, most of the time anyway, but that doesn't mean there aren't occasional upsets. *You* are something else entirely, which is why I can't really be seen speaking with you openly. And that's why I wanted to meet you away from the City where we could talk. Only you ran off.'

More people were coming up the path and Boaz took Ruth's elbow. He quickly stepped aside, away from the thoroughfare.

'I'm sorry for scaring you,' he murmured. 'I can't talk any longer – I'm breaking rules of etiquette by speaking to you now. I hope you don't think I'm being rude. I'll try to find you again tomorrow, out in the field where we can talk together more easily.'

Ruth nodded, not knowing what to say, as Boaz stepped back on to the road.

'Your woman's house is that way,' he said, gesturing towards the nearest row of houses. 'Not long 'til the curfew anyway.'

He nodded goodbye and turned away towards the centre of the City. Ruth walked in the direction he had indicated, found Naomi's house and went inside.

It was not long before Naomi returned, bringing with her a flaccid skin that she said contained a small amount of milk. She found more of the bitter, blood-red berries that she had dried out and gave them to Ruth with some bread and a sliver of cured meat. Ruth could not remember having two meals like the ones she had enjoyed in the past two days. It was only when she had finished eating and drinking that she noticed Naomi had hardly eaten and had not finished her milk.

'I'm not hungry,' she said lightly. 'I had some water earlier, and that has kept me going. You look as if you need it more than I do anyway, Ruth.'

'Naomi, can I ask you something?' Ruth began, and Naomi inclined her head to listen. 'A boy, no, not quite ... a *man*, young anyway, started speaking to me today when I came back from the field, but he said he was breaking the rules. Then he had to go. What rules did he break?'

'I don't know. There could have been a number of reasons. Perhaps he was important, or perhaps the opposite: unclean. Perhaps he thought *you* were unclean. How old was he? I suppose he could be ready for marriage, but that wouldn't stop him talking to you – unless, of course, he was a *very* important person. Maybe a Chief's son or nephew, or a favourite of the Minister ...'

Ruth interrupted. 'But why would that stop him from speaking to me? I've hardly seen anyone close to my age since I've been here. We never had this rule where I come from.'

'Well, the City is different from your tribe. Here the Chief's family is still very important. Even though children are rare, it is vital for the Chief to marry his own off carefully. What did he look like?'

Ruth felt that she ought not to make enemies by getting strangers into trouble, especially if strangers like Boaz really were Chiefs' sons, so she gave a vague and inaccurate description and entirely failed to mention a name. Naomi shook her head.

'Ruth, I don't know who you mean. Point him out if you see him again, won't you? Anyway, you should be careful. A daughter is a valuable asset, not to be wasted on anyone's son. Your father ...' but Naomi pulled herself up short. Then, realising it was too late, continued, '*Your father* should set some rules for you, too; he doesn't want to waste your potential on anybody. A son means difficulty, but a daughter is valuable currency in a place like the City. A father does not want to misuse his daughter by spending her on a poor marriage.

He could get far in life by giving you to the right man – if you are worth a great deal, that is. I think he could get a lot for a girl like you, as long as you have it in you to do what is expected of you.'

Naomi gave Ruth an odd look that seemed, in one moment, to express regret, sorrow and memory mixed with fear. Ruth shifted uncomfortably where she was sitting; leaning against the wall, she could feel the cold creep into her through the heavy depth of sand that was the floor. Without needing further prompting, Naomi immediately unfolded a bed cloth and draped it across Ruth's back. The girl grasped the edges and pulled them close about her, whispering her thanks. She stared at her feet, her mind full of questions. There were almost too many to ask, and so far she had not had any answers. Where to begin?

'Naomi, where did those tapestries come from? And why are they holy?'

Naomi paused in preparing her own bed. She gave half a smile in reply, and thought for a moment before responding.

'Those tapestries are closely guarded by the Order. They tell the story of the City, and the desert, and how there is so much life here. The Minister will never allow the Cityfolk to see any more than what you saw today. But,' she added, a bright light suddenly blazing in her eyes, 'I believe there is more to the tapestry. There is more, because the story of the City is the story of the tribes, yours included. And you know better than any of us here what that could mean.'

Ruth did not know, and Naomi's sudden zeal frightened her.

'But why are they holy?' she asked.

The light instantly left Naomi's eyes, and the years of City life returned to her face.

'To the Minister they are holy because of what he can do with them,' she explained. 'The Cityfolk tell their stories in word and song handed down from parent to child – well, they used to – but only the Minister has the story of the City in pictures. Those tapestries were made a long time ago using crafts unknown to us. But since then, beyond living memory, the Order keep that story to themselves, only telling us what makes us afraid.'

'Afraid?' Ruth cut in.

'Afraid, yes. Afraid of sand, afraid of thirst, afraid of death and the ever-growing desert. That is why the Minister calls the tapestries 'holy'. And that is why the Order keeps them secret.' Naomi became earnest again. 'But you know a different life, a life of plenty. You and your father …'

She trailed off, realising that mentioning Dan could bring another barrage of questioning from the girl. But Ruth was silent, a small child sitting under a threadbare cloth, as if filled with a deep and ancient sorrow. She wanted desperately to be away from here, far away. She didn't know where. The recent days had been too much for her. She threw a glance at Naomi's doorway, where the light was dying and the sand was chilling in the encroaching night. Somewhere out there her father was sitting or standing or lying on the same dusty sand that trickled in the through the door of Naomi's house.

Ruth felt profoundly alone again, and her small body shivered beneath her bed cloth. Her mind turned back to their first sight of the City, when her father had seemed so excited. Everything would be all right; they had escaped certain death in the madness of the open desert and would find safety and new hope in what had been a place of legend. In her mind she retraced the steps down the dunes and across the plain towards the first pasture where the Miller men and women had been working. She remembered the darker, greener plants that led them from the place of death to the City, and unswervingly to the spike. She reflected on what it had been like to walk among such beautiful vegetation, to feel the brush of the leaves against her legs, to smell the scent of the crushed foliage in her hands. The world seemed vast and beautiful, and she felt as though the short weeks that she had followed the way through the desert were the most precious moments of her brief life.

Now it seemed as if the large, expansive world was moving on without her; the dusk was settling and she would have to chase it to feel a new dawn again. The world of the City was closing in; the stars, tiny points of white light quivering in their cold heaven, had disappeared as the small cell of sand, brick and patched roof shrank in her mind to the shallow pit that was the floor of the house. She remembered her father again, but thinking of him seemed exhausting. She forced herself to remember the miraculous path of plants, but the effort became painful; it seemed she was drinking a bitter cup that left her weak and sorrowful.

Ruth came back to herself enough to sense that night had long fallen and that she had curled up in the bed cloth. Naomi was not far away, sleeping. Ruth lay motionless and listened. The City was much quieter than the previous night, still and virtually silent. There was no noise of men talking and laughing and snoring as before, nor could Ruth hear the crunch of cold feet on freezing sand as folk moved about the City. Apart from the other woman's lulling, gentle sighs, the world seemed mute as if holding its breath. Moments passed. The silence waited.

Ruth sat up, unsure if she had just heard something – but something too quiet for her ears to acknowledge. Was she imagining things, or was someone calling her? She stood up, pulling the largest of the bedcloths around her shoulders to curb the night's frozen air. Taking two steps across the house floor to the doorway, she gently lifted the edge of the hanging cloth. The night was bright from the large moon that sat some way above the eastern dunes. Nothing stirred, and still all she could hear was her own breath, drawing lightly, frostily, in and out.

Without even looking back at Naomi, Ruth stepped up and put one foot outside the house onto the sand. It was cold and hard, tempered by the freezing gnaw of bitter exposure to the open sky above and the numbing depth of sand below. She stole inside again and wrapped her feet in some of the smaller bedcloth strips, folding them into useful lengths.

In a moment she was outside once more, creeping through the rows of decrepit houses, not knowing where she was going.

CHAPTER SEVEN

THE CITY FELT DESERTED, as if Ruth were the only person in the whole world. No, not quite, she reflected. She felt it was more as though she was the only *other* person in the world; on some instinctual level, she seemed to know that there was one other person abroad in the night besides her. She felt a stinging apprehension, so earnest it was almost indistinguishable from fear. Who was out there?

'I must look!' she whispered to herself.

In the same instant, Ruth felt her yearning suddenly come into focus, as if she had looked up at the sky and could navigate by an unseen sun. Her thoughts turned immediately to the north-east, so she set off in that direction, winding her way around the houses and tents. Nothing moved; the silence breathed. As she crept out from the last line of low houses, she looked up to the eastern dunes. Her gaze followed the line of sandy hills that climbed one above another, until it seemed to lift her into the starry heavens. The darkness seemed to lessen as the sparks of silver-white filled her consciousness with a sense of awe for the celestial ocean.

Ruth's mind, captivated by what she saw, allowed her feet to find their way through the tents and towards the eastern dunes. She reached the edge of the City and stopped. Her eyes tumbled through the stars, rolled uncomfortably down the dunes and came to a stop on the plain before her. The gulf of pastured desert that swept out from her toes to the feet of the far slopes seemed suddenly huge, as if she could only hope to cross the distance in great strides. She listened again, hoping to hear someone call her name as she hoped they had before, but no one did. The silence remained expectant; waiting.

She shuffled her feet and looked up to the high, moonlit silhouette of the eastern dunes' peak. There was nobody there. Yet she felt she ought to go, to step out onto the seemingly pathless plain where Herders and Millers wound themselves around the City in a daily migration to nowhere. No tracks crossed this valley's floor. No, that was not true either; there had been a path, the one that led her and Dan to the City on the first day. That path had led them out of the absolute desert, from a place of nothingness to this place, the City. A voice inside her, a voice that Ruth thought she recognised to be her own, told her that the City was not a good place. It was forsaken; cruel. She felt sorrow well up inside her, as if it shouldn't be like this. The City was supposed to be something else. But what, she knew not. Would the answer be out in the dunes? Dare she go?

She stood on the City brink for a time, long enough to miss her chance to step beyond the confines of the settlement. The cold crept into her and she shivered. Then she turned back towards Naomi's house, but, as she did, her gaze swept northward. And her heart stopped.

On the edge of the settlement loomed a dark shape. It was the form of a man standing still and staring out across the plain towards the east, as if he were waiting for the sun to rise, watching where she had been watching.

Ruth recovered herself and stepped swiftly back within the line of tents, out of sight. Curiosity begged her to creep closer, to see who the man was, but she fought the impulse. It would be dangerous, she reasoned, but, as the pull from the east faded, she still felt drawn to the lonely figure. Something told her she was in no danger. She paused, wrestling with her instincts: the shadowy man *should be* dangerous but somehow was not. Yet she did not move in the direction of the watching stranger, held back by the same hesitation that had prevented her from moving in the direction of the eastern dunes.

She turned to go back to Naomi's house, feeling suddenly exposed and foolish. For the first time that night the danger seemed real, and she fled swiftly along the route she had taken, returning to the house of the woman who had been so kind to her. As she ran, her gaze once again rose towards the stars, only she found that her eyes were transfixed instead by the grey-brown spike that sat atop the holy mound, and the dull form of the Minister's tented palace slinking sullenly around it. She didn't stop until she reached Naomi's house, and as she went she realised the source of her unease.

Other eyes were keeping watch in the night; something was gazing at her from the wings of the shadowy tent. She could feel it. She did not breathe easily again until she was safely indoors and hidden beneath the blankets.

The new day began very much as the previous one. The men rose early and encircled the holy mound to receive the Gift; the ritual was repeated by the women a short time afterwards. Naomi reminded Ruth of what to say and do and the girl followed the instructions as best she could. Before long, the two of them were walking out towards the fields behind the other goatherds, but Ruth went with a sensation that there was something missing in the east. The sun was rising as usual, but underneath its early morning glow she perceived an absence. Something had *gone*, moved on. The feeling hung over her for the entire morning and, as she tramped around the City circuit, driving the goats, she thought of little else.

Before long the sun rose high and grew in strength, prompting the Cityfolk to retreat to their shelters and cower in the shade, away from the scorching eye.

The rest time passed slowly in silence. Naomi dozed, preventing Ruth from both talking about her unease and taking her mind off it. Eventually, the signal came to leave the shelters, and the workers went back to the fields, their feet bandaged against the hot sand.

Moments after Naomi returned with the herd, a young man presented himself to them. Though he inclined his head respectfully towards Naomi, he kept his eyes firmly on Ruth.

'You are required to come this evening to present yourself outside the House of Salmon,' he said. 'Come immediately after your labour is done.'

He gave Naomi another nod and left them before Ruth could respond. She looked to the other woman for an explanation that did not come, so she asked, 'Who was he, and what does this mean? What is Salmon?'

'He was a messenger from the House of Salmon; Salmon is the foremost Miller Chief in the City.'

Naomi paused, checking the weight of her words. 'I do not think that he wants to see *us* as much as he wants to see *you*. Salmon has sons and nephews, some of whom are unmarried. I would guess he aims to buy you.'

'*Buy* me?'

'Yes, and I think you are valuable in more ways than one. He may think that the danger you bring is outweighed by your value. Your father will be a rich man.'

'My father? You mean he will come, too?'

'I should think so. He owns you after all, and you don't need to worry about being from another tribe. Millers marry Herders in this place, although I have never heard of anyone marrying one of your tribe. If Salmon has a kinsman lined up for you then you will get away from the Herders as you'd like – you'll become a Miller.'

'But … I am a Miller …' Ruth began, puzzled.

Naomi continued heedless. 'Though we ought not to get ahead

of ourselves! You are still a child, are you not? And we don't know what is in Salmon's mind.'

For the rest of the afternoon, Naomi spoke very little, but from the moment they returned to the herding work, Ruth could see the older woman's mind turning the matter over and over, a hint of a smile on her lips.

At last, the long afternoon came to a close and Naomi turned the herd and took the animals across the pastures towards the west.

She turned and called to Ruth, 'Meet me at our house. I'll join you there shortly and we'll go together to the House of Salmon.'

Ruth did as she was told, pondering the disquiet in her heart. The pain of the unexplained absence in the east was dull and fading to memory, and she knew that she ought to consider the pressing matter of this evening. But it was easier, she found, to wonder who the figure had been out in the City last night. She knew only a handful of people here out of at least a few hundred, so she could not hope to find his identity quickly. Nevertheless, she was taken up with the thought of who it could have been. She would go out again tonight, to the same spot, and wait. She would have to keep herself hidden from the watching eyes on the holy mound.

At that realisation, she instinctively looked up to the tented spike atop the sandy hill. It was relentlessly there, unmoving and prevalent in a world of shifting sands. It was powerfully inert yet horribly stunted, limited and hunched, as if it were all it could ever be; just there. She could not deny that it dominated the imagination of the people in the City. It made them helpless. She, too, had become powerless but in a different way. There were many souls in the City, each with a place in the hierarchy, and she was not yet one of them. The interests of the ruling Order seemed to supersede all other freedoms. The curfews, the Gift and the daily duty of circling the City in journeyless migration held her in, and she felt as if the horizon had shrunk to an impenetrable wall of sand that closed around her. She did not belong here, but perhaps that would be taken care of this evening. Either through enforced sale and marriage to a Miller, or by creeping out unseen to the eastern edge, she would find her place.

As she approached Naomi's house, the young man who had intercepted her yesterday stepped onto the path beside her. She acknowledged him but kept walking.

'Greetings, Ruth!' he began cheerfully, trying to pre-empt her hostility. 'I'm sorry I couldn't meet you out in the fields as I said. Things have been moving – and moving quickly – since we last spoke. Quicker than I could have hoped.'

He smiled again, but to no avail. 'I hope you'll be pleased with what is going to happen.'

'Boaz, yesterday you said you wanted to talk but couldn't speak to me openly,' Ruth said deliberately. 'Now you're here again, hiding things from me *again*. What do you want? Do you mean to buy me?'

At this Boaz looked surprised, as if he'd been caught by an unexpected punch.

'I just want to talk to you,' he said slowly, 'and if buying you is the way to do it, so be it. I don't want you to stop being who you are. If anything, I should be the one to join *your* tribe, not the other way around, and if it costs me everything I have then I will pay that price. I was drawn to that road in the sand, the road of living plants, when I first saw it. Since that day I have ached to leave this place, but I can't. There is life here that keeps us all trapped. I don't expect you to understand, because you came off that road and you know what it's like to walk alongside the living water in the desert where there is only death. Why you are still here in the City, I don't know. If I were you, I would …'

Words failed him for a moment, then he continued, 'I … would leave. I would walk out onto the dunes and find my way into the wilderness. It is too dangerous here, too small. Do you ever want to leave this place?'

Ruth's eyes immediately widened and she leaned forward to speak but, in the same instant, she heard a firm yet reverential voice come from behind Boaz.

'Forgive me, sir.' It was Naomi. 'I beg you, please, to leave us now. Ruth and I must make preparations.'

Boaz turned to Naomi and nodded. 'Very well,' he said and, looking back at Ruth, whispered, 'I will see you shortly. We'll talk more, I promise. Everything will be all right.'

Naomi spent some time fussing over Ruth; tying back her hair; washing her eyes with a little water that she'd saved; beating the dust out of her clothes. Finally she drew out a small square of white fabric that she unfolded and draped over Ruth's head. One corner covered Ruth's forehead down to the arch of her eyes. It was beautifully soft against her skin. Naomi tucked Ruth's hair underneath the rest of the cloth that hung over her shoulders, stepped back and smiled.

'There. We're ready now.'

Ruth put her hand up to her head, reverently touched the gentle fabric, and ran her finger tips all over it, being careful not to dislodge it.

'What is this?' she breathed.

'Wool,' Naomi answered. 'I thought you'd know that.'

At that moment the curfew cry went up, the harsh, almost inhuman wail cutting through the dusk to hurry everyone into their houses or tents. Everyone, that is, except Ruth, Naomi and the special escort of Salmon's men.

'Naomi!' came a voice from outside. 'Come; we must go.'

Naomi tensed, resisting a surge of excited agitation, and then composed herself. She gestured at the doorway and Ruth lifted the cloth and stepped up and out into the night.

There were three men waiting for them. In the dying light Ruth could see that they were dressed well in skins and woven hair shirts. Each had, hanging from his straw-weave belt, a millstone held on a length of cord that indicated his allegiance to the Miller tribe. The stones were more than ornaments; they were heavy weapons that could be thrust or thrown hard into an enemy, puncturing and crushing soft flesh. They were slightly more unwieldy than the Herders' knives of horn, but the stronger Miller men could apply the brute weapons with a firm finesse that ruptured muscle and cracked bone. Ruth recalled how Dan had demonstrated such a skill on their arrival in the City, and how it had immediately established him as a force to be reckoned with, even with only one good arm. She impassively remembered that she had not even heard whether or not the man Dan had crushed had survived the experience.

The men turned away from Naomi's house and led them through the rows of houses towards the main path. When they reached it, they headed north towards the centre of the City and the holy mound. Ruth followed them, excited and fearful, unsure if she would see her father or Esar. Even though the curfew confined people to their houses, the City was full of noise, as if it were a different place from last night's quiet and watchful peace. The air itself seemed disturbed and feverish.

When they reached the foot of the mound, Ruth sensed movement at the mouth of the tent but heard nothing. Her escort did not climb the sandy hill but followed the path around it to the north-east. Ruth's excitement skipped again when she realised they were going towards the quarter of the City where she had seen the lone figure watching for the dawn.

But before they reached the outer ring of tents, the party turned north and made their way further up than Ruth had been before. The houses were much the same: low, sandy structures of half-ruined, half-repaired bricks with patchwork roofs. And still there was that unsettling sensation of clamour and noise coming from the dwellings around her. She felt watched, as she had in her moments of fear the night before. Tonight the City had eyes that followed her.

They approached the largest house Ruth had yet seen and one of the men went inside. In an instant, he returned.

'The Chief has taken his court out on the plain,' he said, more to the other men than to Ruth or Naomi. 'Come,' and they turned out towards the east again.

As they walked on through the houses, the feeling of claustrophobic inevitability encircled Ruth more strongly. She felt an impulse to touch the woollen cloth that covered her. The moment she did so, a deep calm stirred within her, a previously unrealised acceptance that she was unshakably secure in something she could not understand. She let her hand drop and, within a heartbeat, the glare of the City's dark watchfulness fell again heavy on her mind.

The women found themselves leaving the City's boundary and walking out into the plain, towards the eastern dunes. Ruth felt her steps become more eager, in spite of her apprehension. Naomi seemed possessed of a new vitality, too; her footfalls were purposeful, as if she marched open-eyed towards a moment of decision.

In the last rays of the dying sun, the dunes stood proud before them, challenging all who dared to come and climb, but as the small party took each step, the sandy hills looked more and more like the dying embers in the fires of Ruth's childhood. She remembered the ashes fading from orange to grey; she remembered the slow crumble and collapse; and she remembered the faint warmth dwindling to an aching cold.

Likewise, the dunes caught the last warm glow of the sun which, as it sank, left longer and longer shadows that advanced unwanted up the lower slopes, finally smothering all colour from them. As the brightness and heat of the day faded, the unpleasant uproar from the City intensified, and Ruth could sense its colourless, heatless intensity even from the outward plain.

She looked down again at the plain in front of her. Night was falling, and they had been summoned to an exposed spot of sand and dust. Even the grass did not grow here. She saw the low flame of a campfire with a figure crouched near to it. Fire was an expensive luxury, and she was surprised and amazed by its presence. However, this discussion would be short, if it was indeed a discussion of any kind. If Naomi was correct, and Ruth was to be sold into marriage, then there would be a brief, ritualised time of bartering, followed by another ritualistic exchange – the handing over of a portion of the final bride price. Once that was arranged, the wife would be given to her new husband.

Before the small fire had burnt low, Ruth could be a woman sold into marriage.

As she and the others approached, more questions pushed insistently at her. Why was the meeting to take place in the open, yet at night? It couldn't hope to be secretive in such a location *and* with a fire. Why would Salmon go to the trouble of lighting a fire and burning precious fuel for a marriage transaction? What could they accomplish out here that they could not accomplish in one of Salmon's houses?

At last they reached the waiting party. At their approach, a man stepped out of the shadows around the fire and placed a log of twisted straw on the flames. The darkness immediately retreated and Ruth could see that there were a number of men present. They were all standing, except for one – the figure she had seen near the fire. This man was wrapped in goatskins with only his hands, feet and turbaned head exposed. He was sitting comfortably upon a large stack of straw logs, which to Ruth seemed to be a massively abundant fuel supply and completely inappropriate for the small meeting fire. What, exactly, did they plan to burn with so much fuel?

The man raised his arm and two other men stepped forward to help him to his feet. Ruth realised immediately that this must be Salmon, the old and powerful Chief. Once on his feet, he came towards the women and spoke, first to Naomi.

'I bid you welcome, worthy woman. Please, make yourself comfortable near to the fire.'

Naomi did not speak, but bobbed in obedience and went over to the flames.

Then the man turned to Ruth. 'And welcome to you, special one. I hope you will not disappoint us. Come, join your friend.'

Ruth sat next to Naomi. It was some time before the old man was resting comfortably on the fuel supply again. He had one of his men put another log on the fire. The brightness flared and the darkness retreated once more. The dull throb of the City pulsed behind them as they sat facing the old Miller.

'One of my kin has noticed you,' he said slowly to Ruth. 'He has spent a disproportionate amount of his time wearying my ear with talk of you. There are only two things I can do to prevent him from driving me mad: one is to cut out his tongue,' Salmon smiled, half-laughing as he spoke, 'the other is to meet you for myself and decide on a less painful course of action. That is why you are here. I am sure you have guessed that the man I am talking about is my son.'

He paused, watching Ruth closely, and Naomi shivered next to the small fire.

'Another log, please,' Salmon said. 'Immediately.'

After a further watchful pause, he continued, 'My son tells me that you are a special one; that you, only a girl, came from the furthest reaches of the desert. He says you have done the impossible. He says,' and the man spoke more slowly now, 'that you walked out of death itself to join us here in the magnificent City.'

Ruth felt his eyes firmly fixed on her, prompting her to respond.

'It is true, sir, that we came out of the desert,' she said, hardly daring to meet his gaze.

'And what were you doing in the desert?' he rejoined.

'We were chased there. Herders. We … they … wouldn't stop coming after us. We left the pastures and went into the desert.'

At this the old man nodded and folded his hands in front of him. Ruth found it surprisingly easy to tell him everything; the words came tumbling out.

'Yet here you are, having escaped both from ferocious enemies and from the merciless desert. How did you accomplish such a feat? How did you not dry up? How were you not burned under the hot sun?'

'We followed the way through the desert. On a path. A Wonderful Path.'

'Ah!' said the old man, raising his hands as if he had just smelled a delightful scent. 'A Wonderful Path. But tell me, child, you did not do this alone. Who was your companion?'

'My father, sir.'

'Your father. And where is your father?'

Salmon leaned towards her with a look of vivid compassion. For the first time in their conversation, Ruth felt permitted to raise her eyes to his.

'He's with Esar, in the tent on the mound.'

The old Chief did not seem surprised by the news.

Ruth shivered suddenly and Salmon raised his voice to the nearby men. 'Bring more fuel and blankets for these women.'

Within moments, Ruth felt the soft folds of a large and fine blanket settle on her shoulders. The light flared again and a suggestion of heat brushed her cheek.

'Your father is with Esar in the Sanctuary tent. My dear child, I have no adequate words of comfort for you. But let that be; we have matters that demand our attention.'

He inclined his head to one side and called into the darkness. 'Boaz? Come to me, my son. There you are. Sit by me, please.'

The young man stepped into the light and took his place on the floor beside his father. He positioned himself with his father on his left and Ruth on his right, so that he could look at each as they spoke. For the moment, he kept his eyes fixed on Ruth. He appeared much as he had at their first meeting, although his clothes were of an even greater quality than before, as befitting the son of the highest Miller Chief. He did not yet wear a turban, but kept his hair knotted behind his ears, and neither did he have a full beard.

Ruth looked closely at his face and, across the distance between them, saw into his eyes. They seemed to speak in whispers of pride mixed with expectation, as if something wonderful could happen at any moment.

Salmon glanced at Boaz, gestured at Ruth and spoke again.

'Show me,' he said.

Chapter Eight

BOAZ ROSE TO HIS FEET and approached Ruth.

'Please stand,' he said, holding out his hand.

Warily she took it and climbed to her feet. He led her to the edge of the firelight, next to where Salmon sat, and let her hand go. Then he bent down and picked up one of the tightly bound logs of grass straw that fed the flames. Unbinding an end, he took the frayed log and moved backwards and forwards in front of the fire, sweeping a large area of sand free of footprints. Puzzled, Ruth looked to Naomi who signalled by her expression that she did not understand the evening's strange events either. Boaz stood to one side of the freshly swept area and took a deep breath.

'Father, you see before you trackless sand in an arid part of the plain. You know in the wisdom of our fathers that, as no water reaches this place, life cannot come here. Not even the authority of Esar can command life to visit all the dry places that lie in the wide expanse under your eye. Yet the wisdom of our fathers has no place for this girl and a tribe like her people. We have allied ourselves and our people to the Minister's way for many generations, and we have found the alliance to be unevenly balanced. Too often, we work for little part of the plenty that they so freely promised us. I beg that you will watch me closely.'

Boaz paused in his carefully rehearsed speech, returned to Ruth and again offered his hand. She shot an urgent glance at Naomi, who returned it with a look of excitement. Boaz stepped between them and led Ruth to one side of the smoothed ground. Pausing only to nod reassuringly to her, he walked smartly across the cleanly brushed sand, drawing Ruth alongside him. Then he turned towards his father and spoke.

'I beg, Father, that we wait a while.'

He motioned that Ruth might sit if she wished. Salmon indicated for another log to be burned and, as the brightness once again pushed back against the ever-encroaching gloom, Ruth looked at the imprints they had made in the sand. She could see her own light and slender footprints alongside Boaz's deeper, broader tracks. Moments passed and many more stretched into the cold night. The fire died, was refuelled, and died again in a pattern that repeated several times. Still nothing seemed to happen. Ruth looked to Boaz, who was downcast.

'Son,' Salmon said, breaking the watchful silence, 'I do not see anything.'

'Father,' his son replied, 'I pray you will wait a while longer.'

Again the solemn party kept watch, unspeaking. It was a shorter length of time, however, before Salmon spoke again.

'I do not see anything, Boaz, and my bones feel the cold. Tell me, what am I looking for?'

'We are looking for a sign,' Boaz answered, the lost delight creeping back into his face. 'I believe that Ruth and her kind hold the key to something very precious; something that would lead us into a new way of life – a life that we could live to the full!'

'Could this "sign" free our people from the Minister?' Salmon returned.

Boaz nodded gravely.

'And do you suspect Ruth's father has been taken by the Minister for this same reason?'

Again, Boaz nodded, more gravely still.

'Is that why you were so eager for this girl to be brought before me?' the old man questioned again, and Boaz smiled.

The old Chief grinned broadly.

'You are the wisest of sons; come to my arms!' he cried, and dragged himself to his feet unaided.

Boaz stepped towards him and as they embraced, Ruth turned back to Naomi.

'What is going on?' she hissed, but Naomi did not reply, except by flashing her eyes and frantically waving the fingers of one hand in a gesture of 'don't ask'. Ruth did not obey. She turned back to the Chieftain and his son and addressed them both loudly.

'Sir, Boaz, what do you want with me?'

Salmon turned to her and was about to respond when Boaz caught his eye. Something unspoken passed between them and the old man slowly turned and took his place once again on the soft pile of fuel.

Boaz did not answer Ruth immediately, instead going to collect one of the straw logs. He extended one end into the flames and it caught quickly. When he held it at head height, it illuminated the other men standing around the small conference. He walked back to the lines of footprints and brought the fiery head of his torch down low, as close to Ruth's imprints as he dared. Feeling emboldened by her few words, Ruth felt free enough to step towards him.

'Ruth, you have already told us you came from the desert on the Wonderful Path,' Boaz said. 'What you have not told us is *how* the Path came to be. I wanted to show my father what it was that kept you alive in the desert – the same force that could free our people from near slavery under the Order.'

He paused, hoping Ruth would respond. When she did not, he pressed on, staring hard into her eyes.

'Ruth, I believe you are one of *them*. You are one of the ones who made the Path and can tell us about the real power in this desert. I believe you can tell us about Rain.'

'Rain!' choked Salmon in surprise. 'Now, there is a name I have not heard in years! This girl couldn't possibly know Rain. I heard about him from my grandfather when I was a boy! He would be the oldest man who ever lived!'

'Father, I doubt very much if he is the same man now as then. Perhaps his great grandson walks in the desert in his footsteps. I believe Ruth does indeed know of Rain. I believe she can teach us his ways.'

Boaz spoke with soft fervour and kept his gaze on Ruth, but she did not know what to say. As the moment stretched, the young man dropped his eyes from her.

'Well,' mused Salmon aloud, 'I suppose if there is a Rain, he could be the descendant of the man from my days. It is not uncommon for tribes to choose their leader by blood; ours would not be the only one like that. Tell me, son, how is it you know the name "Rain"?'

'I listened to the old songs and stories in the City. There is still a whisper of him among the oldest folk.'

'Sir,' came Naomi's voice out of the quiet, 'this isn't the only time Ruth's people have been here. They came long ago and I hold in my heart the truth of those days, passed on from mother to daughter, from the time of my many times-grandmother. For who can remember except the very old?' She looked at Boaz. 'Who, except those who listen to songs?'

Salmon stared at her and, as he spoke, his voice revealed his interest. 'Dear lady, do go on.'

Ruth bit back her own questions, sensing Naomi's coming revelation might answer them. Naomi smiled sadly.

'I do not think you would thank me to tell the full tale of those days. I will just say that I believe there is a Rain because I could have been one of his people, if only fate had trod a different route across the desert. Rain came to the City with his people. The singers of songs say he was returning to it as he had founded it long ago, but I do not know about that. When he came to the City, strange and wonderful things happened. Curious grasses with broad, soft and sweet-smelling leaves grew up everywhere. Tough little plants grew quickly where there had only been dust, and from them sprang blood-red berries dripping with colour and juice. The plains that had produced only dusty, brittle grass burst into colours unheard of.

'And there was more water than was needed for drinking. There was enough to make the mud bricks from which your house is built. There was enough to wash the dust off your face at the end of the day. They say you could pour it from a gourd into a skin bowl to wash your face but,' and she laughed as she spoke, 'if you held the gourd up high above the bowl, when you let the water fall, it would split the sunlight! The water would show all the colours of the sun! Who has seen such things?'

Naomi laughed again brightly, as if these were her own memories, and those around her who listened felt lifted out of themselves for a moment.

She continued, 'These people were neither Herders nor Millers. They were a Third Tribe. They were strange and different, yet they had some unusual lore about growing grasses and finding water. When they tended the land, the grasses grew thick and green. The fields were not grey and brown like ours, but became bright green at times and dark green at others. The Millers and Herders forgot their quarrels and walked among the grass as if they were friends. The old songs say that you could stand at one end of the valley and see nothing but green, and when the wind blew up, white seeds would fly over the land. The earth was not dry and dusty but dark and rich. The scent of it, mixed with the leaves, made you feel alive.'

There she paused, unable to go on.

Boaz spoke next. 'Some things you say I have heard in the songs and some are new to me. Yet you were not there. How do you know of all this?'

Naomi turned her head towards him, as if hearing the sound of his voice was a strange and new experience. She spoke slowly and sadly, as one newly awoken from a good dream.

'This is my memory, given to me by my mother from her mother down the ages. I remember those days and they feed me.'

'You have not told all,' Salmon interrupted, excited beyond patience by a story he had not heard. 'What became of Rain and his people?'

'The Order murdered them. Or, at least, the Order murdered Rain, his Chiefs, and many of the men. They were staked out under the hot sun to burn in the midday heat. They roasted to death. Some of Rain's remaining people escaped into the desert but nearly all of the women who remained were forced to marry into the City's tribes. They became the mothers and grandmothers of Herders and Millers. They were instructed to forget the ways of Rain. But they did not forget.'

Ruth saw in Naomi's eyes a fierce determination that she had not noticed before in the older woman. They flicked up towards Ruth and transfixed her.

'The Order took your father, Ruth,' Naomi declared gently. 'They took him when he came off the strange desert path. And I am so afraid.'

Ruth's voice gagged for an instant in her throat before she found it. 'You think they will *kill* my father?' she cried.

Naomi did not need to nod her reply. Ruth felt her innards writhe; she sensed hot pinpricks on her face and she wanted to be sick. She had been so hopeful of seeing Dan tonight, yet had been so quickly swept up by the strange turns of Boaz's speech and Naomi's story that she had quite forgotten him. And now, only now, Naomi hinted that she feared he would be burned to death.

'But he isn't one of them!' she entreated Naomi and the others. 'He isn't one of the Third Tribe! Neither of us is!'

'You have to be!' Boaz blurted out, confused and surprised by her words.

He snatched up another log and thrust the tip into the fire. It caught immediately and the young man twisted quickly back to the area he'd carefully swept before leading Ruth to walk over it. He strode to the lines of footprints and brought the flaming torch down to within a few hands' width of the sandy surface. Illuminated in the fleeing darkness, Ruth could see his heavier footprints next to hers. They looked unremarkable. Boaz stared wide-eyed at them, searching for something he could not see.

He turned back to Ruth, anger rising in his voice.

'You are one of them! Where is the water? Why do you hold back?'

Ruth stepped away, mutely afraid of this change in the gentle Boaz.

'If you're not one of them,' he continued, his voice hollowing with disillusionment, 'why do you wear this? This is wool – from *their* flocks!'

As quick as thought, Boaz snatched his free hand forward and tore the wool scarf from Ruth's head. Her hair fell down around her face, partially hiding her frightened eyes.

'I'm not who you think I am!' she sobbed. 'I'm a Miller, born of Dan, child of Millers!'

Boaz paused, his face displaying a conflict of emotions. Gentleness returned to his eyes. He ran the wool through his fingers, seemingly unable to continue. After a moment he stammered his apology and held the fine cloth up to Ruth as kindly as he could.

'Forgive me. I have behaved badly,' he said. 'I am sorry you are not who I thought you were.'

'This does not belong to me,' Ruth replied. 'It's Naomi's.'

Boaz turned towards the older woman.

'Where did you get this?' he hissed at Naomi, confused yet still angry.

'It was passed down from mother to daughter since *they* came, long ago,' she explained, evenly. 'It is all I have, but I gave it to you,' Naomi continued, pushing Boaz's arm back towards Ruth. 'Take it from him.'

Ruth put out her hands to take the cloth and, the instant her fingers touched the soft, woven surface, Boaz let go.

A man stepped quickly out of the darkness to Salmon's side and whispered something in his ear. The old Chief raised his head to address his son and the two women.

'We are about to receive visitors. The Minister, himself, is coming here now. What has been said tonight cannot be made known. None of you will speak. Do not disobey me in this.'

He thought for an instant and spoke again. 'There is only one way out of this. My son, pick up the cloth. Ruth, kneel. Naomi, stand to one side of her. Do it now.'

They moved quickly, and arranged themselves as the old Chief instructed. Ruth's heartbeat throbbed in her ears as she waited in the agony of expectation for what might happen next.

Boaz leaned towards her as far as he could and whispered softly, 'I'm truly sorry, Ruth. Forgive me. I rested my hopes on you without even bothering to understand who you are. I had … I had something for you.'

His words faltered, as if he did not know how to proceed. She looked up at him, glad for the distraction from her own nerves, and encouraged him with her eyes to continue. Boaz reached into the folds of his robe and pulled out a cloth that, when unwrapped, protected two short wooden staves. They were thin, weather-beaten and probably very old. He carefully enclosed them in the cloth again and handed them to Ruth.

'Put them away now, out of sight. I'll try to see you again in the fields. We'll talk then. Keep them safe and unseen.'

Ruth nodded, but immediately her attention was drawn to the far edge of the fire's light where a party of men had just emerged. They were eight in number, all robed in the black cloth of the Order. Esar was at the head.

Dan was nowhere to be seen.

'I hope we're not interrupting anything, Salmon,' Esar began pleasantly. 'Though this is a strange time to meet. What a lot of fuel you will use for light and heat! It is so dark.'

He gestured at one of his men to add fuel to the fire. The light immediately flared and, as it did so, Esar seemed suddenly to notice Ruth, Naomi and Boaz arranged in their strange drama. Salmon looked on in silence, his eyes everywhere.

Esar acknowledged Boaz first, and then nodded to Naomi. Ruth he ignored.

'Boaz, are congratulations in order? This looks very much like a betrothal! Only,' he added, looking back to Salmon, 'I do not recall authorising a betrothal. Perhaps my memory is failing me, Chief Salmon, but I do not believe you have negotiated the right to obtain this property,' and he waved his hand towards Ruth, 'for your son by marriage.'

Esar let the point hang in the air for a moment and then continued, 'Because that is what this meeting is about, isn't it? A marriage?'

Salmon waited, and then replied without the least hint of hurry, 'Yes, Minister, we are negotiating a dowry ahead of a proposed betrothal. It has not happened yet. You have joined us at the close of tonight's business. We have not sued for permission because the time is not right. I am very glad you have come, Minister, because we need to involve the girl's father from here onwards.' Salmon craned his head to see who was among Esar's party. 'Her father is currently in your care, is he not? Did you not bring him?'

'He is not here,' Esar answered. 'He remains in our care for the moment, but it matters not. It was unnecessary for him to attend tonight's *unexpected* meeting because we have been doing some negotiation of our own. Your evening is wasted. Dan has already agreed to give his daughter to another. To one of his brothers. One of the Order. Salmon, your son will have to take a wife elsewhere.'

Naomi foresaw the girl's reaction, so she grabbed Ruth's hand

and gave it a sharp tug to distract her from speaking up. Ruth recovered herself and opened her mouth to protest, but another pull on her hand, coupled with a withering glare from Naomi silenced her. Salmon spoke again.

'Which of these is the fortunate man?'

'Haman,' Esar pronounced, 'our latest Initiate into the Order.'

At his name Ruth's mind raced back over the strange days in the City to their arrival. So much had happened, she had almost nothing but vague impressions. The memories were of blood; of the wet snap and reek of breaking bones; of cries; the violence of feral men. Then they cleared and she saw him, simultaneously emerging from the darkness of her memory and limping out of the night's blackness into the fire's illumination.

Before her stood a half-broken man, reeling on a splinted leg and clutching at his side where hidden injuries uncoiled. His face was torn with pain and anger and the living threat of revenge burned behind his eyes. He was a wreck of a man, wrapped in the black cloth of the Order. Esar seemed delighted with him.

For the first time that evening, the Minister spoke to Ruth.

'You are *reparation* for the sins of your father. Payment,' he added, as she did not seem to understand, 'for the unjust injuries inflicted upon Haman when you arrived here.'

Without hesitation or a moment's thought, Boaz spoke up.

'If it's a question of payment, can she be redeemed by a greater payment?' he called to the Minister, emphasising the last two words.

Esar ignored him and Salmon did not show any reaction.

Boaz tried again. 'Are you prepared to negotiate?'

Esar, amused rather than surprised, only gave it a moment's thought.

'No.'

He turned to leave with the Order members, but for a third time Boaz was insistent.

'If you will not negotiate, will you set the price?'

Esar turned back to him. 'You can redeem her, but these are my terms: for every man, woman and child that makes up your people, you will offer one bag of bread, two bags of flour and six bales of straw. What you cannot produce, you can obtain by trading with the Herders. Finally, water taxes for all Millers will double. Permanently.'

He smiled as he said this, staring past Boaz into the shocked face of Salmon.

Then he was gone into the night, but from out of the darkness he called, 'You have two days to answer me! Goodnight!'

Salmon was incensed. Through gritted teeth he hissed at Boaz, 'Foolish boy! Will you ruin us? You can't pay for this! *We* can't pay!'

Boaz acknowledged his father's anger with a glance, but he turned to Ruth and in a low, insistent voice said, 'We'll talk more. Go now, and don't worry. Third Tribe or not, I don't want you married to Haman!'

He smiled lamely, and then went back to his father to placate him. Ruth watched Boaz go to the old man, who slapped his son smartly across the ear. She thought that was the end of the discussion, but the quiet, furtive argument and negotiation went on.

Naomi led Ruth back through the night to the City. The dry frost of the desert darkness had undermined the heat of the day and spread unseen across the sand. Ruth and Naomi moved quickly to avoid the cold, but Ruth was more anxious to get inside their little house to shut out the weirdness of the evening, the Order and the talk of the Third Tribe. It had been too much for her to anticipate, too much to understand. Naomi, Esar and Boaz each seemed to have separate plans for her and her life in the City. Whom could she trust? Salmon was unreadable, and Naomi's story was not fully told. Boaz had tried to expose her to Salmon as the keeper of some deep secret that could give the Millers a great advantage over the Herders and the Order if it came to a war. He had been so zealous, so intense, that a seed of fear had been planted in her. If he misdirected his passion, it could destroy the careful balance of peace in the City.

Yet he had also been gentle and reassuring. He had mastered his emotions, and he had given her a gift which she had yet to look at more closely. In the morning, when there would be sufficient light, Ruth decided she would inspect the strange pair of little sticks to see if she could work out their meaning.

Ruth and Naomi were soon among the outer tents and then the houses of the City. Ruth noted the dull thump and beat of the settlement's intimidating energy; there was no stillness to this night as there had been on her exhilarating and impulsive night walk east towards the dunes. Then, the City had slept soundly, as though it had never slept before. This night, like some others, was feverish – the township seemed to moan and turn in its trench like a sickling, uncomfortable, inconsolable and troubled.

But things were happening in the darkness. Esar was about his business and this concerned Ruth. She was relieved to get into the low house and dissolve underneath the blankets in attempted sleep. Naomi did not speak. She seemed glad not to, and for once Ruth agreed.

Before she slipped under the covers, Ruth carefully laid Boaz's small cloth bundle containing the two rods to one side, next to the clay cup Naomi had given her, so that she would not roll onto them and break them in the night.

Ruth awoke early. When she turned to look at Naomi, she saw the older woman's eyes were open and fixed on her. They greeted each other but said no more. Ruth felt a number of questions rise in her but she could not quite form them properly, and was afraid they would tumble out in a torrent of misapprehension. The two of them dressed and readied themselves for the Gift ceremony. Naomi lifted the hem of the door drape to leave, but Ruth could hold the questions in no more.

'Naomi …' she began, and Naomi hushed her.

'Ruth, there is so much to say after last night. I don't know what you must be feeling but let's have the Gift together, and then we'll talk. Please don't think badly of me.'

Her voice trailed off as she fought with her desire to say more. Ruth nodded, and turned away to pick up the clay cup that she had left next to Boaz's sticks. She crouched to pick it up, but her hand was drawn instead to the rough staves. Her fingers ran over them and she felt the coarse grain of the wood. She knew it had once been alive and growing, and the polished shimmer that the sand had wrought in places along the hafts suggested the twinkle of moisture and life. She felt that the pair of sticks had come to her through many owners and across great distances. The City did not seem so huge and overpowering; there was, or had been, life outside its boundaries. Beneath her, the ground suddenly felt very deep and broad. The Minister did not rule everywhere. Ruth cursed herself for forgetting so quickly about everything that lay outside the shadow of the City's central spike.

'Coming?' called Naomi from the doorway as she disappeared outside.

Ruth dropped the sticks back onto the cloth wrap, snatched up the cup and followed her. The men were already walking out to the fields so the two of them hurried towards the City centre. The other women were forming the line around the holy mound and they took their places. Ruth kept her eyes down, occasionally flashing a glance upwards to see if Dan or the terrible Haman were with the Order's group. To her disappointment and relief, neither men were with the Minister and his assistants.

Esar did not acknowledge her, but merely droned his chant with seemingly sightless eyes. The ritual went as it had done before, but by now Ruth had grown used to the bitter fluid that the Order distributed. She swallowed it with just the slightest of grimaces and only lifted her eyes when the black-clad men moved on.

She and Naomi went back to the house as quickly as they could, both eager and anxious to discuss the previous night's events. Naomi drew back the door curtain and stepped inside with Ruth right behind her. She went straight to her small arrangement of alcoves and shelves to stow her precious clay cup away carefully, and Ruth returned to her corner to do the same, stepping over the two sticks that she had put down on her way out. As she did so, her toe brushed the edge of the cloth, which lay underneath the staves. The material was cool; quite cold. The night's chill had passed and the sun was rising; this cloth was unnaturally cool.

She bent down to place the cup somewhere safe so that she could investigate properly, and suddenly caught a scent she recognised from a time or place she couldn't quite bring to mind. There was a quality in the air and a heavy richness that denied the savage dryness of the desert atmosphere. There was a taste and texture to it, yet it was fresh and pleasant to breathe.

Ruth left the cup to one side and turned fully to the staves and the cloth. The sticks lay upon the material, one across the other in an X shape, just as she had dropped them. The cloth itself looked darker than first thing this morning. Ruth touched it and withdrew her hand quickly. It was wet. She lifted a corner carefully with the tips of her fingers and the sticks rolled off onto the sand with a light clatter. Ruth lifted the rest of the cloth and held it aloft. Moisture ran down from the top corner by her fingers to the opposite corner in partially concealed rivulets, following the weave and threads of the cloth. The moisture pooled at the end and a large drop swelled until it was too big to remain, and it fell onto the sand below.

Thud.

Ruth's heart quickened and her mind shuddered and danced. She looked in fearful amazement at the floor beneath the suspended cloth. The droplet had not fallen on dry sand; the ground was dark with moisture, no longer dusty, and where the centre of the cloth had been the sand had begun to subside in its heaviness. A small hollow had developed underneath the material … and water had collected in it.

Chapter Nine

RUTH LOWERED THE CLOTH and replaced it on the wet floor without speaking or giving any sign to Naomi that something was wrong. With a trembling, hurried hand, she picked up the two staves Boaz had given her and tucked them into her robe out of sight. Before she turned to Naomi, she retrieved her clay cup and slipped it beneath the cloth so that it might catch some of the rising water. Ruth did not understand why she didn't simply show Naomi the tiny wellspring that had appeared in her house, nor did she know how she could hide it if it became any larger, but something within her whispered to her that she must not. Terrible things could happen if this strange occurrence became known to the Order, and Ruth remembered the stories of midday burnings under the irresistible sun. Yet water was water, and it must be caught, preserved and used sparingly.

Even so, no matter what she saw in visions, water did not bubble up from the depths of the earth; nor did it fall from the sky. Ruth felt pulled in many directions, torn, and to end the internal dialogue she turned away from the hidden spring. However, she sat directly in front of it so that she might hide it from Naomi.

The older woman was still rearranging her corner of brick shelves and alcoves, but when she sensed Ruth's eyes upon her she turned to her immediately. Ruth did not hear much of what she said. She was aware that Naomi spoke about Esar and Dan and Haman, of marriage, and of Boaz and Salmon's strange meeting, but she could not draw her mind from the water that was a few hands' breadth away. She could sense its cool freshness; she could smell it changing the air in the low, dry house. Her throat silently rasped for it; her tongue longed for the moisture; on some unfathomable level, beyond mere survival, it moved her.

Naomi was animated in her talk. Somehow Ruth managed to smile, nod and frown at appropriate moments.

When she finally came back to the conversation, she registered Naomi saying, 'Then we're agreed. When the sun is high you will visit Boaz and plead his help. I will do the same with Salmon.'

Ruth did not reply and struggled to know what response to make. Naomi tried to reassure her.

'Don't worry. Even though Boaz is disappointed you're not one of the Third Tribe, I'm sure we can get him to come around. We'll stop this marriage to Haman yet! He will not have you. I'd rather die than let him have you.' Naomi grimaced as she mentioned the twisted, menacing man's name. 'Who knows where this could lead? If Boaz redeems you from this bargain, then who knows? Oh, we must go! It is time.'

They left the house without looking back and hurried towards the fields where the herds awaited them.

'It may be that we'll see him when we pass by some of the Millers this morning. That'll make it easier to find him when the sun approaches its peak. You can speak to him then,' Naomi continued as they went. 'Boaz, as the Chief's son, will be watching over the workers in the fields. Let's look out for him.'

Ruth and Naomi took their flock and drove it around the City in the familiar grazing loops of recent days. It was not until late in the morning, when they were preparing to go to their shelters, that they finally saw Boaz. He was not out in the fields, but came from the City directly towards where they were grazing their animals on the eastern side. He had another man with him whom he had evidently instructed to help Naomi with the goats. Boaz approached Ruth.

'Good news, Ruth,' he smiled. 'You will be a Miller once more. Come.'

He gestured back to where he had walked from – the City.

Ruth hesitated, unsure exactly where in the City Boaz would take her. Naomi spoke up in an attempt to cover the girl's uncertainty.

'Don't worry about me, Ruth. I can manage; I've got some help. You go on!' she said, smiling broadly.

Ruth dropped her eyes and stepped towards the Chief's son, unwilling to raise her hopes of escaping Haman. Boaz gestured again towards the City and together they found their way back to the main path on the side that would take them west, towards the centre. But when they were within the line of tents and out of sight of the man he'd left to help Naomi, Boaz seemed to change. Thus far they had strolled quite casually, but now Boaz paced off the path, turning suddenly north with a new excitement that showed itself in his voice.

'Ruth, come with me, please!' he pleaded, putting out his hand to her. 'Let's go this way.'

Ruth did not give him her hand, so he strode away from the path without her. She cast her eyes up to see the position of the sun. It was getting very high; they would have to find shelter soon. Why would Boaz take her around the north of the City at such a strange time? She followed with nervous interest, but it was not long before she felt the temperature of the sand rising; soon it would become unbearably hot. Boaz seemed to be pretending not to notice. He led her towards the north east side of the settlement, to where the tents were more derelict than elsewhere and the houses seemed to have been dismantled. Ruth hopped behind him on the burning sand.

Suddenly Boaz ducked into a low tent on the very edge of the

City. Ruth followed and found herself in a well-tended and comfortable shelter. The floor was even and recently dug out; the frame of ancient wood, bone and twine seemed secure and the sand-bleached fabric was carefully patched. There were skins half buried on one side of the floor to keep their liquid contents cool. In the centre was a woven mat of grass stalks. There were even some of the precious bales, the kind that Salmon had burned with such breathtaking extravagance. Next to them were firestones, and some kindling of cut hair and grass heads.

Boaz expected Ruth to comment on what she saw, but she didn't. Instead he guessed at what she might be thinking and responded to that.

'I brought all this here myself, and – yes – my father's people know about this place and they know I come here. But they're not expecting me to come here today. They expected me to bring you straight to them before the burning hours began. Oh, don't worry. They want to make you one of their own – a Miller, I mean … but I wanted to speak to you first, and to ask you some questions. Maybe I can answer some of *your* questions?'

Ruth did not reply, still acutely suspicious of Boaz and his intentions. He uncovered one of the buried skins and handed it to her. Then he fetched one for himself, sat down at the far end of the tent on the edge of the mat and began to drink.

Ruth felt the weight of the skin in her hand. It was heavy. She sat down, not quite opposite Boaz, and opened the end. The initial breath from the unsealed skin brought her the scent of fresh water, much like the sweet smell that had lingered in the air around the little well in Naomi's house. This was good water, if a little bitter. She drank, and the same passionate craving for life beyond survival bolted through her, and for the first time since leaving the Wonderful Path, she felt her thirst diminishing.

Ruth drank as quickly as she could and in a moment had consumed half the skin's contents. Yet as soon as she stopped, the heat and dry dust prickled her throat. An acrid sourness clung to her mouth, but it was still good water.

'Thank you,' she said, recognising the value of Boaz's gift to her. Then, after a pause she asked, 'Where did this water come from?'

'As a Miller Chief, my father must look after his people,' Boaz replied. 'He buys water from Esar at great cost, just like everybody else, and so Esar can keep his charges high. There is no other source of water and my father has declared that his people will never go thirsty as long as he lives. He has kept that promise so far, and that is why he is still the Chief. A younger man could fight him and win, but no one can stand up to the Order like my father.'

Boaz's words fell easily from his lips in a wave of admiration and well-earned respect.

'The water you've just had is from Salmon's own supply. Unlike the Herder Chief, Father helps our people buy water, but he can only afford second-rate quality in great enough quantity for them. He saves enough to buy a little of the clear, clean water for himself. And for me.'

Ruth held the skin up before her. 'Esar *sells* this?' she said in disbelief.

'Yes, of course. Didn't Naomi tell you? All the water she's given you she's had to buy.'

'Oh,' Ruth murmured, thoughtfully. 'Where does Esar get it?'

'His palace. The place on the hill. The *holy mound*. It is from there that he summons water to the fields and causes the grasses to grow. Only the Order members are permitted to go inside. I don't know how he does it, but Esar can raise water out of the sand to bring life to this plain. It would be all desert, otherwise.' He paused. 'Anyway, you should know all this. Didn't Naomi tell you anything?'

'She did, but I missed some of it. It's all so strange.'

'Is it? Is it, Ruth? Yes, I suppose it must be strange to you. I know you're not one of them – one of the Third Tribe. If you were, you would be used to bringing water out of the dust.'

Boaz sighed and Ruth softened.

'I'm sorry that I'm not one of them,' she said. 'I'm a Miller. I'd never heard of Rain before yesterday evening.'

'It's all right. I should have guessed. Little things – quirks of behaviour. I suppose you're just different from how I imagined them. I've been following stories about Rain for some time, years actually, and when the plants appeared, coming up out of the south, it was like a dream. Then you came. You and your father. I was so keen to meet real followers of Rain that I forgot to wait and see if you were his people at all. When Esar took your father, I thought that was it! I thought the Minister knew Dan was one of the Rain-men and what you could both mean for the City …'

His voice trailed into the silence of his unspoken thoughts. Then he began again.

'You've not shown any signs in the few days you've been here, but … I don't know … last night, I thought you would bring the water out of the desert. You'd show what it is you – or rather *they*,' he corrected himself, 'do when you walk the Wonderful Path.'

'What do they do?'

Boaz looked at her sideways, half hoping that she was just playing with him and really knew. But she wasn't; she didn't know.

'You yourself know what it was like on that Path. It led here, and things started to grow. When that happened, the Minister declared it was his doing, and he'd decided to bless the City. But things kept on growing and growing and before long there was enough food for everyone. And it was more than just grass. Strange, small seeds – berries – grew on odd plants, and they became soft and full of sweet water. The very day you arrived, the Minister instructed the Order to pull the plants up. They stopped growing straight away.'

'Why would he bless and then destroy his own blessing?' Ruth asked.

'Maybe it wasn't *his* blessing,' Boaz said, with a mischievous smile.

'Then who …?' Ruth began, but Boaz had already answered her by laughing with delight.

'*Them!* The Third Tribe! *They* did it – and you followed them! Do you see what this means?' he grinned.

Ruth shook her head uncertainly, and Boaz calmed himself. He paused suddenly in the rush of his excitement and seemed to slip away somewhere else, recalling others' memories that he had learned by heart. To Ruth he appeared to grow, as if gazing from the heights of the old pasturelands down onto the vast and beautiful landscape. Slowly, almost tasting the words, Boaz spoke.

'The old singers say that the burning sand will become a pool, the thirsty ground bubbling springs. Where death once walked, grass will grow. And a highway will be there; it will be called the Way, the Wonderful Path.'

Boaz talked in a pulsing flow of sounds, and Ruth was not sure if he was speaking to her or repeating the words for himself. The words felt old and yet fresh; new yet familiar; and more supple and wonderful than the brittle chants of her nomadic tribe's evening firesides. Her short years seemed long, and as she focused on the gaping void between her songs and his, she was suddenly touched by the deepest ache she had ever known. Boaz's words filled her mind and she felt a surge of unbidden emotion. She forced it back down into the pit of her stomach and had a strong need to speak, just to distract herself. Then the sound of Boaz's voice dissipated and the world was dry dust once more.

'Well, I'm not one of those … one of *them*,' she said. Her defensiveness rose of its own accord. 'So what do you want from me?'

'Nothing,' he replied. 'Nothing except to help you. The thought of you marrying Haman makes me sick. He is a cruel man. I want to stop it. You are not one of *them*, so maybe you could be one of us. A Miller.'

'I am already a Miller! As I've tried to tell everyone since I arrived!'

'I know, I know. I'm sorry. I meant that you could be known as a Miller *again*. People think you're one of them, you know – one of Rain's people. Anyway, I want to make you a Miller.'

Boaz stopped short, as if there was more to say. He shifted to one side awkwardly, picked up a skin and drank deeply. He handed it to Ruth and she spoke hesitantly.

'Naomi said you might want to "redeem" me. What does that mean?' she said.

Boaz half blushed, and answered quickly. 'It's a bit complicated. Your father has given you to Haman. I don't know why or for what price. Haman has the right to you. If I were to redeem you, it would mean that I'd have to buy Haman off so that he'd give up his right to you.'

He paused, thinking, but could not find his way around the subject. 'I'd have to buy you,' he said.

Ruth nearly spat the water she was drinking onto the tent floor. She managed to control herself but instead almost inhaled it, and began to choke. Boaz guessed what she was going to say.

'Look, I don't really like it, but I *really don't like* the thought of you being given to Haman. Do you want to be mauled by that beast? Am I worse than he is?'

Ruth's choking subsided sufficiently for her to answer. 'No. I'm sorry. I just don't want to be traded at all. Out in the pastures, people got married through a kind of agreement with some sort of dowry, but it wasn't quite like this!'

'I know. I'm trying to make the best of it. The problem is that Esar thinks you're one of the Third Tribe. Your price will be high.'

'So we'll have to tell him I'm not.'

'No, that would be bad,' Boaz responded thoughtfully. 'Very bad. Remember that they have your father and they think he is from the Third Tribe, too. If they discover he is not, I don't know that you'd ever see him again.'

Ruth blinked in horror. The sound of Boaz's words was like

looking directly into the late morning sun. She felt blinded by pain, and she could not protect herself from the fire. It seemed as though the world had been taken from her and she was left fumbling in a place of intense light and dark and burning. She had hidden herself from the brutal reality of Dan's deadly incarceration since the Minister had taken him, but now the dark shapes of fear crept silently out from the corners of her heart and revealed themselves. Even so, her fierce impulse to act overtook the paralysis they tried to force on her.

'We must do something!' she cried, casting her eyes wildly about the tent for something – anything – to use as a weapon; anything to pin her hopes to. There was nothing.

'No, Ruth, we can't fight. Or at least we can't start a fight. The Herders would side with the Minister to win his favour. They would win; we can't match the Order and the Herders together. We must try to buy you and perhaps buy Dan, too, if he is still alive. Although,' and Boaz spoke to himself more than to Ruth, 'buying you will bankrupt us all.'

He hardened his resolve. 'Still, we must try. This is what I will do: I will take my inheritance from my father, the Chief, and I will redeem you. This will mean that we may have to be married. But I will find enough to meet the price.'

'Can you get enough?'

'I *will*,' he said with steely determination.

'But what if you can't?' Ruth insisted.

'Then I will make trouble. If I can't buy you, I will buy time. If Esar thinks he can get more wealth by putting the marriage off a few days without actually putting it in danger, then he will. In that time I will make this all right. But,' he added, 'we won't need that time.'

He took a last gulp from the skin and reburied it. 'It's nearly time to go. Just one more thing: please don't go walking about at night any more. I worry that the Minister is watching you. If he catches you breaking the curfew, all will be lost. I don't want to think about what he'd do to you.'

'Is that what you were doing out that night? Watching me?' Ruth demanded, accusingly.

Boaz did not seem able to answer. Instead, he appeared confused and struggled to explain.

'No … I … I don't know, I wasn't watching you,' he frowned. 'I was just … out. Something was going on but I didn't know what.' He sighed. 'I went to look to the east. I don't know why.'

He straightened up and moved across to the door. Lifting the hem, he assessed the position of the sun and the glow of heat from the exposed sand.

'I think we'll be all right now.'

Then, he turned to look at Ruth and said, 'Trust me. I will do everything to stop this. Just trust me.'

Ruth and Boaz made their way across the hot sand as the Cityfolk emerged from their hiding places. The people moved out to the fields again or to other duties, and the pair headed towards the Miller Chief's house where Ruth was quickly presented, and just as quickly sent out into the fields without much ceremony. There was work to be done, and Ruth found her hands falling into the old pattern of harvesting grass, although she worked slowly at first, adapting her movements to leave more stalk than she'd been used to. It would not be long before the Herders would tramp over this area and their goats would feed on what remained of the growth.

The Millers moved quickly, working alone. They were spread out across the broad smears of grass, their bodies hunched with busy arms, and each with a bag of collected grass heads flapping at one side. There was little opportunity to talk, but when Ruth periodically straightened up to stretch her back, she found others had fallen in with her rhythm and their looks and eyes seemed to be friendly enough. The work was tiring but not difficult, all of them having lived lives of this doubled up, half-stagger toil.

In the middle of the afternoon, a boy, much younger than Ruth, came around from Miller to Miller with skins of water.

'What's this?' she asked him.

He seemed unsure how to answer, as if she had asked a stupid question.

'Water,' he said.

'Where's it from? How much is it?' Ruth was worried.

'It's from the Chief. And you're earning it now. By working.'

Ruth drank and the water was bitter, but not too bad. The boy moved away to the next Miller.

The afternoon wore on. Ruth saw Boaz briefly. He worked for a short while but was soon fetched away by some business. Ruth hoped he was making plans to redeem her, and she fought the doubt within her by throwing herself into that hope. By the end of the afternoon she could think of nothing else. Boaz must succeed in finding enough money to redeem her from Haman. She silently vowed to take her life rather than give it to that twisted, crushed, hateful man. Under the orange smoulder of the receding sun, she shivered in terrible anticipation of hearing his voice, seeing his darkness and collapsing under his brutality.

Evening came with a dreadful inevitability and Ruth became inconsolable. Naomi worked at comforting her, labouring against the dual trials of grief and fear that shook the young girl. Ruth felt the pull to the east as an unnatural hush descended on the City, but the quiet made her cries all the louder and she buried herself into the bed cloths and tried to sleep. Her cup was still beneath the damp cloth and the staves were not far to one side, yet they lay forgotten in the sand. The noise of the City returned. Ruth slept, exhausted by fear.

She woke in the night. All was still, as if listening or waiting. Ruth looked up at the roof above her. The cloth was edged with silver in the moonlight, and the light filled the fabric; the moon must be very high. She was sure it had not yet risen when she had gone to bed, and she could have sworn it was not due to be high for some days.

She lay still, again listening to the pregnant silence and the waiting world. Something powerful but gentle seemed to be prompting her from within, so she pulled herself round and up onto one elbow. Then she lifted herself onto her knees, being sure to keep what warmth she had around her wrapped close in the bed cloth. She stretched out one leg, tentatively placed her foot on the cold floor and held it there. Moments passed; she did not move. Cold quivered through her foot and seeped into her ankle. The bed cloth seemed warm and inviting, and Naomi's breathing soothed her. She remembered Naomi's talk of murder, and thought fearfully of Haman lurking in the darkness. Then she recalled Boaz's words and his plan to save her. His plan seemed more tangible than the moonlight.

Ruth cast her eyes up, almost apologetically, at the silvered roof above her and sank back down again into the small space that had been her bed. She buried herself in the cloth and, as she disappeared into an empty, dreamless sleep, the sounds of the City returned and the silver light slipped away.

CHAPTER TEN

RUTH AWOKE IN THE GREY DARKNESS of the early morning to the sound of a disturbance. A woman nearby was weeping in long, low howls. Her cries were immediately answered by a man who roared incoherently. Their voices were joined by others and in almost no time, voices all over the City were crying, wailing and shouting. Even the far-off goats, sensing danger in the disturbance, could be heard bleating.

Ruth shot a glance at Naomi who was awake with wide and fearful eyes. They were framed by a face as white as frost. She was doing her best to suppress the shakes of pure terror that threatened to overcome her. Feet thudded past their door and the noise prompted Naomi to action. Spurred on by her panic, she scrabbled at the pots and cloths that held her supplies of food. She fumbled and struggled until Ruth, not sure what was happening, helped her.

Under the crying, shouting and wailing, Ruth cried, 'What's going on?'

'I don't know,' came the urgent reply. 'Something happened in the night.'

Naomi poured the few remaining red berries out of a pot next to a scrap of bread that lay on a cloth spread out before her.

'I woke in the night,' she continued. 'It was quiet but something was calling in the darkness. I wanted to look but I was afraid. And now this. I don't know what it was but I *felt* something going on. I had the same feeling once before only …'

Naomi looked up at Ruth and hesitated, suddenly seeming unable to choose her words well enough to tackle the difficult subject.

'That was when … that was the last time … your people were here.'

'My people …?' Ruth began, but Naomi cut her off.

'Ruth, listen to me. I believed you when you said you were a Miller, but you lied.' She raised her hand to hush the girl. 'I saw your cup. You drew water up into this house. I wanted to talk last night but you couldn't. Anyway that doesn't matter now.'

Ruth shot a glance over to the strange little well that had sprung up in her corner of the house. It was uncovered with the cloth folded and placed to one side. On top of the cloth, the staves lay next to one another. The cup was nowhere to be seen.

More voices joined the clamour outside and the sensation of panic and activity seemed to shock the low house.

Naomi continued, 'Don't ask me how I know that this disturbance is because of your tribe. I simply know deep down. I should hand you over to the Order but I will not. We have very little time. Eat this now,' she said, pouring the last of the goat's milk from a gourd into a cup and pushing the hastily assembled meal of bread and berries towards the girl. 'And then you must run. Ruth! Eat it!'

Ruth listened for a moment to the growing tumult and then looked hard into Naomi's face for some sign of betrayal, but she saw nothing; nothing but urgent, desperate love for her battling with almost overwhelming fear. She ate as quickly as she could while Naomi made further preparations for her escape.

Naomi leapt to her feet, grabbed Ruth's skin bag and dropped the folded cloth from the well, the staves and a bundle of food into it. She retrieved Ruth's cup from her alcove, considered it for a moment, then carefully lowered it into the bag. She felt for her own water skin and held it up.

'It has the water from your cup in it,' she said. 'It smelt so fresh. I wanted to keep it but … you must have it. Oh, Ruth, why did you lie?' she cried suddenly, but her look spoke of sadness and apology – as if this was all somehow her own fault.

Naomi dropped the gourd and broke down. Ruth jumped up and went to her.

'I'm sorry, Ruth, I'm so sorry,' she gasped through her sobs. 'I don't understand any of this. I feel as though I've failed in my care of you. And now you have to run away. You have to run; you have to run or they'll take you, they'll take you,' she repeated, her hands clenching into little bony fists.

Naomi continued to talk but it was more to herself than to Ruth. 'Maybe it's because you're still a child – only now you've got to go out into the desert without much water. I'm so sorry.'

'Please don't cry. It doesn't matter, I'll be all right,' Ruth replied, saying anything to placate her. She looked up to the doorway as the sound of more feet hurried by. 'Oh, please don't cry! If we're in danger we must go. *We* must go, now.'

Ruth pulled Naomi to her feet, grabbed her bag and the gourd and pushed back the sand-scourged cloth that hung over the doorway. People were darting in and out of the houses around her. Most seemed to be going north-west into the centre of the City. Taking her chance when it came, Ruth led Naomi out of the low house – but Naomi stopped immediately, staring in horror at the ground outside her door. There were footprints in the light, dusty sand. Ruth, neither looking nor caring, tried to drag her away but Naomi was rooted to the spot.

Ruth glanced down and noticed that the footprints were dark and well-defined, as if the broad feet that had made the impressions had been … wet. She bent down to touch the crumbling shapes, but pulled her hand back as Naomi began to kick them into nothing.

The older woman sprang into action, almost dancing with fear, as she frantically scuffed out the trail that led right to her door.

Ruth's eyes darted up and down the tracks that headed back the same way they had come: to and from Naomi's door, coming and going along the same path.

'I never dared dream I'd live to see these!' the older woman cried, hysterical. 'But if *they* see them they will kill us!'

'Naomi, there's no time! We must go now!' Ruth implored her.

She could hear more shouts rising over the roofs of the houses. People seemed to be coming towards where they stood. She heard the dull stamp of many feet on sand and lunged again for Naomi's hand. She caught the older woman off balance and pulled her between the low sandstone structures towards the outer ring of tents. They might not get to the far dunes without being seen, but they had no choice but to try.

Ruth ran east, sprinting where she could, hauling Naomi along with her and racing towards the rising sun. It was not yet above the dunes but soon it would fall over the wind-worn summits and flood the plain with light. If they made their break for the slopes then, Ruth thought, it might dazzle all who looked that way and cover their escape.

The two women moved as quickly as the older one could manage. They were soon slipping through the ring of tents towards the tufted blotches of pasture that broke up the desolate expanse between the settlement and the edge of the mighty dunes. A voice called a warning to the south and was answered by others; Ruth dragged Naomi away from the sound, turning sharply to the north. Swiftly they weaved their way left and right through the lines of tents but, to her surprise, Ruth found they were following what seemed to be a well-defined path. The sand was firm and easy to run on, and she saw that the dark, damp footprints that had stopped outside Naomi's door had trailed the same way.

She looked up. Two Ordermen were striding purposefully along one of the wider paths that led to the central spike of the City. She stopped dead and pulled Naomi down behind a tent as the men marched past. Then she got up into a crouch, ready to run when the way was clear. Naomi spoke.

'Ruth, did you see? Men from the Order are out, and they're armed. They had their truncheons! I was right – your people were here in the night and the Order will not stand for it. Ruth, we must get you away!'

Questions flooded Ruth's mind but her blood, crying out for flight and survival, quashed them in a surge of fear. Everything had changed. Boaz could not help and there were greater dangers than Haman.

Ruth realised her fear of the Order had grown quickly since they had taken her father. The men in dark robes had tamed the beastly goat-men and they excelled in instilling a new kind of fear, a kind that came from unseen cruelty. The unearthly conical horn that thrust up over the holy mound's dark tent was coldly sinister, but the members of the Order lurking beneath lent a twisted human shape to the feral brutality of the Herder folk. Haman seemed like the cruelty's runt when compared to the malignant Esar.

The moment to move came. Ruth pulled Naomi up again and dashed across the City's thoroughfare and in amongst the tents. She turned east once more and ran on. In both directions, coming and going along their route, the encrusted shapes of the same pair of feet went before and behind them as they ran. Whoever it was that wove through the City in the night, stopping outside their door, must have returned along the same route as they now travelled. Where her feet fell on the imprints, Ruth felt the cool, damp sand press against her skin. It invigorated her; she felt fresh and eager.

Then a new sensation arose within her, one that she could not have anticipated or imagined: it was a beautiful, flowing breath that streamed in through her nose and down into her very core. Its fragrance grew around her as she ran along the strange path and, as the sun broke over the eastern dunes, she felt Naomi's pace quicken unbidden beside her. Ruth shot her a glance and saw that the morning light made her look stronger, and both older and younger in one moment. The years fell from her as she ran, yet she looked ever the same; new but enduring.

Ruth looked back to the path and it turned north again. Feeling a strange confidence, she took her chances and followed it. The sense of cool refreshment grew in her and she went quicker than before, unseen by searching eyes.

But then, just when she felt she knew where she was going – out onto the eastern plain and to the safety of the far dunes – the path veered suddenly in towards the centre of the City. Fear writhed within her and Ruth's footsteps faltered.

Unswervingly, the imprints clearly marched into the City and directly towards the holy mound.

'No,' she murmured, half to herself. 'We can't go that way.'

Naomi looked along Ruth's gaze back towards the settlement, but she did not see what the girl saw.

'Of course we're not going that way!' she muttered. 'We're getting you safely away from here, not back into danger! Come on, let's keep going. We can go together. I want to leave all this.'

The two women left the path of footprints and continued east, through the last of the tents and towards the dunes. The ground was suddenly hard under their feet, and the compacted sand of the City's outer ring thudded into their legs and made their bones ache. When they reached the last knot of tents, they paused. Ruth cast a quick eye out onto the blotched pastureland, squinting in the low sun.

Fairly certain she could see no one on that side of the settlement, she turned and whispered to Naomi, 'The sun is up. Let's run now straight to the dunes. It's a long way, out in the open.'

Then Ruth stopped. She could suddenly see something new in her companion; a new strength, a new determination.

'I can do it,' the older woman whispered back, earnestly, 'but I don't think we can go together. I'm slowest – I must run first. If I'm seen then you can hide and I'm the only one who will get caught. If I am not seen, you can come after me. Then, if you are spotted, I have a head start and you can try to catch me up. Our chances are better that way, I think.'

Ruth nodded, smiling at Naomi's good sense.

Naomi continued quietly, 'Duck into one of these tents – no one will be in them now – and pull up the hem and watch. When I get half-way to the dunes, you come as fast as you can.'

Ruth slipped inside the nearest tent and did as she was told, lifting a tiny part of the hem away from the sand so that she could see out onto the plain. The sun was still dazzlingly low and she whispered a hoarse 'good luck' to Naomi, who was now crouching as low as she could. In a moment she was gone from the safety of the tents' low cover and out onto the unforgiving openness of the broad, flat valley bowl.

Hardly had she gone a stone's throw when a high, keen shout went up nearby and was immediately answered from all parts of the eastern side of the City. She had been spotted!

The sound of feet on sand thudded across the ground towards Ruth. A moment passed and she saw a dark shape dash out of the tent line onto the open plain – a member of the Order. The man ran after Naomi who, seeing the danger, fell shrieking in utter panic. Before Ruth could find her voice, he was on her, grabbing and punching and kicking her helpless, prone form. Four more black-clad Ordermen arrived and dragged their comrade off the seemingly unconscious woman. Two men hauled her upright and the party turned back towards the City's centre at a brisk, triumphant march.

Ruth panicked quietly under the cover of her tent. She tried to move but could not; she racked her brain to work out what to do, but found that only the same half-formed thought rose and died, then rose and died again. The draw of the distant dunes vanished, and before Naomi had been taken very far, Ruth knew that she could not leave her to the Order. Though she was friendless and alone, she would put herself between Naomi and the dark gaping mouth of the holy tent. If the woman who'd cared for her was taken inside, Ruth knew she would not return.

She ran her fingers over the internal ribbing of wood scraps and bone that formed the tent's skeleton. She did not know or care if this shelter was inhabited. Wasting no time, she found the longest, stoutest haft of wood and tore it out, leaving a broad split in the tent's flank that quickly collapsed into a wider hole. The stick was largely straight, with a slight bend at one end and it varied in width. She held it naturally at the thinner end, where it was the thickness of her wrist; the other end was slightly wider, more like her elbow. The weapon was shorter than her outstretched arm but it had a balance of weight that encouraged the arm to swing it. It was almost as if the ancient wood, held in place for so long as a piece of tent, had come to thirst for movement and the eager strokes of battle. Ruth tested it, slicing it through the air. A dark sensation of pleasure swept up inside her.

She left the tent and ran parallel to the road along which the Order members had taken Naomi, moving quickly, head down, ever listening for the sound of hurried feet, and watchful for dangers ahead and around. She approached the line of houses that marked the inner circle of the City. Her eyes darted everywhere, terrified but keen for an encounter with the dark-clad enforcers of Esar's law.

In a moment she could hear the clamour of a mob, and then saw a great mass of people – perhaps the City's entire population – pressing forward around the holy mound. Esar was atop the small dune, waving his arms amid the cries and bellows of the crowd below him. He was appealing for calm. None came, and he turned his back on the people.

He picked up the Gift Jug that stood by his feet and held it close to himself. Still the people did not quieten. He stepped towards the tent's doorway, which hung lazily in the gathering heat of the morning. A few in the crowd guessed his meaning, but the majority continued to shout. He took another step. More of the crowd realised what he meant, but they were few. He took still another step. This time he held the Gift Jug out at arm's length and poured some of the dark waters onto the dusty ground. The fat, dark drips twinkled as they fell, and when they struck the dune they shattered messily. Sand stuck to their glassy sides before the liquid sank broodingly into the dust and vanished into the air. Many in the throng were instantly hushed, transfixed by the perverse beauty of Esar's act, and the threat that lay within it.

Esar took another step towards the doorway, then a second and a third. The crowd's murmur dissolved but, when he did not turn back and kept walking, their voice grew again in volume.

Only now it was very different. Gone was the anger and outrage; it came as a pleading, imploring wail of unified voices.

Ruth knew, across the gap between them now filled with desperation and fear, that Esar was enjoying the moment. He had changed their anger back into dread and he could toy with them. Turning to them he smiled, as would a benevolent father at his disgraced favourite.

'You are all early!' he said, with mock surprise. 'I am not ready to give you the Gift yet. You have disturbed me with your shouting.' He frowned at them, disappointed. 'Who can tell me what the cause of all this is?'

His question was not to be answered except by Chiefs, so the people kept quiet. Esar looked to one of his Gift-giving lieutenants, who scanned the assembly for a spokesman. The man settled on someone and strode off the mound into the assembly, his arm outstretched, pointing.

'You will speak.'

Esar's deputy drew a man with him as he returned to the hillock. It was the turbaned Herder Chief that Naomi had spoken with when Ruth had first gone out to work in the City's fields. His rough beard and goatskin attire were common enough, but the unusual star brooch atop his turban set him apart and made him unmistakable. Esar called to him genially.

'My friend, come up here,' he said, smiling. 'Come and tell me what this disturbance is all about.'

'Minister,' the Herder Chief began, nodding respectfully, 'I am told that people were taken from their homes in the night. They have disappeared.'

'Really? How many?'

'Two men, four women, and a child. Some of these were Herders, but some were Millers.'

'I see. And where have they gone to?'

'We know not. There was no blood. They could only have been carried off asleep or … or they went of their own will.'

The Herder Chief looked away. Esar darkened.

Ruth crept around the edge of the Cityfolk, careful not to come too close. The club flickered restlessly in her hand.

'Who took them?' Esar enquired, a serpentine calmness slithering beneath his voice.

'We don't know for sure.'

'And who do you *think* took them?' Esar continued quickly.

The Herder Chief hesitated and Esar glared.

'The others,' the Chief responded evasively. 'The other tribe.'

'Who?' Esar barked.

'The blood drinkers,' the Chief conceded.

Esar smiled.

'The Third Tribe!' somebody shouted from the crowd.

'The Water-men!' someone else called.

Esar flicked his hand and another lieutenant gestured broadly to the black-clad Ordermen to search the two voices out of the throng. Then the Minister raised his own above the assembled mass of Cityfolk. A fight broke out in one quarter of the crowd.

'There is no Third Tribe. Those old songs are lies! Instead, I tell you the truth. There are monsters there in the desert. Your families are in danger. There are blood drinkers out there! They may be among us, even now. Sympathisers will be dealt with. You will see how.'

By now his men had found the owners of the dissenting voices, and they dragged a man and a woman out of the crowd to the foot of the mound and threw them prostrate before Esar. Other voices were shouting in the mob, this time angry and thirsting for revenge.

'They took my wife!'

'They took my boy!'

'My husband!'

The people bristled angrily yet fearfully. Ruth could feel the hot prickles of civil war piercing the calm veneer of City life.

Esar appealed for quiet. Then he addressed the pair prostrated before him.

'You have sinned against me and against your fellow men,' he said, raising his voice for all to hear. 'What have you to say for yourselves?'

Ruth crept around the perimeter of the crowd, edging closer to see more clearly. She thought she recognised the woman as one of the Herders.

'I'm sorry,' the woman sobbed, terrified beneath Esar's gaze.

'And you?' he said lightly to the man, who pulled himself up and lifted his eyes to meet the Minister's.

Ruth gasped. It was Boaz.

'You can't win, Esar,' the young man said from his lowly position. 'Whatever you do, you can't win.'

Esar appeared to ignore him. He turned to the terrified woman who crouched before him.

'You're forgiven,' he said, before kicking her savagely on the side of her head.

She moaned and fell to one side.

'Crawl away, child. You're forgiven. And *you*,' he hissed, finally addressing Boaz, 'know nothing. I know what you tried to do that night. Conspirator! It didn't work because it will never work.'

Esar sighed loudly and walked away from Boaz further up the mound, before turning to the crowd, as if he'd just remembered something important.

'We have this one – this *sympathiser*,' he said loudly, pointing at Boaz, 'and we have one more. Another was caught trying to flee into the dunes.'

He turned and spoke quickly to one of his men, who strode into the holy tent that encircled the sandy spike on top of the mound.

'We will ask her what happened to your families and, if she can't satisfy you, you will decide her fate. I think I can trust that the right decision will be made.'

The man to whom Esar had spoken suddenly dashed the tent's entrance flap aside and stood wide-eyed in the doorway.

'She's gone,' he murmured, terrified.

Esar opened his mouth to reply but his follower spoke again.

'Minister, she's gone, and ...' he stammered, '... and there's someone else here.'

He gaped, stunned, and was unable to say more for a moment. Then, 'Help,' he urged, coming back to himself. 'Help!' he cried again.

Esar gestured quickly to the Ordermen nearby who had begun to encircle the crowd. They pushed their way to the mound, climbed it quickly, and ran into the tent after the alarmed man. One passed close to Ruth, and her fingers whitened around her club but she let him go.

In a moment they re-emerged, and they brought with them a man. None of them dared touch him, but circled around him ever watchful for a sudden move.

The man was young and of unremarkable height and build. He had a broad, sprawling beard and sun-bleached hair. He was dressed similarly to the Ordermen and, though his robe was cut like theirs, it was made of a lighter coloured material. But that was not why it looked different. It was stained and marked all over, and it appeared to have been sewn back together many times. It also seemed cleaner, brighter. The garment was the wreck and remains of a fine robe, but its quality still shone through. Ruth forgot herself when she looked at him. She felt she had seen him before.

When Esar saw the man, he almost exploded.

'You dare violate the holy tent! How dare you?' he demanded. 'What have you done with the criminal?'

The man did not reply. Esar fumed.

'Where is she?' he screamed.

He took swift paces towards the man and spoke to him sternly. Ruth could not catch everything he said and neither could the Cityfolk, who were becoming at once alarmed, enraged and entertained by the disappearance of one offender and the appearance of another. Conflicting and confused voices began to argue in the crowd.

'You are the one responsible for this!' Esar yelled, shrieking over the top of the growing clamour. 'Speak!'

He pointed his fingers accusingly, his outstretched hands curling into claws. 'This is your doing!' he repeated, angrier than before. 'You are one of them, aren't you? You're responsible!'

'I am,' came the man's reply.

Ruth was sure she had heard that voice before. It was not attractive or easy to listen to, but it was distinctive and it cut across the uproar effortlessly.

Esar took one final step towards him and slapped him hard in the face. Ruth felt the blow echo across the dunes and its noise shuddered in her ears. It was as if somebody were trying to shake her awake from a deep and testing sleep, a sleep filled with tortuous dreams. The clamour of the crowd dwindled to nothing and the people looked on in silence, uncomprehending. Esar stared at his hand for an instant, then spun on his heel.

'There will be no court here,' he shouted, incensed.

He turned to his lieutenants.

'Stake him,' he said darkly, but loud enough for all to hear.

The silence of the crowd lay unbroken under his voice. He gestured at Boaz. 'This one too. Stake them both out.'

There was immediate uproar: some cheering, some wailing, shouts of triumph and screams of anger. From the back of the crowd, louder than all others, came the voice of Salmon, hysterical and livid.

'My son! My son! That's my son!'

The grizzled old Chief howled as he hobbled towards the holy mound, flanked by his grim-faced servants.

The Cityfolk fell on each other, tearing and clawing and punching. Many fled in different directions, some keen to protect their property and loved ones, others afraid for their own lives. Mostly the men stayed: Herders, Millers and Ordermen, lunging and kicking at each other in the spreading brawl.

Ruth dashed towards Boaz, who had leapt up and was now struggling against three Ordermen. They were dragging him up the mound towards the tent's gaping mouth. Salmon and his followers were armed with horn knives, clubs and millstones, and now they waded into the fighting. The unarmed Herders and Ordermen dropped back in front of them or fell under their attack and were trampled in the dust.

Taking advantage of the distraction, Boaz knocked down one of the Ordermen holding him in a spray of blood, and Ruth crippled another, a sickening crack coming from where her club struck the man's hip. Together they turned on the last one, who thought better than to take them on and retreated up the hill. Ruth made to follow him, but Boaz called her back.

'Ruth! There's no time!'

'But Naomi! We can't leave her!'

'No – she's gone! She's not there. There's no time – we must go, *now*!'

'But my father – what about him?'

Boaz shook his head. 'He's probably dead. I'm sorry. Esar knows. He knows you're not one of them.'

Boaz took her by the arm and pulled her back down the slope away from the holy tent. The Ordermen had regrouped with the Herders and they seemed to be fighting together against the Millers. Boaz snatched up a fallen millstone and dropped his shoulder into an oncoming Herder. The man fell winded and Boaz leapt over him and ran on to where his father's group fought, a tight knot of Millers against a larger number of enemies. The old tribal wounds of the City were opening with fresh blood.

'Run, boy! They're going to burn you! Run!' puffed Salmon, staggering back from the fighting.

'I can't leave you!' Boaz cried as he and Ruth approached.

'You will! I'm old. Anyway, I'll cut a deal. The Minister's got his price for everything.'

Boaz nodded and in a moment Ruth found herself racing with him towards the eastern dunes. They charged between the houses and on into the tents. Cityfolk were scattering across the whole settlement, diving into their homes to gather their precious things and to arm themselves. The fear of the Order's reprisals for this civil war was subsumed by the urge for immediate survival.

Ruth and Boaz felt it, too; the sickening, quickening reaction of fight or flight. It was time to run.

A Herder stepped onto the path in front of them and they raised their weapons. The man put his hands up in surrender and leapt quickly to one side, but Boaz could not avoid him. The two of them glanced off each other, crashing heads and arms and knees in their collision. Boaz fell on top of Ruth and the other man fell onto a tent, disappearing in the clatter and tear of the ancient structure collapsing. Boaz tumbled over Ruth and rolled on his side, groaning. She was quickly back on her feet, urging him to get up. She dropped her club and grasped his arm with both hands. Pulling him into a sitting position, she tried to tug him upright.

A broad, muscular arm suddenly encircled her waist and yanked her way from him. She was lurched sideways and upwards off her feet; there was hot breath on her neck and she heard the wheeze of the effort. It was Haman.

'I thought you might come this way,' he rasped, 'and here you are.'

'Let go!' she yelled, flailing her arms and kicking back with her legs.

He hugged her close and she could do little to reach him with her small fists, but she did better with her feet. Haman winced as she made sharp contact with his good leg, but she could not move him.

'We were going to be married, remember, but since you have to leave, you can take your wedding present with you!' he crooned, squeezing her ribs savagely.

He raised his free hand in front of her face so that she could see what it held: a length of horn that he had been working into a Herder's knife. It was not finished, but the naturally sharp tip was keen.

'Hey, Boaz,' he called to the stricken man, who was trying to pick himself up. 'Good news – you can have her. She's yours. But this,' he said, flourishing the unfinished dagger, 'is my price.'

With that, he dropped his hand in a flash underneath Ruth's ribs, and brought the knife's conical point up into her side with gleeful force.

Ruth screamed, unable to comprehend the terrifying sensation of the twisting puncture. She struggled fiercely and wept aloud. The world lost its quality of feeling. The colours seemed different and the sounds blurred.

Ruth was aware that Boaz roared in anger and had thrown himself from his crouching position onto Haman's crippled leg. She knew next that Haman had dropped her, and that Boaz was on his feet holding Haman upright by the throat and pouring his rage into the man's face through the millstone clenched in his fist. Next, she knew that Boaz had picked him up bodily, and thrown the wrecked figure onto the upturned points of the broken tent that protruded from the ground like teeth, and that he hung there, a wretched, twitching remnant of a man.

She heard Boaz's voice next to her, and felt him lift her up, bag, club and all. She sensed that they were moving again, and there was heat on her face and a fire burning in her side. And she could hear Boaz breathing fitfully as he carried her out of the City, across the plain, up into the dunes and away.

CHAPTER ELEVEN

RUTH AWOKE IN THE HALF-LIGHT of dawn or dusk; she didn't know which. She felt warm and very tired, but also she knew in a way she couldn't explain that she was safe.

She let her eyes run over her surroundings. The low sun streamed in through a wide doorway and fell across a broad, even floor, and dust motes danced gently in the beams. The room appeared to be long and thin, and she did not immediately understand how the walls and roof were made. She could see no joins between any bricks or thatch in the roof. Everything looked solid.

Ruth lay at the opposite end of the room to the doorway on comfortable cloth bundles that felt as though they were stuffed with straw. There were a number of other such mattresses piled up against the wall to one side. She pulled herself up onto her elbow and winced as a sharp pain twisted in her body. Reaching down, she found that she was bandaged just above her waist. The bandage was thickest behind her right elbow. A memory stirred, but she was not ready to face it.

There was a skin of water by her bedside, just within reach, but Ruth did not feel thirsty. She caught herself in that thought and wondered at it. She had always been thirsty, as long as she could remember; as long as she had been alive; and now she wasn't? Was there something wrong with her? Questions crowded in but she was too tired to address them so she pushed them aside.

She picked up the skin, unstopped it and brought it to her mouth. Its scent made her shiver. It was cool and fresh as if it had never known the cruel sun; as if made of night and starlight; and when she shifted the skin in her hands the water gulped and gurgled within. The sound was like a promise of life. She drank. Cool, clear and clean liquid sweetened her lips, flowed across her tongue and seeped down into her, seeming to reach the tips of her fingers and toes. She smiled and drank for the joy of it, and there was no urge to finish the skin; she had had enough. She stopped it again and replaced it on the floor.

She looked out towards the door and the sky beyond. She could not see anything distinct, just the vast blue haze that twitched and jumped in the heat. She felt fresh and clean and more tired than ever before, and sank beneath the cloth cover into the warmth of rest.

When Ruth woke again, it was the heat of the day, though she reflected that she did not know which day it was. The soft beams of light that had earlier coloured the room's floor had retreated back to the threshold, confirming her sense of time. The sun was high. It was the burning hours.

She rolled onto her side and then, in one further effort, pushed over onto her hands and knees. Gingerly she raised herself up. The pain returned in force when she stood, but it was manageable. Her muscles protested at the exercise, but Ruth preferred to move about and explore her surroundings. She put out her hand onto the wall for support and slowly made her way towards the doorway. The sand was cool beneath her bare feet, but as she approached the room's entrance, it warmed pleasantly. Her fingers brushed the smooth surface of the wall and there were, indeed, no joins or cracks between bricks – no visible bricks at all. It was as if the wall were one block of solid sand. She looked up at the high ceiling above her and, although it was irregular and less well defined, that too looked like one continuous piece.

Stepping as far as she could towards the entrance, she gazed out. Before her lay the entire world. The dunes rippled down and away from her door into an infinite sky. The land fell away beneath her and glowed white and deep orange in the high sun. In the nearer distance, gigantic dunes crowded each other but looked like tiny clumps of sand, the vast space belying their size, whilst endless plains of dust encircled them and mocked their proud height.

Dark pockets of fury peppered the space between Ruth and the horizon; she realised after a moment that they were sandstorms venting their ire. From the safety of her vantage point they seemed as petty little nothings, yet she knew she would feel differently beneath any one of them. It was the height and vastness of her view that made it easy to smile at them.

In the far distance, the horizon blended white-on-pale with the hazy sky. She watched for some time, but the heat radiating from the sand outside her threshold pushed her back further into the shade. Cautiously, she lowered herself once more onto her bed, careful of her wound, and within a few moments was asleep.

In the late afternoon, Ruth woke for the third time that day. The sun had swung far to the west and its lowering beams lingered on one side of the doorway. She drank again, enjoying the simple, vital pleasure of it. Only when she put the vessel down did she realise that it had been full when she'd picked it up to drink. Somebody must have refilled the skin. Somebody had done that while she was asleep.

Unsure whether she should be disturbed by this, she slowly got up and moved around the room to see if there were further signs of another person. Her search revealed nothing, as if someone had come and gone with only that single task to perform. Still, she was pleased to find her bag and club. Opening the bag's neck, she pulled everything out.

The staves were there, wrapped in their cloth. She inspected them. There was a sensation she felt when holding them, too vague for thoughts or words, and although she couldn't express it, she felt good to be touching them. The sand-weathered wood told a story she could not understand, but she liked to listen. Why Boaz had given the sticks to her she did not know. They hadn't had an opportunity to talk about them and she didn't even know what they were. She resolved to ask him.

But where was Boaz? She suspected this shelter was his doing, so he must be all right. She didn't worry and turned her mind back to the contents of the bag.

She picked up her cup and Naomi's small parcel of food. Then she placed the fragile vessel to one side where she wouldn't knock it over or damage it, and unwrapped the food. There was a small hunk of bread, a crumb of cheese and a handful of the dark berries. She ate mournfully, turning the kind woman's fate over and over in her mind. What had happened to her? Had she really escaped the Order's grasp, or had she been stretched out on the burning sand and tied to stakes to await the rising sun's fiery glare?

Ruth felt gutted by her own sense of safety away from the City, and a well of emotion, swirling with anguish and betrayal, bubbled up inside her. She thought of Esar and the brackish foul liquid of the Gift. Everything in the City was wrong. It was not supposed to be like that. She knew it must be changed, put right. Her fierce self raised its defiant head in this internal conflict. Naomi had been more than good to her; and Ruth would do all she could in return.

She finished her meal and drank again. The search for another person had been fruitless, which meant her curiosity remained unsatisfied. Coupled with her need to act, she knew she had to find out where she was.

She stepped outside onto the cooling sand. The sun was in the low western quarter of the sky, and she thought she had enough light left to explore her immediate surroundings. The view had changed in nature. Now gleaming beams brushed the dunes with myriad colours. Here, golden-brown swirls showed warm, grassy smudges on the dune side; there, the sand seemed pink, with starry, mineral shimmers; and in places there were colours unknown to her.

She looked back to the doorway, and saw that the dune was like no other she had seen. Its peak was out of sight to the north, hidden by the gentle, rolling nature of its sides. It was huge, and she knew why the plain below her, with its handful-sized dunes, appeared both small and gigantic simultaneously. She was high up on a desert hill of unthinkable size, looking down on the world below. Her shelter was cut out of the dune's very side, yet the sand did not collapse on the long, low cavity.

Ruth touched the ragged, weather-beaten edge of the doorway and followed it along, away from the opening. She found that it was solid rock heavily dusted with sand, probably carried up from the valleys and plains below by the errant winds. She dug deep into the recesses of her memory and brought up two words from the fireside legends of unrecoverable times: *mountain* and *cave*. In the ever-changing and uncertain world of nomadic tribes, snatching a living from treacherous and unfixed sands, the Miller folk had dreamed of something that didn't move. They'd fixed their hopes on the legend of mountains, towers of infinite, immovable rock; like the fingertips of gods not yet swallowed by the sand. But the Miller folk believed the sand swallowed everything sooner or later, so they kept their dreams to the harmless songs of evening, when a more pressing danger was darkness and quiet, foreshadowing death in the lonely places of the world.

Yet here Ruth was; on a mountainside, by a cave.

She followed her feet some way around to the west before

returning to the cave. Then she explored the same distance to the east, and returned once more. There was no sign of any other hollows, so she sat in the cave's mouth and gazed over onto the plains. Most of the dust storms had died out far below, and there was little of distinguishable form or shape to look at in the oncoming evening. Ruth felt her strength had returned a little so she was not content to sit and wait for nightfall; she had enough time to make one further excursion. She could see what was below her, so her natural choice was to head upwards.

She started with a grimace. It was one thing to walk a short distance around the side of the mountain, but pulling her body upwards one painful step at a time made her reconsider with every footfall how far she would go. Still, she pressed her hand onto her side and pushed on regardless. She climbed a little way, and reached what she hoped would be the top, but it was just a low, convex summit that had kept the next peak hidden as she climbed. There was another above her and she did not feel strong enough to tackle it. Instead she lowered herself gently to the ground and lay waiting for the stars. It had been so long since she'd seen them.

The first appeared high in the deepening blue. She sensed it appear more than saw it, as if its tiny dawn in the evening sky were too feeble for the eye to catch. It was some time before the next came, but after that she recognised more and more blink into the old familiar dance.

'Ruth!' somebody shouted.

She jerked upright, startled, and suddenly afraid and excited that she'd slipped into another vision.

'Ruth! Hey, Ruth!' The voice came again.

It belonged to Boaz.

She turned and searched the darkening slope behind her to see him. He came quickly, half-sliding and half-striding down a steep section to meet her. There was somebody else with him, although a little higher up and moving more carefully. Ruth squinted into the gathering gloom and saw to her delight that it was Naomi. Boaz reached her first, eager to see her. He stepped towards her, but pulled himself up just short of embracing her.

'Hey!' he began. 'How are you feeling now?' He grinned broadly and shifted a bundle on his back.

'A bit sore,' Ruth replied, aware that there was so much she should say to him. 'I think I know what happened in the City, but I … there's so much missing. Where are we?'

'Let's talk about that when we get inside. It'll get quite cold up here now the sun's going down. But that's why we've got these.'

He swung his pack around to Ruth. She could not see clearly in the intensifying gloom, so Boaz told her what it was.

'Wood,' he said, as solemnly as his broad grin would allow. 'Wood to burn! There's fields of it. Up there. I've never seen anything like it. Oh,' he added, 'and here's Naomi.'

Ruth's faithful nurse and friend stepped joyfully towards the girl and embraced her.

'I'm so glad to see you're upright and moving. I was so worried,' she said, softly, and Ruth felt the damp of Naomi's tears on her neck. 'Let's get inside.'

Night fell quickly as the sun disappeared behind the mountainside and dropped into the far western dunes. The three went back to the cave and Boaz put down his bundle just outside the entrance. Naomi busied herself inside, arranging the mattresses while Boaz prepared the fire. He would not let Ruth help, so she sat to one side and watched as he broke the smaller sticks into splinters and arranged them into the beginnings of a blaze. He found his flints and soon short flames were springing up amongst the dry grass and the kindling he'd made. He piled on some of the sticks and let the heat and flame increase. Before long, the crackle and spit of the healthy fire had lulled Ruth into tiredness. With drooping lids she nodded over the food Naomi put in front of her and ate slowly.

They all ate in silence and were content to stare at the lick and dance of the flames until the meal was finished. It was only when Naomi gave Ruth the water skin to drink from that she came back to herself and was fully awake again. The scent of the water within the skin prickled her senses and unclogged her mind enough to rouse her. Boaz added larger logs to the maturing fire and in doing so sent a column of red stars spinning up into the empty reaches of the quiet night. Naomi's and Ruth's eyes met, and the girl saw the shadows of the bruising on Naomi's face that spoke of her beating.

'What happened?' Ruth blurted out in her awakened eagerness to know.

'It's all quite confusing,' Naomi began. 'I don't really know *how* I got here but I know what I saw and what I did in the City that day.'

Ruth interrupted. 'They had you … They beat you … They were going to kill you!' she said, jumping ahead, but Naomi took back the tale and started again.

'You saw them beat me and take me away. I was hardly conscious when they brought me into the City and up to the holy mound, but I could hear that a crowd was gathering. People were angry. There was a lot of shouting. The Ordermen dragged me through the mob and up to the Sanctuary tent. I thought I was going to die. I was sure that they would take me in there and kill me, or they would bring me out and kill me in front of the Cityfolk to appease them.

'A man, one of the Order, opened the entrance to the tent and the others threw me in. I fell down inside and lay still. I was so afraid I couldn't move. Then somebody touched my shoulder and helped me onto my feet. I thought it was one of them come to take me out again and hurt me, but this man looked different. I was still terrified, so I backed away but there was nowhere to hide. He put out his hand towards me and beckoned me over to him. Still I didn't move. I just wanted the sand to open up and swallow me. Then he called me by name and his voice sounded very hard. I thought I'd better obey so I went towards him. He took me to the tent wall and then he gripped the material in his hands. He ripped a long tear in the fabric, said, "Come, you can go this way. I'll deal with them," and nodded behind me to where the tent's proper entrance was.

'I suddenly felt very brave and I went through the hole he had made. He said, "Just keep going. That way. Don't stop. I'll send help." So I went. I went as quickly as I could away from the holy tent. I didn't see anyone as I left the City, and it was not long afterwards that I saw, rising up out of the desert, this mountain. Once I'd spotted it I couldn't take my eyes off it, and I knew I had to get to it somehow. I crossed one dune, then another, then another – and I found I could keep going. My feet seemed to be following a path only they knew, so I let them. They led me here. Then, later on, Boaz came, carrying you.'

Ruth listened open-mouthed to Naomi's strange tale. Then her questions came tumbling out.

'Who was that man? What happened to him? Where are we? How did we get here?'

'I can answer some of those questions,' Boaz cut in. 'Where are we? We're a long day's journey on foot from the City, due east. Naomi got here by walking. You got here because I carried you.'

Boaz anticipated her thanks and waved it away with his hand. 'It's all right. I couldn't leave you. I'm just amazed you survived. The wound looked deadly. But Naomi saw us coming and helped me bring you up here. I was tired so she cleaned you up.'

'You'd lost a lot of blood,' Naomi added, 'but Haman had made a bad job of it. His knife got stuck outside of your ribs. Still,' she added, 'you've survived where others would have surely died.'

As Naomi spoke, Ruth unconsciously touched the bandage.

'Thank you. Thank you, both,' she murmured quietly. 'Is he …?'

Boaz guessed her question. He frowned.

'Haman paid for what he tried to do. I thought you were dead, so he

… I killed him.' Boaz spoke the words without pleasure.

'Good,' Ruth replied simply.

'I didn't want to, but I couldn't stop myself,' Boaz went on. 'He hurt you, and then suddenly it was all over … I've never done that before. Killed a man.'

'He wasn't a man,' said Ruth, bitterly, remembering the crooked, brutal eyes that lurked within the broken, hateful face.

'I think I should check your wound, see how it's healing up,' Naomi said, and went to fetch a fresh dressing.

She returned in a moment and gently moved Ruth into a more comfortable position. Boaz made himself busy with the fire and Naomi pulled the folds of Ruth's robe aside, unravelled the old bandage and gingerly stroked the edge of the current dressing. It fell away lightly and revealed a long, thin gash. The wound looked clean and dry and pink, and the skin seemed to be knitting itself back together nicely.

'I've never seen anything like this,' she said. 'It was turning bad, so I cleaned it with some of the water you brought. Since then you're healing well. You'll be back to normal before long.'

She smiled. Ruth smiled back at her.

'Thank you, again,' the girl said softly.

The silence stretched and she looked from face to face, awaiting the answers she had already requested but feared to ask for again. Although Boaz had finished poking the fire, he did not meet her gaze. Naomi tried to look away but could not, the weight of Ruth's two questions that remained unanswered dominating the fireside.

'I don't know for sure who the man in the tent was,' Naomi said ponderously, considering each word carefully. 'But I *think* I do.'

'No, we don't know,' Boaz cut in. 'None of us saw him for more than a few moments and he didn't say much.'

'It wasn't what he said that told me who he was,' Naomi continued softly. 'It was what he *did* that told me. I am sure, even if

I can't say anything to prove it to you.'

'Who was he, Naomi?' Ruth asked eagerly.

'Rain,' Boaz blurted out, as if to say it quickly and be done with it. 'She thinks he was Rain.'

The quiet of night returned out in the darkness and the fire rustled warmly. A few lazy cinders floated on the gentle rising heat and flicked upward towards the sky, while the glowing logs subsided softly as the silver-pink ash beneath shifted.

Ruth did not speak. The world seemed so vast, the stars ever distant and the darkness infinite. Yet here, within the tiny glowing ring of a mountainside fire, Boaz had spoken a name that was unlike any other. The universe contracted to the spot of tiny campfire that burned before them, this light that danced so merrily in the massive darkness. Ruth felt her breath in her throat, and she knew she had it in her power to give voice to this mysterious name: *Rain*. In the instinctual core of her being, where she understood that the world was not as it should be, she knew what the name meant. But she could not say so, any more than she could tell how many grains of sand there were in the desert. She spoke.

'Rain?'

'Yes!' Naomi said happily. 'I know it was him.'

'It doesn't make sense,' Boaz cut in, dismissively. 'Rain is supposed to be a Chief with a people – a people he is supposed to lead and look after – and what does he do? He gives himself up to the Minister and the Order, the very ones who want him dead!'

'But …'

'No, Naomi, he gave himself to them and now they've probably killed him. His people are left alone. They'll have to choose another leader, if they can, but it might lead to infighting and death before anything is sorted out. Can you imagine what would happen to the Millers in that place if my father, the Chief, threw away his life like that?' Boaz scowled. 'It doesn't make sense.'

'I don't know, Boaz,' Naomi went on in a tone of desperation. 'Perhaps it was one of his sons or close supporters acting on his behalf?'

'I don't think so! Why would a Chief like Rain give up his son to die for you? Or for me? Who are we to him? We've never even met him!' Boaz sounded exasperated, as if this was ground they had covered before. Naomi turned away, equally frustrated.

'I can't tell you, except that I know it was him!' she insisted, fiercely, and Boaz let it drop.

Ruth wasn't sure if she should say anything, but she knew she couldn't stay quiet.

'I don't know if this man was Rain because I've never met him,' she began, focusing on Naomi and making a point of not looking at Boaz, 'but if the stories you've told about him are true, then he must have been nearby. Boaz, you said enough in the City to make me think you believed in Rain. So what about now?'

Boaz looked uncomfortable, and pained.

'I did believe,' he cried. 'And I believe now! But that makes it worse because Esar will have had him killed. So it has all gone to nothing.'

The words hung in the gathering cold. The fire had been left untended too long. Boaz stepped towards it and added some of the broken scraps of wood and then the last of the larger logs.

'I don't want to talk about it anymore,' said Naomi.

'What about his people?' Ruth asked, attempting to brighten the mood. 'If it was Rain, and if he has a people, wouldn't they be nearby? Couldn't we find them?'

Naomi and Boaz looked at each other. Ruth sensed something pass between them, a rippling excitement that whirled across their faces from one to the other and back again.

'What?' Ruth asked, smiling in anticipation.

'This wood came from up there,' Boaz returned, 'on top of this mountain. You wouldn't believe what you can see from there. I said there was more wood. Well, there is – there's loads of it. I brought down only a tiny part. There's grass. There are bushes, but not those little shrubs that grew in the City in those recent days. These are bigger. Some of them are taller than I am. The ground is different. The sand has changed into something else, something darker and richer and more alive. At least …' he hesitated, 'it *was* alive. It's all dried out now, but you can see what it must have been like.'

'If it's dead, what use is that?' Ruth said, deflated.

'Don't you see?' Naomi answered. 'It wasn't always dead. There was life there, but now it has gone. Or perhaps I should say, moved on.'

'And we think we know which way it has gone,' Boaz added, with a joyful, conspiratorial grin. 'We think there's a path up there. We walked a little way along it today, before we met you. We were back late because we went further than we meant to. Naomi and I only went to get some wood and see what we could find, but then we saw it: a narrow row of plants that had sprung up, heading away from where we were. It was as if the water that had made the wood grow up and flourish had moved on, but as it went little plants grew, marking the way.'

'I don't know if they go with the water or if the water goes with them,' Naomi said, 'but the two do go together. The Third Tribe were up there. They were up there recently, but they've gone and we mean to follow them.'

Ruth stood up quickly and immediately regretted it. She grimaced and gripped her side, muttering, 'We've got to go now!'

'Soon, Ruth. When you're better.' Naomi soothed her, and helped her sit down again. 'Although I am amazed how well you are. Perhaps we could go tomorrow or the day after.'

'But won't the plants have disappeared by then? When we came to the City there were plants, but then they were gone.'

'I don't think that will happen out here,' Boaz said. 'There's no one pulling them up this time. When you came to the City off the path, Esar ordered his men to root up any sign of them. Naomi gave you berries, didn't she? Well, those came from some of the small shrubs that sprang up just before you arrived.'

'How could they grow so quickly?' Ruth asked, incredulous.

'We don't know that, either,' replied Naomi, 'but I think there is so much life waiting to be released that when the chance to grow comes, it makes up for lost time.'

'We can't be sure of anything, Ruth,' Boaz said, looking sideways at Naomi, 'but there is something in what Naomi says. I think the wood growing on the mountaintop is there because the Third Tribe stayed here some time. Not too long, but longer than a few nights. Maybe it was long enough for life to grow up very tall.'

Ruth's eyes lit up as a thought occurred to her.

'I saw footprints in the sand that were wet. In the City, I mean,' she said to Boaz. 'Water came up through them. And those staves you gave me made water rise up into the corner of Naomi's house. What are they? Where did you get them?'

Boaz grimaced again, as if Ruth had raised another awkward subject.

'I took them,' he said slowly, 'from a dead man. It was a few years ago, when I first heard about the Third Tribe. Some of the Herders had supposedly caught one of Rain's people – or at least they claimed they had – but instead of taking him to the Minister as they were supposed to, they killed him. Afraid of Esar's punishment, they buried this stranger. No one knew where, but eventually I found out and I went to find him.

'His hands were clamped around those staves as if they were the most precious things in the world. I thought they might hold some great secret, but nothing happened. When I gave them to you, and you appeared not to recognise them, that confirmed my fears that they were good for nothing except firewood. Now? Who knows? But I would guess there is more to them than we realised. Maybe they'll lead us to the Third Tribe.'

'Do you think so?' Ruth asked eagerly.

'Perhaps, if only we knew how to use them,' Boaz said matter-of-factly, denying Ruth's hopes of a short cut to meeting Rain's people.

'Did they stay here? In this cave?' she yawned, tiredness suddenly taking hold of her once more.

'I think some came here in the heat of the day,' Naomi responded. 'But the cave is far too small for a whole tribe. Maybe there are other shelters nearby we've not found. The mattresses were here when I came. They must have made them.'

'But why did they leave them?' Ruth exclaimed. 'Why would they leave such valuable things?'

'Perhaps they moved on in a hurry,' Boaz suggested.

'Or perhaps they didn't need them,' Naomi said, simply. 'Perhaps they had … enough.'

Ruth looked from Naomi to the fire and then to Boaz. This was all startling, exciting and strange. With a loud crack, the last of the logs split in a burst of sparks. Her eyes followed one as it was sucked forcefully up into the chilled dark of the night. Picking up a handful of sand, she let it run through her fingers. It was cold, very cold, yet the night had hardly begun. She felt sorrowful, and stiffly climbed to her feet.

'I'm going to bed,' she announced, a half-formed sadness numbing her voice, and she went into the cave.

Ruth selected the mattress she had slept on before, and folded herself within the cloths. Before long she was warm but the physical sensation did not comfort her. She turned away from the wall and looked out towards the cave entrance and the fire. Naomi was gathering her things and readying herself for sleep. Boaz still sat by the dying embers. The low light from the ashes cast a sunset glow up onto his chin and eyebrows. He seemed lost in thought.

Ruth looked past him out into the blackness and moaned quietly. She closed her eyes but there were no dreams to be found. Darkness encapsulated her and she remembered her father, and the gaping maw of the holy tent's entrance; she remembered Esar and his black-clad followers; she remembered the fear of death, stories of dry bones and parched corpses. The formless black was infinite above her, and the hungry chasm of sand unending below. She screwed her eyes up even more and mewed in tiredness and fear. But still sleep did not come.

CHAPTER TWELVE

RUTH LAY AWAKE THROUGH the long watches of the night. She turned over and over again the events of recent weeks and months, and could not find any sense in them. Life had been brutal but simple. Now it was still brutal, but the simplicity had gone. Her mind was full of restless questions that refused her sleep. Their voices were inescapable and they were hardly comprehensible, but as Ruth listened and fretted over them, a theme appeared in the frantic confusion of too many thoughts: would she go with Boaz and Naomi to follow the Third Tribe, or would she go back for her father?

Soon this question was shouting louder than all the others, and she did not want to answer it. She longed desperately not to hear it, but it prompted her endlessly and something stirred inside her. High above, the wheeling stars marched on, and as the night deepened before starting at last to shallow, within her one of the conflicting forces found new strength. She tried not to listen but it pumped at her ears until she couldn't ignore it. The impulse beat its fists on her mind and tried to shake her violently. The more she pushed it away, the harder it came back. And the dominating voice grew and grew until she could bear it no more. She had to speak out.

In that crucial moment, under the dragging weight of worry,

strangled and deafened by fearful cries in her head, and unable to escape the image of Dan lost in the darkness – something whispered.

Ruth!

The clamour of voices faded.

Ruth!

The whisper came again. And the voices vanished like smoke.

'I'm … I'm coming,' she whispered back, swiftly rising to her feet and dressing.

Before she knew it, she was at the cave's doorway. The air was fresh, and the faintest hint of wind brushed her cheek. There were scents on the breeze. The moon was high, and the land before her was silvered. She could see well enough to leave the cave without fear of getting lost in darkness. With one fleeting look back at her slumbering companions, Ruth stepped lightly across the level patch of ground where Boaz had built the fire. The cold of the chilled sand made her hurry, and she half thought of returning for cloths to wrap her feet but something urged her on. She did not know where to go, but the motion of limbs and travelling felt right.

Ruth turned uphill and set her mind on the mountain's hidden summit, however many false heights it lay above. She started swiftly, and found there was little pain in her side. The first brow she gained quickly – and that was when she heard it.

A muffled beat. *Dumn.*

The atmosphere crackled. Ruth felt the hairs on her neck rise. She stood absolutely still, hardly daring to breathe. Nothing happened. There was silence, except for the half-suppressed rasp and wheeze of her own tiny breaths. Just as she lifted her foot to move on, it came again.

Dumn.

It seemed to come from further up the mountain. Shorter instants passed before the next, but this time she heard it twice: *Dumn-dumn.*

Ruth broke into an eager, unthinking, reckless run up the side of the mountain, desperate to find the source of the sound. The pounding of her feet on the sand was almost immediately matched by a constant rhythm of fast-paced beats, *dumn-dumn-dumn-dumn-dumn-dumn-dumn-dumn*. Her heart raced ever faster, and it was echoed in the relentless pace of the pulsating, primal music.

Ruth passed the second peak, untiring, then the third and, after a sharper incline, found herself crashing through high grasses and occasional shrubs. The sounds drove her onward until, her legs finally burning, she drew herself to a hurried stop at a vast cliff edge, throwing herself backwards to avoid going over the sheer face that vanished beneath her. The dust kicked up by her sudden halt floated lightly over the perilous abyss and the music vanished.

Ruth collected herself. She could hardly take in what lay before her. This was a sight like no other: she swayed in the power of the view. It moved her. The expanse of the landscape reached her through senses beyond her eyes. She smelled the swirling chasm of air and sensed its unconquerable size as it broke upwards on the mountain like an invisible, silent dust storm. She heard the deadly potential in the empty space beneath her as tiny pebbles of sand flitted off the cliff edge and disappeared silently into the gulf. As they warmed in the growing light, the emerging colours on the distant valley floor were laid out in front of her and she could almost taste them. She felt that if she only dared, she might reach out and remake the dunes beneath her, pull the horizon closer, or perhaps push it away. Instinctively, she sat down, feeling unworthy and too fragile to stand in such a place. She pulled herself around onto her belly and crawled to the edge of the cliff, to the very point where it fell away.

Unlike the way the world rolled back from the cave's entrance, it plummeted from this place. Feeling more secure laid flat, Ruth gained sufficient confidence to choose what to look at and her sense of wonder blunted. She squinted into the fleeing gloom, making out distinct shapes far below. There were spots of light down there, tiny and still, encircling a larger focal light. The booming roll began again, *dumn-dumn-dumn-dumn*, more powerful and vigorous than before, and the spots of light began to twirl below. The primal pulse blasted up the cliff face and paralysed Ruth, hypnotising her. The lights moved and swayed and darted in the rhythm of the beating; they danced and coiled, bending in two opposing circles that turned against each other. They entwined and unwove in a curling whirl. Then, at some mutually understood signal, the drumming suddenly stopped and the lights stood still.

In the new silence Ruth breathed, as if for the first time. In and out her breath moved, in cleansing draughts, and she caught them again in her throat when the sun broke over the eastern horizon and dazzled her. A single voice, clear and pure and high, refreshing as water, rose up to her from below. In a wordless song, it greeted the dawn in a chant that filled Ruth's heart and vision with wonderful, unknowable mysteries. The song returned to some apparent refrain, and other voices, high at first and deeper later, joined the hymn. The morning song filled the space between Ruth and the singers, and she ached to know the words. She opened her mouth and made some noise, anything, to join them, but all that emerged was her crackling, hoarse whisper of many desert years. She quickly fell silent, momentarily saddened and ashamed by her effort. But the feelings passed and she was soon entranced once more by the rising harmonies.

She could hear the voices of men, women and children on the distant floor below and wanted to leap up and join them, but the way down the mountainside was unknown to her and she could not be sure of reaching them. In any case, she couldn't leave without Naomi and Boaz, but neither could she drag herself away from the sight and sounds before her. So she lay yearning on the cliff edge, peering down to where the figures of tribesmen and women – the Third Tribe – stood singing. They were real; they were here and she could see them. Rain or no Rain, they were here. She would find them and follow them. That must have been why she had come. That was the only thing that made sense.

The sun was rising quickly, and the golden light of early morning raced down the cliffside. The tribespeople below renewed their vigorous drumming and dancing, one powerful deep voice rising alone and then joined in chorus by all the others. The chant was accompanied by claps in unison, and Ruth felt the whole body of Rain's people – an entire tribe – beat their palms together in powerful affirmation of existence, and a bold welcome to the rising sun. The sunlight finally reached the bottom of the cliff and they sent up a final cheer – then there was silence.

They were still for a moment but then all moved in different directions on their own errands. The celebration was over. Perhaps they were breaking camp; perhaps they were moving on.

Ruth forgot all else except to fetch the others. She rolled onto her side and pulled herself up, grimacing as, surprised by pain, she found her side was sore again. She clutched at her ribs and they were tender. She moved as quickly as she could, back across the remarkable field of wood and down each long and painful slope to the cave. The effort exhausted her and, when she stepped into the cavern, she saw Naomi standing over Boaz, shaking him awake.

'Boaz! Wake up! Ruth's gone!'

'What?' Boaz said loudly, as he came around. 'Ruth?'

'I'm here, it's all right,' Ruth said, coming from the entrance right up to them.

Naomi spun around, delight remaking her face. After embracing Ruth, she recovered herself and smiled bashfully.

'I am foolish,' she said. 'I panicked; I thought … I don't know, I was worried. I thought something had happened.'

'Something *has* happened – but I'm fine. Everything is fine,' Ruth replied, and she sat down heavily on a nearby mattress.

Naomi frowned. 'Here – drink. You look pale.'

'I'm fine, really. I've seen them. They're not far.'

Boaz sat up suddenly. 'What? You've seen who? *Them?* Where are they?' He leapt up, cloths and all, and hastily dressed.

'They're on the other side of the mountain,' Ruth smiled. 'Right down in the valley below. There is a big cliff there. I …'

'We know it,' Boaz cut in. 'We nearly fell over it in the dark yesterday, just before we met you.'

'Well, that's where they are, at the bottom,' Ruth said.

She looked expectantly at Boaz, as if he were going to rush out of the cave and immediately race off after the Third Tribe. Instead he sat back down on the mattress.

'That changes things a bit,' he remarked soberly. 'We don't know the way down that side of the mountain. It might take us a whole day or maybe more to get to the foot of that cliff safely.'

'We've still got to go, haven't we?' Ruth pleaded.

'Yes, of course,' Boaz said, 'but we wouldn't get very far if we went without taking suitable supplies. I thought you meant they were here, close by. I was ready to run after them.'

'Let's get our things together, shall we?' Naomi suggested, and she and Boaz busied themselves about the cave, collecting bags and water skins and scraps of food. Ruth tried to help, but Naomi pushed her gently back onto the mattress.

'You can help us best by resting now,' she said firmly. 'You'll need your strength if we're going to climb down a mountain.'

At last they were ready. Boaz shouldered his pack and took Ruth's bag and club in his hands. Naomi carried the single skin of water. Their plan was to climb up onto the wooded plateau that was the mountain's peak, collect wood for fuel and more weapons, and then explore the most likely way down to where Ruth had seen the Tribe. From there they would track them and hope finally to catch them.

Even with Ruth's injury slowing them, Boaz thought the three of them could easily follow and catch up with an entire people.

They left the cave before the sun reached their side of the mountain, gaining the first of the false summits quickly and without too much pain for Ruth. The climb to the second was more difficult for her, and she dropped behind slightly. Boaz and Naomi were walking ahead and did not notice at first. When Boaz turned to offer help, Ruth refused it and waved him on.

Naomi reached the plateau first and caught her breath. Boaz arrived next and sat on the edge of the slope, looking down to Ruth who was not far behind.

'Boaz,' Naomi began slowly, 'what's that?'

He stood and went to her. Ruth caught them up and her eyes followed Naomi's sun-squinting gaze past the wood, across the flat terrain and towards the far distance. In the heat haze, something looked not quite right; the distance and distortion were playing tricks with their minds. Either that, or the world was changing.

Something was in the sky.

'Impossible,' whispered Boaz, scarcely daring to believe what he was seeing. In the far distance, many weeks' and months' march from the mountain to the east, where the sun was rising steadily, a shape hung in the air. Naomi attempted to describe it.

'It's like … grass seed. Like grass seed when it blows on the wind. Once, in the City, there was a different kind of grass that would go to seed in white heads of perfect softness. The breeze lifted them in clouds and took them; they floated slowly, gracefully. This is like that seed, only whiter, brighter and bigger – as if thousands and thousands of seed heads are floating together in one place.'

The others listened, silent, rapt. This thing that floated high and clean and vast above the desert was tumbling in slow motion, rising, reforming and rising again. It seemed to be growing, spreading and moving, and its shadow transposed its ongoing transformation into dark shades on the desert below.

Ruth stared, transfixed by a memory of a now distant time when a gang of Herders chased two Millers out into the absolute desert where they would surely die. She had seen a sight like this before, in a vision, and here it was. She feared and yearned for what it could mean, but she said nothing.

Without talking, they moved on towards where Ruth had seen the Tribe dancing. Boaz was sufficiently aware of their needs to collect a small supply of wood for fuel and a larger length for a club. Ruth and Naomi did not make such preparations. In a moment they were carefully approaching the cliff edge. When they looked down, they could make out the ashen spot that marked where the central fire had been, around which the Tribe had danced.   Boaz was quick to spy a long, thin line of people on the move. They had already travelled a good distance, but because of their huge numbers, they stretched out a long way from first to last. They were moving north-west, seeming to bend around the mountain on its lower slopes. Boaz thought he could guess which way they had travelled down this side. It was not, as Ruth imagined, where a shoulder of rock jutted out just north of where the three stood. Although it looked easy there at first, anyone descending that way would soon be confronted with long, sheer faces and impossible drops. Just to the south, however, where Boaz pointed, was a large spur that was much squatter than the northern shoulder, and it looked possible to zig-zag down a series of broken hillocks protruding from it.

'The only trouble with that way,' he frowned, 'is that it'll take us a long time to begin the journey downwards. It's some walk to the top of that climb. It will take more than the rest of this morning to reach it and then, after the burning hours have passed, we'll have to finish that leg and then try to climb down hot sand. We could camp tonight at the bottom of this cliff where the Tribe camped.'

Boaz paused, grimacing a half-smile in anticipation of the

response he would get before continuing, 'There is another way. We could stay up high, up here where we can see where they are going. We could walk along this flat top first north and then west, always keeping an eye on where they are heading. I am hopeful of finding a way down towards them and we might even head them off. There may be a gentler route somewhere for you, Ruth.'

He offered the idea and let it hang in the air. After a moment, Naomi responded. She looked at Ruth hard.

'Sounds good,' she said simply, but Ruth was not convinced. Her gaze flicked uncertainly from Naomi to Boaz.

'If we go wrong,' Naomi continued, 'we can just come back. It isn't as if their tracks are going to disappear over night. And I don't like the look of *that* way down.'

Boaz's plan seemed to work. They found the route north flat and easy, and then it declined to a slope shallow enough for Ruth to manage. There was only one steep section that slowed them considerably: a sharp, shingle incline down which they slid painfully. Ruth grimaced and grunted, but her complaints were involuntary and she tried to make the best of it. Naomi became tired, too, as the morning passed and, with the sun rising ever higher, Boaz began to look for a suitable place to shelter. Just as it became painful to walk on the hot sand, he found somewhere.

They had descended a flank, and the harshness of the mountain's stone ribs began to mellow into dune valleys between protruding, bony ridges of rock. It was at the end of one of these gorges that they found their shelter: a boulder of unbelievable size lay cracked and broken, and a quarter of the way around it, there was a fissure in its belly where the stone was collapsing and undermining itself. Into this cave they went. The crack was more than twice the height of a man, and Boaz, Ruth and Naomi could stand shoulder to shoulder comfortably within it. The heart of the rock had crumbled, leaving a pebbly antechamber to one side of the main split. Here they made themselves as comfortable as they could to wait out the burning hours.

The heat rose. Only Boaz slept. Naomi tended Ruth's wound and found that it was still healing well. Her own bruises had come up vividly and the deep tenderness was more bearable.

They rested for some time, not speaking much. Ruth drifted on the edge of sleep, but when she came round from her nodding heaviness, Naomi's curiosity gave way.

'Ruth, tell me again about the cup and that water. In the corner of my house there was a water well. Your cup was in it. I know you've not wanted to talk about it, but there's too much I don't understand about it … and about you. What happened?'

Ruth did not know how to answer. She had been avoiding the subject since leaving the City. She did not understand either. Why would a well suddenly spring up inside a house? It made no sense, yet somehow she was supposed to be responsible for causing it. She sighed.

'I don't know. It just happened. When I went to bed that night, I put Boaz's staves down next to me, with their bit of cloth. Everything was as normal in the morning, but when we came back from the Gift, the cloth was wet and the water was there. You were so convinced that I was one of *them* I didn't know what to do, because I would only let you down. I didn't say anything, hoping it would just go away. But it didn't.'

'How did the cup get there?'

'I put it there because, even though I wanted to hide the water, I couldn't let it soak away. It was too precious.'

'You made the water come.'

'No,' Ruth insisted. 'It was just there. It wasn't me.'

'Then who?'

'Rain?' Ruth suggested.

Naomi frowned. 'Do you think he came into the house?'

Ruth shook her head. 'No. It was only an idea. Those sticks Boaz gave me may hold the answer.'

Ruth dived into her pack and brought out the wrapped staves. She unwound the protective cloth and held them, one in each hand. There was a quality to them that spoke of age and experience, as if they had been further and seen more than Ruth, or anyone else who might have touched them. Ruth had sensed that whenever she picked them up. But today something was different. There was more; something new, something that gave them weight and energy. They impelled Ruth to move, to explore and to discover. They seemed to point her onwards to something greater.

Her hands shook. The wooden rods were pointing forwards together as if something was calling them. It scared her, and she dropped them. They plummeted lifeless to the floor with a clatter. One fell and bounced near Naomi, who picked it up and inspected it with finger and thumb. Ruth retrieved the other, and passed it to her. Naomi looked at them closely.

'How do they work?' she asked.

'I don't know,' Ruth lamented.

'I think they are tools for finding the water,' Naomi said. 'If the stories of my grandmothers are true, perhaps Rain's people use them for following underground streams. Maybe that is what the Third Tribe does. They look for water with these.'

'Those staves didn't find water,' Ruth asserted. 'Water found those staves. The water came up exactly where they were.'

'Yes. But … Oh, I don't know.' Naomi let it drop. Then she grinned suddenly. 'Perhaps we can ask the Tribe when we see them!'

Naomi eventually slept out the rest of the burning hours. Ruth could not; instead she fidgeted and couldn't get comfortable. She retrieved one of the staves and absent-mindedly turned it over and over in her fingers as her mind and body tried to slip into sleep, but it did not come. She got up and moved about the small cell of rock within

which the others snoozed and found that her ribs did not hurt as
much as before. Picking up the water skin, she drank a little, surprised
again at how full it was, then fetched the other stave from beside
Naomi's sleeping form, and held the pair lightly in her hands.

Ruth could swear they wanted to move. They seemed to quiver.
Or was it Ruth's fingers that made them quiver? She could not tell,
but she couldn't dismiss it either. Something was happening.

The heat was marginally less so Ruth resolved to look outside. As
she stepped over her bag and water skin, she felt suddenly unbalanced
and swayed. The staves crossed each other in her grasp and fell from her
hands. They bounced with a noisy clatter off the water skin that lay
beneath her. Unsure of what had happened, Ruth picked them up and
went to the cave's opening, leaving her other possessions behind her.

Heat glowed from the ground but without the fierce intensity of
midday. The hottest part of the day seemed to be passing quickly and
Ruth tested a toe on the exposed sand. It was bearable. Boaz and
Naomi were both sleeping deeply, so Ruth stepped outside. As she did
so, she knew that she was under a shadow. She looked up.

Things were not as she had expected at all. The sky above her
was filled with more of Naomi's seed-clouds. The first one they'd seen
on the far horizon had multiplied, and the resulting herd of clouds
had swarmed across the vast expanse of desert to the mountain and
Ruth's rock. The sun was still very high, but the clouds hid it, and
lessened its ire. They were beautiful and unnatural to Ruth, like
creatures from another time or world. They seemed like living dunes,
ever turning and changing as did the sandy hills, but more quickly
and majestically. These strange, regal presences floated on the highest
breeze as gently and tenderly as breath. They cast shadows as soft as
the best of sleeps, and dimmed the painful brightness of the sun on
the rocks and yellow-white sand. She marvelled at them and forgot
herself – until her hands suddenly twitched as the staves moved.

Ruth stared at them for a moment until they jerked again. She felt the instinctive urge to step forward. She did so, and the staves seemed to move differently, if indeed they'd moved at all. A dialogue began, Ruth's steps responding to her study of the sticks and how they made her feel.

She moved around in an odd way: sometimes sideways, sometimes forwards, sometimes turning. She wove an erratic path across the cooling sand until she reached the base of the giant rock, on the north side, away from the mountain's heights. There was a dent in this side of the rock big enough for one person to crawl into. She bent to look into the little cleft and, as she did so, she heard an eerie and unfamiliar noise. The sensation from the staves faded.

The noise reminded her of the rattling gourd that Esar's attendant used in the Gift ceremony, but on a larger scale. She stood up and listened. The sound echoed around her on the valley's sides. It grew suddenly and kept increasing in volume until the bouncing, crashing clamour overtook its own echo and became terrifying in intensity. The earth shook and small pebbles around Ruth's feet danced the early steps of a stampede. Ruth couldn't understand what was happening, so she hurried anxiously around the side of the rock towards the larger fissure where Boaz and Naomi slept.

A wall of moving sand and stone was racing towards her from higher up the valley.

She stepped back involuntarily, unthinking and not knowing how to protect herself. As the avalanche swept on towards her, Ruth took more steps backwards before turning and running to the far side of the massive rock. The narrow, high-walled valley stretched out before her and she knew she could not outdistance the flooding boulders. She dived sideways, hopelessly afraid, entirely unprepared, and threw herself against the rock wall to hide within its shadow. The crashing and rumbling continued to grow and, just before it became a deafening madness, Ruth heard Naomi calling her name. She shouted back but it was too late to make herself heard.

The quaking earth shuddered as the crashing, plunging river of stone thundered into the far side of the mighty rock. There was an explosion of sound, and the avalanche came on, splitting into two streams that rolled around, past the cave, past the edge of the rock and on past Ruth. The debris poured on its way and splayed out around Ruth's protective bastion, leaving only the tiny triangle of unravaged ground where she cowered. Then the noise began to lessen, and a screen of dust obscured everything.

As the veil slowly cleared, Ruth saw that all the sand beyond the rock's shadow had been flayed with stone, splinters and debris from the avalanche. Everything within the protective shade was largely untouched. Dust swirled as it settled, and Ruth was completely caked in it.

Finally, silence reigned. There was not a sound to be heard – but only for a moment.

A flicker of breeze raised the dust into eddies and began to grow in strength. Soon it was a powerful gust that built and built to become a sandstorm. The wind rushed down the narrow valley in the avalanche's wake. It blew up the dust, sand and smaller stones in a deadly, tearing, and choking gale.

Ruth dragged part of her robe up over her head and covered her face to shield her eyes, nose and mouth. She dropped to the ground in the whirling tumult and rolled up against the protective rock, pushing herself as far into the little cleft as she could. But her back remained partially exposed, and she couldn't escape the agonising scouring of tiny stones and sand.

As quickly as it had arrived, the wind was gone. When Ruth surveyed the scene, she realised that the heat was rising, and rising quickly. The last of the clouds raced overhead and surrendered the sky back to the hot sun. It was still the middle of the day, and the falling brightness cast a burning, dazzling glimmer on the devastated mountainside valley. The sun, denied its usual intervals of fire and heat, was making up for lost time. Ruth was outside in the deadliest part of the burning hours.

She felt the savage, desiccating kiss on her face and hands immediately, and feared the imminent burns. Picking her way across the field of debris, she headed in the direction of the shady cavern and its safety. As she approached, she heard coughing and someone calling to her. She reached the cleft in no time and Naomi pulled her inside from where they could examine the chaos.

Ruth!

'Yes?' she replied, looking at Boaz.

'I didn't say anything,' he said, puzzled.

'You did,' she responded, equally bewildered.

Ruth! The small voice came again.

And the vision struck her more powerfully than the avalanche, as all around her vanished into darkness.

Chapter Thirteen

Ruth could not see anything in a darkness more complete than any she'd ever known. Every night had stars, but this was a night without any light. It was alive, or rather she sensed there were things in the darkness that meant she wasn't alone. The air was rank and she breathed it with growing distaste. She heard a strange splashing sound that beat a poorly kept rhythm on saturated ground. This fall of water seemed vile as it plopped and slapped, but Ruth could not think why. She listened harder, and found that there were other spots of falling water. They gurgled and splashed at innumerable, scattered points across the darkness.

She was cold. Ruth found that she was sitting on a hard stone floor that sucked the heat out of her muscles as she crouched. Lifting herself with the heels of her palms, she found to her disgust that the floor was not wet, but slimy. She brought a hand up to her face but could not see it, and when she smelt the smear of dank slime, she gagged. It was like cold, wet death.

She rose to her feet carefully and attempted to brush the putrid dampness from her robe and hands. They felt contaminated – she was unclean. She put her arms out in front of her and edged forward, testing the ground with a foot before moving her weight onto it. Such care did not prevent her from stubbing her toe on a low platform of rock and it was all she could do to stop herself from howling. She lifted her foot and placed it forward even more cautiously, finding that she could step up onto the platform; in fact she could step up onto a second platform, and to one above that.

She climbed the three steps carefully and her groping hands found a wide, high doorway. The darkness was complete. She did not know if she was moving from the inside to the outside or from outside to within. She didn't know where she was. With a flicker of fear, she realised she was completely alone. She didn't dare to call out, and she knew instinctively that her chances of surviving this dark pit were slim.

Despair rose within her and she let go of the hope of seeing the sky or breathing dry, clean air. Her soul writhed, and a moan forced itself upwards from the deepest place of her own darkness. It drifted mournfully into the unknown gap and was heard by no one. There came no answer. This strange and black place was the complete opposite of the glaring, dry desert that she had known all her life. Yet she knew it was equally perverse, unnatural and strange, and she would die here, forced to extend her suffering by the compulsion to lick the rocks for moisture and bear the foul bitterness of the slime. Or perhaps it would poison her and speed a welcome death.

She stood in hopeless silence, her body hanging on its frame, mindlessly upright in the futile gesture of standing above the muddy floor which beckoned. She stepped forward again, and again. And yet again. Moving thus in her careful way, at length her fingers brushed a waist-high edge of rock. As she edged towards it, she found that it was intricately shaped. The top edge was continuous and stretched out in front and behind her further than she could reach. Her hands found their way down and she discovered that there were tapered legs of stone spaced at intervals to support the beam above. When her hands reached the floor they discovered, apart from the creeping slime, that on her own side there was a floor, but on the other side of the legs there was nothing. She was on another cliff edge, but between her and the precipice was a wall.

Ruth sat down, this time given over to the cold muck that splashed her legs and soaked her robe. She reached out and explored the floor with her hands. It was made of large slabs that felt like rock, but there were straight seams between filled with a softer material. She forced her finger into one decomposing vein and dragged up a handful of muddy gravel. Pulling herself onto her feet again, she slumped over the low wall, then flung the gravel over the abyss to listen for its landing on whatever was below. Within a heartbeat there was the ripple and splashing of many small stones hitting a liquid surface. Ruth smelled the intensified dampness in the atmosphere and knew there was a great mass of water beneath her. She reached downwards but could only grasp at the air.

Her despair returned, stronger than before, and she buckled beneath it and slid back to the floor. Alone and in the dark, she could only turn in on her fears. She could not fight the blackness or find the strength to overcome it. It swallowed her and robbed her of herself; it was impersonal and unknowable, ignoring her where she sat. She moaned, uncaring of any dangers that might lurk in the darkness. She wept. She sobbed – and someone moaned back.

Out in the darkness, somebody cried.

Ruth stopped her own mourning and listened. It was the deep, low groan of exhaustion and fever. It was a whine fading to its own bitter end. Her heart sped up and her breathing became light and quick.

There was somebody there.

She climbed to her feet again, and padded forwards with arms outstretched. Every few steps she paused to listen, focusing on finding the direction in the black world of dripping water.

As if awakened from a dead sleep, the wailer cried on with gathering intensity. Ruth bumped into a large obstacle that sloped away from the left down to the floor on her right. She half-climbed over it, half-edged around it. In doing so, she found it to feel like wood. It smelled rotten, and was soft to the touch. Something ran over her hand and she pulled it back in fright.

Ruth shuffled on as quickly as she dared. The cries were louder now but she found there were three more obstacles of the same nature to traverse. She edged onwards, and found herself up against a wall. Moving slowly along it, she stumbled forwards with a heart-stopping jerk and discovered a stairway heading downwards. It was broad, and each step deep. They led away – into what she did not know. The quality of the air was subtly different here, thicker, heavier with moisture, and it rose up the black stairway from a pit of the unknown. The moaner cried from below, and Ruth knew she had to go down. She went slowly, bumping her head on the stone mantle.

She forced herself on, and stepped out again. Her feet splashed when they landed, and rods of icy cold shot up her legs and shocked her bones. Her toes numbed quickly, and she danced on the spot, compelled to move by fear and yet afraid to go any further. She stumbled quickly backwards and sat on the low steps away from the water. In her inaction and strong sense of loss, she despaired. The moans intensified her own sorrow, and she choked on her grief.

Suddenly, she raised her head, her hackles up. There was a stirring above her and she heard the rhythm and stomp of heavy feet. She leaned out of the stairwell into the cavity above the water. High above her, somewhere in the darkness, someone was moving about.

She heard the crack and fizzle of flints lighting kindling. Somebody coughed, and then the tiniest hint of red light crept onto the edges of Ruth's perception. There were innumerable footsteps on wood and stone. Whoever it was was descending from a great height down many stairs into this forsaken place. The light grew in shades of orange and fierce red that pushed back the fringes of the darkness. Then it disappeared. But the steps continued and their sound echoed around this cavern of unknown size.

In a moment the light had returned, edging away the blackness into a powerful gloom. Ruth raised her hand in front of her face and could sense movement just before her. The flickering light increased slightly and she began to make out features of the room. An ankle-deep flood of water covered the floor, running a little way towards the opposite wall. The moaning came from over there.

The light increased again, and grew strongly above her. The torchbearer was heading towards Ruth's stairway.

She stepped forward into the icy water, felt her way to the stairwell's doorway. She followed her way through the door and edged along the wall to one side of it. Perhaps the torchbearer might not see her. She might slip by whoever it was and climb up to where they had come from. There might be a way out. Perhaps she could escape.

The padding of feet and the orange glow descended towards her. The light grew in the strange place of stone, darkness and water.

In the dull illumination, Ruth saw a massive beam of wood, thicker than her body, taller than a man, extending up from the floor to join a broad panel, also wooden. The vast panel was set into the wall with a thin ledge before it, and many supports reinforcing it. It was holding something back. And beneath the skeleton of beams, cowered the shape of a man. As the torchbearer reached the doorway to one side of her, the prone figure raised his head.

It was Ruth's father, Dan; or rather a shadow of him, more gaunt than she had ever seen him. He stared into the receding blackness from hollow eyes. He was hunched and listless; distressed, yet hardly aware. He moaned pitifully, and arched his spine. His face contorted, revealing that he had lost teeth since she had last seen him. He raised an arm and stretched it towards her.

'Father!' she cried.

'Ruth!' came the reply, and in that moment everything became pale and bright.

Ruth emerged from her state of collapse soaked in sweat. She was panting. The air was dry. She looked wildly around, disorientated, and only calmed at the soothing voice of Naomi. She felt a hand on her forehead, smoothing her hair. Boaz stood to one side, white-faced. Ruth realised she was on the floor. She rolled onto one side and tried to get up. She felt sick. Her ribs ached. She coughed and Boaz brought her some water. She feared to try it, but at last she did and it was cool and calming. It comforted her, and she felt clean again, although it did not remove the dark memory of her vision. She smelled her hands and touched the hem of her robe. There was no sign of the murky slime. Yet it had been so real. She closed her eyes and the stark memory of Dan's hollow face loomed before her in the darkness; she dared not close them again.

Boaz and Naomi did not push her to speak. She wouldn't have talked anyway, so after resting silently until the last burning hours were gone, they readied their packs and picked their way across the devastation of the avalanche. Ruth barely noticed. She thought of nothing else for the rest of the day but followed the other two mutely as they tried and failed a number of routes down the mountain. Tempers flared between Naomi and Boaz until they finally saw their way down. They would have to cross a number of rocky headlands, but they were now definitely on a course towards the dunes. Boaz's spirits lifted, but Naomi reverted to worrying for Ruth. The girl did not seem to be the same. Wordlessly, Naomi put her arm around her and they walked together quietly.

By mid afternoon they were standing on the prow of an enormous shoulder of rock. They were on the northern side of the mountain, far away from the City to the south-west. They could see out over the flat land ahead of them and, with great excitement, Naomi pointed out the distant shapes of people moving in the desert.

'There they are!' she laughed, her enthusiasm renewed. 'There they are! They're really here!'

Ruth did not share Naomi's excitement, and she wondered why. Here was the answer to all her questions – here was the way to survival. She attempted a smile.

Boaz was impressed with the Tribe's speed. Even with the delays in finding their route down from the highlands, Ruth, Naomi and Boaz had travelled quickly. Yet the Tribe had moved quickly, too, astonishingly so, because, although they had not been climbing across rocky terrain, the distance around the mountain was a good long day's march. And here they were.

Ruth wondered why they had taken the route down that side of the mountain only to come around the northern end, but perhaps they had their reasons. Maybe she could ask them. She tried to smile, but something – a swelling grief – was wringing the happiness out of her.

'We can cut them off,' Boaz said confidently. 'If we keep following this route down and strike out true north before nightfall, they'll come right towards us and we can join them.'

'Well, let's go then,' urged Naomi eagerly.

Their route took them down the mountain to the left hand side of the headland. Ruth tired in the descent and this leg of their journey seemed endless. Naomi's fretting returned.

'I'm sorry,' Ruth said. 'It's not my ribs, I'm just … It's hard.'

She gave up. She could not articulate her feelings because she didn't begin to understand them. The image of Dan's face grew in her mind and punctured her sight from within. Behind this memory growled a low voice, reminding her of his violence, his cruelty and his abandonment of her. The gaunt face floated before her and there it stayed, however much she tried to push it away.

At last they came around the final bluff and out onto the upper heights of the sandy foothills. Naomi and Boaz eagerly looked out over the plain below. There was no sign of the Third Tribe. Naomi scowled but Boaz tried to make the best of it.

'They were definitely coming this way,' he said. 'This can only mean they haven't got here yet.'

'Or they have already passed by,' Naomi replied bitterly, as if it was Boaz's fault. Then, 'I'm sorry,' she added immediately, reflecting on her hard words. 'I just can't wait to see them.'

Boaz didn't say anything and simply nodded at her with a smile.

'Can we rest, please?' Ruth asked quietly.

Without waiting for an answer she allowed her legs to buckle beneath her and collapsed carefully onto the sand bank. She closed her eyes and snoozed. A short while later, she was woken by Boaz.

She opened her eyes and Boaz straightened up from where he had been leaning down to shake her shoulder. Feeling warm and refreshed, she stretched and yawned. But as she came fully awake, she felt the twinge of her side and the ache of her father's memory. It was not long before the effects of the nap were wearing off and the tiredness was returning. She wanted to close her eyes on everything, but there was no way she could. She suppressed the growing need to make a decision. The Tribe was so close, but her father's face ... she didn't want to think about it.

Naomi gave her some water. It was still cool and fresh, and the skin flask again seemed close to full. In the late afternoon, the jutting buttresses of the mountain threw gentle shadows over the landscape. The sun was orange and it would soon sink down to lengthen the lazy patches of shade.

In the east, the Third Tribe was approaching. Ruth glared fiercely into space; she silently demanded why she should have to make such a choice as this.

They walked a little way further onto the last hill, but stopped short before reaching the plain itself. Here they camped, in a prime position to see the Tribe as it rounded the mountain spur, very close to the east. It wouldn't be long; if not before nightfall then soon after the next sunrise.

Boaz was tempted to explore out to the east, but he deemed it too far after a day's walking over the mountain. Instead he dug Ruth's trench and built a fire as the light faded. The Tribe did not appear. Ruth sat next to the crackling logs while they cheerily transformed into orange-grey cinders. She found it easier to clear her mind when she sat by a fire. The hypnotic effect of flames and warmth drew it out of its worries and into a state of calm. She relaxed.

Her thoughts wandered. She looked up at the stars, and they stared intently back. The night listened and waited. She cast her eyes back to the flames, but this time they did not hold her mind so gently. Instead she remembered the flickering glow of the torchbearer's fire, and how it had grown in the vile cavern to reveal the face of suffering – the face of her father. She glanced away into the blackness, and saw the darkness of that terrible place. Shivering in spite of the campfire's warmth, Ruth relived the drip and slap of dank water on slime. That cave was a place of death, and her father was there; her father, the man who, for better or worse, had kept her alive all her years through many dangers. She could not say with certainty what had happened to him, but she was sure that he was still clinging on to life by the fingernails of his ferocity and violence.

Yet he had not always been a man sustained by cruelty and blood. Looking back to her early childhood, Ruth felt the vague stirring of memories, half-lost to the years of suffering, that spoke of happier times with Dan; his treasuring of her; his games and songs; his stories. He used to sing to her of the days of great plenty, and he would tell her of the Miller heroes of old who thwarted the evil Herders.

It was not in the hope of recovering those lost times that Ruth made her decision. It was not even in tribute to those days. It was simply because Dan was her father, and he was trapped. He was dying.

Her mind told her that it made no sense to walk into a place of death, that he was probably dead already. Still, Ruth knew she had to go back for her father. She knew, too, that she wouldn't be able to justify it to the others. But blood is thicker than water, she thought.

She was aware what they would say so she would avoid them; she would go before dawn, before the others were ready and before they could stop her.

They must continue on after the Third Tribe and the new life that was within their reach, but Ruth must return to the City. Boaz and Naomi both seemed to know more about the Tribe anyway – Ruth had only been caught up in it by accident. She would go to the City, find out if her father was alive and, if he was, she would bring him back to the mountain and the safety of the little cave where the mattresses were. They could go back to their Miller life. It wouldn't be so bad … and if Dan was dead, maybe she could still pick up the trail of the Third Tribe and catch them.

She smiled wanly at the others by way of saying goodnight and crept into bed. Before long she was warm under the cloths, but she didn't notice. Still whenever she closed here eyes, Dan's face implored her out of the darkness.

'I'm coming. Hold on, I'm coming,' she whispered to him.

As she did so, something shifted within her, and she felt different somehow.

'I'm coming!' she said again, but with a new, steely determination.

Ruth was up in the glum half-light before the sun broke over the east, and she began packing her possessions quietly. She laid her cup carefully inside its cloth and then into the folds of the skin bag, taking care that her millstones should not crush it. Then she picked up the staves that Boaz had given her. She hesitated, unsure whether she should leave them behind if she planned to renounce all hope of reaching the Third Tribe. She didn't know what they were for so they would only serve as a painful reminder of friends lost and a path not taken.

In the end she put them in her bag, reasoning that she could perhaps at least burn them as fuel. Then she searched around for her club, but could not find it. Perhaps Boaz had burned it. She cast her eyes quickly towards what was left of the dead fire, but there was nothing. Only tiny, crumbling stumps of the mountaintop logs remained. That was a shame; she would probably need a weapon.

She took a long draught from the water skin. She would leave the most part for Boaz and Naomi. After all, she was the one leaving, and she couldn't take their only water away with her; they might not make it to the Third Tribe.

Turning to her own immediate worries, Ruth knew she would have to get around the mountainside quickly and move as fast as she could to the City. She would find water there. She would be all right, she told herself. Her side was still a little sore, but much better than it had been. That was good news for the trek ahead. The journey would be at least a day and some of the night, two days at the most. She would go as straight as she could from the north-west edge of the mountain in the direction due south-west, looking to the horizon for the unmistakable spike that pierced the holy mound in the City's centre. She reflected that she would never have guessed she'd be hoping to find her way back to that dreadful place. But before going there, she would head some way towards the Third Tribe.

She cast her eyes once more in the direction of her sleeping friends, and then walked down the dune to the north to pick up the trail of the Tribe. Naomi, her second mother and her friend, would follow her into any danger, and Boaz would do the same. The only way to force them into safety would be to follow the Third Tribe and plant firm tracks in their direction, then double back to the City without leaving a trace. But she must hurry, and be far away by the time Naomi and Boaz picked up the trail. They should not have to choose – as she did – between chasing a loved one into certain death or joining the Tribe on their way of life. She just hoped that the Tribe would not strike up another loud morning song too soon and wake the others before she was far enough away.

The stars were still discernible in the high, deep blue of the early morning. Dawn had not yet come. The chill in the sand kept Ruth's feet stepping quickly. She started well, climbing and descending the dunes and leaving as broad and deep tracks as her small feet could manage. She pressed on, and to her surprise and slight alarm found a wide sweep of other tracks crossing her way. The Tribe had already passed by in the night and the many footprints before her looked fresh but were gently crumbled by a few hours' breeze. They could not be too far off. Ruth found the deepest, strongest footprints to walk in, and in doing so she mingled her own tracks with the Tribe's. Naomi and Boaz could not fail to think she'd joined them now.

In following the footprints, Ruth discovered new strength. There was a soft, damp fragrance hanging in the early morning air, and the ground beneath her was easy to walk on.

Only a few dunes away she found them.

Ruth crouched on the crest of the dune and looked down. The Tribe's camp appeared much like any other, but it was large, for there were many people. A few were stirring, perhaps restless in the last hour of night, or perhaps they were sentries.

Her heart spasmed. Here they were, and all she had to do to join them was to walk down one side of a dune. But she knew her feet would draw her away to the City and to Dan, so she pushed her feelings down inside herself and crawled away out of sight. She had done enough. Boaz and Naomi would not find her here and it would be too late to come after her because they would already be with the Tribe. So she mustn't waste time; she must go.

She turned south-west, towards the city, and fell quickly into her old ways of discerning the best route between the dunes so that she was not constantly climbing and descending if she could stay level and relatively well hidden. She remembered the pasturelands of her time before the Path, her naïve childhood, when she and her father had moved as a pair among the grass stalks, making and baking bread, trading with other wanderers and fighting only the battles they could win.

Now her feet were taking her into a battle that seemed impossibly one-sided. Ruth was a small, frightened girl, not quite a woman, with a fierce temper but no strength to fight a city full of Herders and Ordermen. Could she find friends among the Millers of the City? She suspected not. There would have been terrible consequences for Salmon rising up against the Minister to defend his son. The Minister would have struck back at him and his people. Even if the old Chief had survived, what punishment must he have endured? Salmon would not be particularly pleased to see the one responsible, at least in part, for that uproar.

But people had been crying and shouting before Ruth had even got up that morning. She realised she still didn't know what had caused the disturbance when she and Naomi had begun their hasty flight. Perhaps there was more to it. Perhaps she could find other allies.

How long had she been walking now? She had come some way around the side of the mountain, but she'd let her mind wander and had blundered into a bowl of dunes. She was in no particular danger but would tire herself getting back on track, as she would have to climb out of the bowl to resume her march. She sighed and trudged up the side of the sandy slope, crossed the crest of the dune and looked out over the plain. The light was now growing and from this vantage point she could see a green line on the sand stretching from east to west: vegetation. The Tribe had beaten them round the spur of the mountain. They had walked around before Ruth and the others had descended to their hillside camp. Either that, or they had passed by silently in the night. Already the foliage was growing in the dawn.

Boaz and Naomi are in for a shock, she thought, but she knew there was nothing she could do about it. Then she looked west and saw in the distance what she could have sworn were the shapes of people. Pausing momentarily, she squinted into the daybreak. It must be the Tribe. Boaz and Naomi could still catch them, and they would have a wonderful feast of fresh green shoots along the way.

The sun broke into the open sky and sent low beams of gold across the plain. The green growth became ever more vivid in the kind light. It would be especially important now to stay low and out of sight. Ruth turned her mind back to the task ahead: the City. She walked on at the fastest pace she could manage. The mountain receded behind her and she found the going firm enough. She would get there.

The City grew in her mind. She would probably not see it until tomorrow, but it lurked just out of sight on this side of the horizon. She didn't know if Dan would even be there. Her last actual sight of him had been when he was taken into the Sanctuary tent on Esar's holy mound. And then there was the vision. She had no certainty that what she had seen was true. It may have been her fears overcoming her. A cave of darkness, starvation, and filth. If her vision was real then Dan was alive, but barely, and only Esar's Order knew where he was. The tent was the likeliest of places to start.

Ahead of Ruth were clouds, Naomi's seed-heads. They gathered in handfuls and snatches here and there as the morning wore on. Each clump was strange and beautiful, but as they built they took on a dual quality. They hung in the sky, both delicate and brooding, as if some elegant strength was about to swoop down and strike. By the time the burning hours were approaching, they filled the southern sky and were sailing over the spot where Ruth had guessed the City would be.

She waited out the heat of the day in the simple pit shelter of her people. She had become so used to houses, tents, caves and rock shelters that she felt suffocated by the grave-like trench in which she lay.

The hours were long but eventually they passed. Ruth did not refill her trench or hide her tracks, but gathered her belongings and forced herself on towards her goal.

Thirst was growing in her. The afternoon became increasingly parched, and walking south into the face of the sun dazzled her. Before long she moved with eyes closed, simply blinking them open quickly every score of paces to check her route. She pressed on and, as her throat burned unbearably, finally she saw the tip of the holy mound's spike. Her energy renewed momentarily and she surged forwards towards it. Still her throat burned. The once familiar sensation again took hold of her. She must find water.

Dusk drew near. Behind her the first heralds of evening winked in the clear skies and Ruth reached the north-east edge of the vale in which the City lurked under dark clouds. She approached the valley's edge on her belly, crawling to avoid sharp eyes that might look up at the skyline. The magnificent and oppressive phenomenon of the clouds dominated the scene. Nevertheless the dull headache of noise still emanated from the City, its own menacing gloom vying with the clouds for supremacy.

Ruth crawled on again and when she was suitably out of sight, she rose to her feet. She walked a short distance along the edge of the ridge, always a little way back, to find a suitable place to camp. The sun was disappearing into the west and the folds of the hills around her were dark. She moved quickly.

Something crunched underfoot, something cold and damp. Vegetation.

They were here.

CHAPTER FOURTEEN

RUTH CROUCHED BY THE CRUSHED GROWTH. In the gathering shadows of evening she could make out the outlines of wilted plants. She grasped one, and found it to be dry. It crumbled in a sudden and total collapse. All the brush around her was brittle and desiccated; it had sprung up in a rapid surge and dried as swiftly. The water that had caused this life to shoot up had moved through here quickly and was long gone.

But what had she crunched underfoot that was damp? A moment's search found a Jacobswell plant, its stout, turgid stalk crushed by her heel. She gleefully tore away the flower head and broken section and put her lips to the stem. She drank, expecting the sweet, clear water of recent days, but instead tasted the warm, stale liquid that did not satisfy. There was no room for thoughts of distaste – she was thirsty and this was water. She drank as much as she could and emptied the plant, then groped around in the dark but could find no other.

It was time to camp. She could follow any vegetation trail at first light, but for now she must prepare for the night. There was still light in the sky and on the higher hillsides. She walked out of the low, shadowy dip and found a higher place to dig her trench and bed down. Before she climbed in, Ruth sat on the edge and watched the colours of sunset roll through the dune-like clouds. There was a darkness to them, but also colour and majestic beauty. She had never seen an orange sky before, only a relentless blue or the inevitable, star-filled black. It was beautiful, even with the edge of brooding intent brought on by the dark and shrouded depths. Here and there between the clouds were tears through which she could see the stars. They, at least, were safe above this mysterious blanket that had grown and thickened with every passing hour as she had crossed the desert. The light finally faded to a sightless red cataract in the far west. Moments later, the sun disappeared.

Ruth had made it to the City quicker than she could have hoped. And she had found water. She resolved to sleep and recover her strength for the early morning when she would descend into the settlement once more.

And what of the Third Tribe? Were they here, and, if so, in what numbers? She had seen a large number – perhaps the entire people – to the north-east, further up and past the mountain where she had left Boaz and Naomi. Ruth guessed that the huge contingent she'd spotted up there must be the largest part of the Tribe, so if any of its members were here at the City they could not be in great numbers. What reason did they have to be near the City anyway? Only death would await them, as it did for everyone. Maybe there was only a handful here, or maybe none at all.

Yet here were the dried plants, a sure sign of the Tribe and its strange ways. Naomi had said that Rain's people had been staked out and burned last time they came to the City, when her great-grandmother was alive. But if they were here now, against all sense, Ruth wondered if perhaps they could help her. There was so much she didn't understand.

Exhausted and full of worry, finally she slept.

The night passed quickly. Before Ruth knew it, it was dawn and the gentle light of morning streamed over the eastern hills, slipped under the broad blanket of cloud and filtered into her shelter through the rough cloth, which by day was her robe. But she had slept for too long and had lost her chance to sneak down into the City in the early hours and hide in one of the many abandoned tents whose owners had long gone. She wondered if it was Esar's persecutions that had turned the City into a lair of ghosts. From her vantage point on the hillside, Ruth saw that the ancient structures were vast in number. She guessed the City had been the greatest gathering of people ever seen, but that must have been at its height. Now the Cityfolk had dwindled to just a few in each tribe. In the shells of the tents, there would be plenty of places to conceal herself. No disguise would work, however, because she was still small, still as a child, and children were rare and recognisable. She would have to be quiet and careful, and keep out of sight. But she was angry with herself because her strategy was now pointless; she had missed her chance today.

She rose and packed her things. Then she filled in the trench and did her best to remove all traces of her having been there. Without a stick to use as a weapon, she did at least have her millstones. There was no water and little food in her pack, but she had a valuable cup that she may be able to trade for anything she might need. The staves were the only useless items: too short for decent weapons, and not in sufficient quantity for proper fuel. She thought about throwing them away or burying them, but instead tucked them into her robe. They hardly weighed a thing, so they were no trouble to carry.

Ruth went back to the dip between the dunes where she had found the Jacobswell plant and the dried vegetation. She had not dreamt it; there it still was, but without its reservoir of water, the leaves of the Jacobswell were wilting quickly. All the other plants were completely desiccated. She searched the area and found little to suggest a recent presence of the Tribe. Perhaps one of them had been here, some time ago, looking over the City. Maybe the water had come over a number of days and fed the plants enough for them to grow. Whoever had brought it must then have moved on and taken the water away, leaving the foliage to dry under the hot sun.

Ruth was on the City's north-eastern side – just where she had felt that strong pull during her night time trespass not long before she and Naomi had decided to run away. If she had gone then and climbed the dunes on this side, as she had so desperately wanted to, would she have found one of the Tribe? Would she be far away with them now? She could almost hear her father's voice inside her saying, 'You're not with them, girl, so don't think about it.'

She looked around for a sign, any sign at all, that might show her where whoever it was had gone, but she could not tell. Frustrated, but unwilling to sit about all day, she resolved to walk either north around the valley's edge or along the eastern border. Eventually, she decided to explore the east side in search of a good way down into the City, keeping out of sight as best she could, but the constant need to remain unseen hindered the speed of her progress.

Without conscious thought, she took out the staves and turned them over in her hands as she walked. There was something pleasant about the feel of the wood with its dents, rough edges and sand-smoothed corners. It seemed to whisper a story of its own, as if it knew of some purpose for which it had been grown, cut down and remade into staves. Ruth sensed this most strongly when she held them lightly, one in each hand, but when she gripped them and turned them forcefully across each other, they seemed to resist and the storytelling stopped. She could move them however she liked but, as impossible as it seemed, the wooden rods *liked* to be held lightly so that they could move with her, not against her. Ruth found herself walking a particular route that she might not have chosen, because the staves seemed to be guiding her. But when she caught herself in that very thought, she reproached herself, and tucked them back into her robes.

The sun was climbing ever higher, and soon it disappeared above the rim of cloud. Ruth found it hard to concentrate on searching the ground for signs of the Tribe with the awesome spectacle of the clouds unfolding and refolding above her in such tremendous pale and dark beauty. She shivered. The temperature hadn't risen. Lost behind the thick cloudbanks, the hot sun was cooled and the day's heat held off.

Ruth carried on but found nothing, until she suddenly felt the strong sensation of exposure. It was as if a powerful eye had spotted her. She ducked as low as she could, more out of instinct than certainty of any real danger, and crept away from the valley's edge into the desert land that bordered it. She rounded a large dune and, sure that she was out of sight, straightened up and put her bag down. Stretching, she then reclined on the side of the slope that looked away from the City and far into the east.

It was not immediately obvious where the mountain was, so she was not surprised that she hadn't noticed it when she had lived in the City. The whole range of dunes on this side built up one upon the next in a rippling blanket that ran as far as she could see to the north, and as far into the south as well. Immediately in front of her lay a series of high dunes with stark valleys, and beyond them a plain of smaller mounds that sloped up into the foothills of the mountain. The mountain itself was majestic; an ancient, unchangeable presence that was too vast to comprehend. Perhaps Ruth, and all in the City, had missed it because of its very size. It seemed somehow to have been absorbed into the other great unchangeable – the sky.

The sun was still on the mountain. More clouds were racing from the east towards the City and tumbling down the near side of its peak. On they came, blown by the unseen wind that moved noiselessly in the upper skies. Where had they come from? Would they break and fall as they had in her familiar vision? She had not had that dream since she had first seen the Wonderful Path or the City. Water had burst out of the floor in Naomi's house, so would it also burst out of the clouds?

Ruth's sense of exposure passed and she crept back towards the

valley and the City. She crawled on her belly to the vale's edge and
looked out over the fields towards the tents, the houses and the holy
mound with the Sanctuary and spike. The Cityfolk were in the fields,
attending the grasses and goats. She watched them for a while, but
then the call came from the City centre and runners were sent out to
fetch them in for the burning hours. Yet it was cool; the unbearable
heat was tamed. There was no reason to go under cover, but still the
people went. With a rush of excitement, Ruth realised that perhaps
she had not lost the day after all! Maybe she could go down into the
City now, while everyone was waiting out the midday hours.

It was some time before all the Millers had returned from their
fields and the last of the Herders brought in their flocks. Ruth waited
until the City's paths and streets were empty. Then she held back a
while longer, just to be sure no one was about.

She slipped down the valley's side and scuttled quickly over the
large expanse of hard plain with its patchy brown clumps of sickly
vegetation. This was the riskiest part and she quickened to an all-out
sprint as her fear drove away caution. Her heart hammered, but there
were no shouts from the City's edge and no eyes seemed to see her
come. Still the heat was low, under the cloud.

She slowed to a silent, careful glide, then came to a sharp stop
some way from the first tents. Pausing briefly, she scanned for life
and movement, and then sneaked forwards to find a derelict tent for
use as her first hiding place. She discovered one quickly – a little way
in – and slipped under its half-collapsed cover. Her heart beat in her
mouth. Still no one raised the alarm.

Ruth looked about the tent for something to use as a weapon.
Where the structure was shattered, she found broken fragments of
sticks and bones that had made up the frame, but they were too small.
Then she looked to the parts of the tent that were still standing, and
the broken sections that remained largely intact. The longer uprights
would be useful. She gripped one of the broken tent poles that still

protruded from the ground and tugged. It shifted and the inner wall of the dugout shelter collapsed. She pulled harder, and it came away completely as the remaining shreds of fabric finally ripped. The pole was usefully thick, but not enough to make a powerful club. Still, its end was sharp where it had broken, so it would be useful for thrusting and stabbing.

The point was deeply stained. At first Ruth thought it was some kind of waxy preservative, but to her horror she realised it was blood, long dried. Her eyes flashed across the upright remains of the shattered tent, scanning the broken stakes. She saw that four of them were splattered with old gore of a past murder. Someone had been impaled upon these points. With grim satisfaction, Ruth realised that this was where Haman had ambushed them. It was here that he had tried to kill her. Boaz had prevented it, and the stakes bore the signs of his triumph.

Ruth did not want to stay any longer in this tent, so she took her bloody stake and bag of supplies and crept outside. She couldn't see or hear any sign of folk on this side of the City, but kept off the paths and crept between tents until she came to the inner circle of houses. Here she paused and listened hard. There were low murmurs coming from within some of the squat, sandy structures. She would have to go more carefully now to avoid detection, but perhaps she could learn something from listening.

'… there's no telling what it could be,' a man was saying, his voice hushed, 'but I'll be damned if it isn't going to be bad on us Millers.'

'Aye,' agreed a female, 'Salmon's failed us! He should have put his people first – us!'

'He's failed us for the last time, remember. We won't see him again now, so don't be too hard on him. It was his boy they were going to burn! You would have done the same for me, wouldn't you?' There was a pause. 'You'd do the same for me!'

'Of course,' came the late reply, 'I just can't help thinking – Boaz has either run off or he's dead … Salmon's lost him anyway …'

'So why didn't Salmon let him burn and save all of us instead?' the man asked, finishing her unspoken question. 'But who would do anything different? It's about survival, yes? You can't ask someone to choose between their son and their people. Family first. And Salmon did us well, you know, before this. He was Chief for a long time, and we did all right under him.'

'I suppose … I suppose it was going to happen sooner or later – the fight, I mean. Between Millers and Herders. Just a shame the Order sided with the Herders.'

'They were always going to, don't you think? I reckon,' and here the man's voice dropped even lower, 'the Minister was looking for a fight. I think he's got other plans.'

'What plans?' the woman, presumably his wife, whispered back. 'Do you think we'll find out tonight, hey?'

'Don't mention tonight!' he said, his voice rising again. 'Taxes have gone up and up – for what? A party!'

'Peace, peace,' she soothed, her voice edged with urgency. 'Don't let's get worked up.' Then she whispered softly, 'They'll hear us otherwise.'

'Sorry, love. Let's talk about something else. What about these things in the sky, eh?'

Ruth continued to listen for a short while, but their conversation was of the strange clouds and their odd ideas about where they might have come from. She moved on, going very slowly, as the slightest movement of toe on sand appeared loud to her. She was terrified of being caught but pressed on regardless.

She crept further in towards the centre. The closer she got, the harder it would be to remain unseen. If any of the Order members were on the holy mound, they would be able to see out over the tops of the houses and down the paths. She would be spotted very quickly. Her only hope was that they would not be out at this time.

Ruth's approach to the centre led her through the last of the houses and very close to the tented mound and spike. Here the dwellings were mostly occupied, and she felt panic rising in her. She wanted to carry on but there was nowhere to go except into the Sanctuary tent or the occupied houses. There was an entrance to the tent on this side, and the cloth was flapping in the feeble breeze. It looked black within.

Ruth thought she heard movement in a nearby part of the City, so she ducked sideways and crouched next to a house wall. The building was occupied, and the people were talking, but Ruth did not hear. She was listening for the sounds of somebody outside, somebody who might find her and drag her into the tent or stake her out in the sun to burn. It was of little comfort that they would have to climb out of the valley to do so; the clouds didn't cover everywhere.

After a moment, she heard nothing more. Perhaps the sounds of movement had simply been the workings of her overactive imagination. Her mind re-focused on her surroundings, and she picked up the conversation going on within the house.

'It'll be fine.' A man was speaking. 'The Minister knows what he's doing. He'll grind them under his heel, no problem. There are hardly any of them left anyway. They're dead or gone. Those remaining will have to like it or leave.'

Ruth heard a number of assenting grunts; there were possibly four or five people in this house.

'Yeah,' another chimed in. 'He'll sort them out. They say he's going to make some big changes. Anyone know what?'

'As long as it ain't taxes, he can do what he likes,' said another.

'Maybe he'll give us their women,' said one more.

'No one knows,' said a more authoritative voice. 'None of us will know until tonight. Doesn't matter to me what he says; the gathering will be worth going to as it is. Plenty of food! Can you ever remember having so much food?'

Then one young voice began to sing. Ruth listened, surprised. 'Oats, wheat and barley grow,' it chanted with childish pleasure –

> 'Oats, wheat and barley grow,
> Can you or I or anyone know,
> How …'

'Shhhh,' the other voices hushed before the song had hardly begun.

'That's a burning offence!' scolded the authoritative voice. 'You know better! Come here!'

There was the sound of a scuffle ending with the noise of a heavy hand slapping someone's head.

Ruth was alerted again to the sensation that she was being watched. She glanced quickly around. No one was there, but it would still be wise to move. Something was happening tonight, that much she knew. Perhaps it would be best to get out of the City before the burning hours were over. That way she could hide out in relative safety and return in the dark. Hiding in the City all day would be far too risky. The only problem was that she had found no more water. She would just have to manage until evening. The man had said there would be lots of food tonight. Maybe she could steal some water then.

She checked her possessions and stealthily slunk away from the holy mound and out through the houses. In no time at all she was back among the tents and preparing for her dash across the open plain. She aimed to return to where she had descended, so that she could be sure it was practicable. There was nothing else for it, and waiting would only bring more danger, so she set off at her quick, light pace.

The City shrank behind her and the dunes ahead grew rapidly. Her feet seemed glad to take her out of the settlement again. Soon they brought her to the start of the valley's steep edge where she climbed using her hands up the side. Her tired limbs shook with nerves from her dangerous expedition. But she had got in and out without being seen and she'd learned something useful. She crept away from the edge and sat with her back to the gentle slope of a dune.

'Hello,' a voice said suddenly from a little way away.

Ruth leapt to her feet, snatched up her short spear and stepped over her bag to put herself between it and the voice's owner. She thrust the spear's shaking point at whoever it was in a gesture of defiance.

It was a man; his head was uncovered, and he was quite old with a great, shaggy beard and pale robes. He was sitting further up along the dune, carefully out of sight of the City but high enough to see far about him. He stood up, and Ruth saw that he wore a dark sash around his waist. There were things tucked into the sash, but he had no bag or weapon. He carried no millstones and that said one thing louder than any other: Herder. Perhaps he was an outcast, a loner left to fend for himself, although he looked well enough. More likely, he was a distraction ahead of an ambush. Keeping her eye on him carefully, Ruth picked up her bag and slipped it over her shoulder. The point of her spear did not lower.

'I saw you coming from down there,' the old man went on, 'so I thought I would meet you here. I'm Peter. And you are …?' He drew small circles in the air with his right hand as if that action would induce her to answer him.

Ruth took no chances. She threw a careful glance over her shoulder and began to back away. Peter frowned.

'Don't go! I'm not here to hurt you. I thought that maybe we could help each other.'

'What could you do for me?' Ruth said, almost sneering as her old hardness, born of a life chasing the seasonal grasses with Dan, returned.

'I could share my water with you. I think I have enough for both of us.'

The man produced from his sash a small water skin. From where

Ruth was standing, it looked full. She felt the dry husk of thirst grate on her throat. She could do without, she decided.

'That's not enough for both of us,' she said.

'That's not all I have. There is more,' he replied with a smile, as if she had suggested something amusing. 'I'll tell you what,' he continued, 'you can have all of this, but,' and he raised his arm, anticipating her next objection, 'I'll drink a little first so you can see it is really water and truly safe.'

He unknotted the cord, held the skin above his mouth and poured. Water flashed in the space between the skin flask and his upturned lips. It looked clear and fresh, like the water from the clay cup. Ruth yearned for it; her mouth and nose longed for the soft flow and sweet scent.

The old man was not a careful drinker. Too many drops went astray and glistened on his beard. He finished and closed the flask, which he then threw towards her. It fell in front of her on the sand with a muffled thud. She edged forward and picked it up. He did not seem to have drunk much – the skin appeared full. She fought her powerful thirst and overcame it; instead of drinking straight away, she put the water skin into her bag and looked again at the old man.

'Do you want something to eat?' he asked.

Ruth shook her head.

'Do you mind if I eat, then?' he added, but she had no time to answer; he had already sat down and was rummaging in the folds of his sash. He brought out a pale chunk of something – Ruth could not quite make out what it was, bread perhaps – and set to work on it. He ate noisily, and seemed to be enjoying whatever it was. Ruth said nothing. She didn't move closer to him or leave but stayed where she was, out of simple curiosity with the man's strange behaviour. No one just gave away water. It was madness.

'What were you doing down there?' he asked, gesturing towards the City.

Ruth remained defensive.

'My own business,' she said simply.

'Very well,' Peter said, with a hint of resignation in his voice. 'Is there anything you will tell me?'

'No. But you can tell me things. Who are you?' she asked tersely.

'I'm Peter. I told you.'

'All right then, where have you come from?' Ruth persisted.

'I don't really know. Perhaps "where am I going?" is a more interesting question.'

He cut across the scowl that he guessed preceded a further question. 'What I mean is, I'm a wanderer. Wherever I go there is sand to the north, sand to the east, sand to the south and sand to the west. It's all death. So what does it matter where I am from? I live in a world of dust and sand. If you really want to know,' he added conspiratorially, 'I'm looking for a place where there is more than just sand.'

CHAPTER FIFTEEN

RUTH LOWERED THE SPEAR POINT.

'So you've come to the City? Then you should know there is just as much sand and death down there as anywhere else.'

'I know,' replied Peter. 'Those sorry patches of grass aren't what I'm looking for. They feed on dead water. Esar gives out water very reluctantly these days.'

'He doesn't give it. He sells it,' Ruth remarked bitterly.

Peter rolled his eyes. 'Ah! It's come to that? He's gone too far!'

Ruth began to suspect the man was too close to the Order to be trusted.

'You seem to know much. You're one of them?' she asked, accusation tainting her tone.

'Good gracious, no!' he said, hiding his discomfort at her question with a smile, 'but folk often think we are.'

'We?' Ruth questioned.

'By "we" I mean my friends and I – my tribe. Years ago – many lifetimes – the Order used to be part of our people. But they betrayed us.' Peter's face hardened under his grey beard. 'They turned against us. They burned us, stoned us and forced us out. They claimed that which does not belong to them. Or any man, for that matter. But this was a very long time ago.'

Ruth caught her breath as realisation dawned.

'You're one of them, aren't you – one of the *Third Tribe*,' she murmured. The words she'd carried with her for some time sounded strange when spoken aloud.

'Yes – the Third Tribe. That is what some call us. Others say we are wanderers. Dowsers. Others say cannibals, others say blood drinkers. There are many names both good and bad, and none of them are right.'

'So what are you called?'

'I am called Peter, but you know that,' he said with a twinkle, unable to resist the tease. 'I think of us as friends – simply friends. But many of us would say we are the Followers.'

'What do you follow? Clouds?' Ruth asked, gesturing with her spear point upwards.

'Not clouds, no. I've not seen many of those before. Certainly not this many at one time. They mean something is happening.'

Peter seemed to fall into thought for a while, and Ruth felt he'd forgotten her question. She lowered her spear a little and asked again.

'It's hard for me to say what we follow,' he answered. 'It is much easier for me to show you.'

Ruth remained wary, but was immediately intrigued.

'Come,' he said, 'and I'll show you.'

He stood and put out his arm in a gesture of invitation, then turned and walked away from her, north up the side of the valley edge. Ruth shifted her bag into a better position and lifted her spear point again towards the old man. He walked around the side of the dune and Ruth followed at a short distance. His footprints were large and well-defined. Ruth half expected to see that they were wet, like the ones she had noticed in the City, but she was disappointed. She rounded the dune and saw that Peter was crossing another and climbing away from the valley towards the broad, parched desert.

They had not gone far when he stopped. He turned and smiled, then gestured onwards again.

'Not far now, and then you'll see.'

'You first,' Ruth said firmly.

Peter pressed on and walked around another low dune and into the dip on the other side. Ruth followed quickly and saw him crouching down, studying the ground. The sand looked unremarkable. He grinned up at her.

'Look at this,' he said earnestly.

Ruth's curiosity finally overcame her wariness and she padded over to him and dropped her bag on the sand. It was cool and its texture felt unusual to the soles of her feet.

'Look,' he said again, his voice filled with awe.

Ruth's heart skipped a beat. Here, on the edge of the merciless desert and high above Esar's valley of sickly grass, was life. Tiny green shoots were uncurling from beneath the surface of the sand. Tender stems and the freshest green leaves pushed their way up into the light. In the sandy bowl between two small dunes, new plants were growing. Even in their immature state, Ruth could see that the leaves would be too broad and the stems too thick for the grasses she knew. This was something else.

'How …?' she said, the question failing in her astonishment.

'Let me show you more,' Peter smiled, and he dug down into the sand.

He excavated a deep but narrow hole and, with each handful, the sand he pulled out darkened. At the depth of his elbow, he stopped and stared into the hollow. He put his hand into his sash and drew out a scrap of white cloth, like the piece Naomi had given Ruth. Down it went into the hole. After a moment he brought it back up again and held it out to her. She took it from him, anticipating with great excitement what it meant, but still could scarcely believe it when she touched the cloth. It was wet. Saturated. Water dripped from its folds and rushed out of the fabric with every touch and squeeze. Beneath her trembling hand, drops fell and scattered in a glimmering shower across the darkening sand. The light seemed to bend around the water and Ruth saw tiny specks of unusual colour flash and change. Then the droplets were gone, sucked into the thirsty sand and dry air. Ruth turned the cloth over and sent another wonderful shower onto the tiny green shoots below.

'You follow this?' she whispered, as if the noise of her voice might break the moment.

Peter simply nodded.

'How?' she asked.

'Go a little way down to where I met you. Then walk back up this way. Tell me what you see.'

Ruth got up and did as he said. She saw three rows of footprints: her own fresh impressions leading back to where she stood, and the double set of hers and Peter's following the contour of the dune to where the old man was sitting. She did not see anything unusual, and walked back up the route she had just travelled. But as she approached the seedlings, she saw that something had changed. She looked closely at one of Peter's footprints. There was a dark spot in the sand beneath the heel. She glanced to the next and saw the same thing, and in the next and the one after that. She looked further on, and saw that the dark spots grew in size and depth of colour the closer she got to the new growth. She bent over and poked the shadowed sand with her finger. It was damp. Water had come back into the desert. It was a miracle.

But there was a doubt in Ruth's mind. She looked from her own small footprints to Peter's; only his were darkened. Hers were still dry. It made no sense. If there was water in the ground here, why didn't it rise up evenly? Why only in Peter's footprints?

He saw her scowl. 'What's wrong?' he asked.

'I don't understand,' she said. 'You can make the water come up.

Why can't I?'

'It's a mystery,' he replied gently, 'but you should know that I can't make the water come. I only follow it. If I could make it come at my will, why would I only make it flow in the desert over here where I sit, and not over there where we met?'

'But Esar can make the water come and go. The Order can do it. If you're the same as them, why can't you?' Ruth's frustration and confusion fed into her impatience.

'As I said, we're not the same. Not any more. They have imposed their power over the water that flows in the desert. Did you taste the Order's water?'

Ruth nodded, and Peter continued. 'What was it like? Remember the colour and taste. Remember the grass that grew from it. Taking power has not improved things.'

He spoke patiently, and she became aware of her rudeness.

'How do they do it?' she asked sulkily.

'The Order? I'm not certain, but they don't do it by walking in the fields. No, the answer to that question lies inside the tent on Esar's mound. In the centre. I'd like to see what really goes on in there.'

'What is that thing in the middle of the tent – that thing like a giant piece of horn?'

Peter shook his head. 'Again, I do not know. I believe it to be a well – a place where they collect water. Somehow they move it from the well into the fields. However they do it, they manage to kill the water.'

'You seem to know the City very well for an outsider,' Ruth said, unable to keep the suspicion out of her voice.

'I was here some weeks ago, with some friends, but we know the City of old. Our people were like cousins to the Cityfolk. How things change. Anyway, when I was last here I camped further up, over there,' and he gestured over his shoulder to the north-eastern side of the valley. 'We wanted to see if anyone in the City would join us, but we knew Esar would have burnt us if we had walked in openly. So we made our way down at night to look around. We found people still remembered the old songs about us, and a few came to join us. They now follow along with us. They've left their old lives behind.'

'You took them in the night?' Ruth said incredulously. 'I was here in the City for a while. One morning there was lots of shouting. People were crying. They said the blood drinkers took people in the night – men, women, children!'

'No!' Peter answered firmly. 'We didn't *take* anyone. They came of their own accord. We can't make anyone come along. All we can do is invite people. You said yourself that only death was down there. We want everyone to have enough to drink and to eat, but if we offer it openly, the Order will kill us. So what are we supposed to do? Drink some of that water I gave you! And then you see if you can tell me that you would be happy for your friends and loved ones to go on drinking Esar's foul water, even though you knew there was a fresh, clean source.'

'I've already had some and I know. You're right. It is better,' said Ruth.

Peter's calm returned.

'Do you have any family, uh …?' he asked, drawing the question out until Ruth filled in the gap.

'Ruth. My name is Ruth. I have a father, Dan. No mother.'

'I'm sorry to hear that, Ruth. Where is your father?' he enquired gently.

'Down there, in the City. That is why I'm here.'

'Is he coming out? Are you going to meet him?'

'No. Esar took him.'

Peter looked shocked. 'Why? Whatever for?'

Then Ruth told him her story of finding the Wonderful Path, of coming into the City and everything since. She tried to keep it brief, but even then her tale took some time to tell. She showed him the cup and the staves, then the cloth, but she did not feel ready to talk about her visions.

When she had finished, Peter remained silent. His old eyes flickered at great speed as he thought hard about she had said, and what could be done.

'You've told me so much I hardly know where to begin,' he said. 'We have nearly met so many times. We've missed each other at almost every turn. I was the one who left those wet footprints in the sand, down in the City. You followed the very path I trod through the houses and tents. This cup and these staves are relics of my people. Your friends, Naomi and Boaz, could hardly have understood where they came from or what they are for. Especially these.' Peter picked up the staves. 'You see, I don't have a cup, but I have my own pair of these.'

He reached into his sash and brought out two weathered and hand-smoothed staves of wood, very like Ruth's. He gave them to her and she felt the same eager energy tingle through her hands as she had with the pair Boaz had given her.

'Listen now to me, Ruth,' Peter went on, 'because there is so much to do and no time to do it. There is something I want you to understand.'

'What?' Ruth asked hurriedly, eyes searching.

'The Way we follow – it isn't just about digging for water and hoping to find it. There is something more. Something wonderful that allows us to find life in the desert and water in the driest places of the world. This is what makes us who we are. We follow, but we do it with these.' Peter held up his two staves. 'Copy what I do, and you may get a feel for what I'm trying to say.'

He stood up, full of haste and energy despite his apparent age, and led Ruth to a dune overlooking the City and the valley.

'What you've got to understand, Ruth, is that there is enough water in the world for everybody. There is enough water to transform the desert in a way neither you, nor I, nor Esar can possibly imagine. Esar, for good or bad, can control a source of water. But he limits it;

he sells it; he kills it. It goes rotten. If he released it, he could turn this whole valley to lush fields, thick, green and fresh. There would be bushes of all kinds, and fruit growing on trees. Oh, trees? They're tall bushes, bigger than men. There would be enough for everyone – there would be plenty!

'But look what he's done! Dying grass, dry land and no life. He buys and sells lives when it isn't his place to do so. Why is this valley dry and dead? There should be a river here. It isn't supposed to be like this!'

Peter was almost shouting now, incensed by the universal betrayal of Esar. He clenched and unclenched his fists. Then, with a great effort, he calmed himself and his tone became more even.

'Sometimes the water stays in one place and rises up in a well, like here in the City. But it also moves. We follow the moving water. There are underground streams and rivers that we can't know about just by looking. We have to be careful. That's where these come in.'

He flourished his staves. 'Take one of yours in each hand.' he said, and Ruth obeyed. 'Hold each at its end, but lightly; don't grip too hard. Do you feel anything?'

'I don't know,' she said. 'Something … but I think it's just me – my hands shaking.'

'That's fine. It is very important for you to tell the difference between your movements and others. Turn to where we left your bag, where our little well is. Do you sense anything now?'

'Maybe. It's hard to tell.'

'It is hard,' he agreed. 'Now try and cross your staves.'

Ruth gave him a puzzled look, but she tried anyway. She gripped the staves and forced them towards each other. They seemed to resist, not allowing her muscles to move them very close. Her arms quivered with the effort, and at last she forced them together. It didn't feel good, but Ruth could not tell why.

'Relax,' Peter said, seeing in her struggle what he had hoped for. 'Do you see the difference? You can't force them. Hold them lightly again, and let's go back to your bag.'

The pair walked the short distance from the valley's edge to the little well. With every step, Ruth felt a pulse of energy tingle through her hands. The staves responded and twitched.

'Do you see what is happening?' Peter asked, and Ruth realised she'd closed her eyes in the intense concentration of it all. She opened them, and saw that her hands were moving closer together with every step towards the nearby water source.

'Let your hands be light,' Peter instructed, prompting her to loosen her grip.

As soon as she did so, the points of the staves twitched towards each other, and her hands were able to return to their more comfortable position in line with her shoulders. Keeping her eyes open, she 'listened' to the sticks and watched them move. Closer and closer to the well they went, and closer to each other the wooden tips became. Peter's were moving the same way, too. They were only a few paces from the water. Suddenly, Ruth's staves jerked wildly and leapt in her hands. She gripped them fiercely, and fought them with all the strength in her arms.

At last, she was standing above the well and the green shoots sprouting through the sand, and the struggle became too much. She dropped the staves and they fell to the ground and were still.

'What happened?' Ruth asked, her voice trembling.

'You tried to hold on to them too hard,' Peter said, calmly, as if this was all completely normal. 'Pick them up, but hold them *lightly*. You'll see the difference.'

Ruth hesitantly bent down to gather up the staves. Immediately, she felt the surge of power through them, then the disturbing twitch and jump, and she gripped.

'Lightly,' Peter insisted, in a half-whisper.

She released her clamped fingers and the movement smoothed. Before her wide eyes, the tips of the staves moved inwards, slowly.

They crossed over each other and stopped suddenly in an X-shape directly above the well hole.

'The X shows you,' she murmured, scarcely believing. 'This is how you follow the water?'

'Where we see this,' Peter said happily, pointing to her crossed staves, 'we know there is water and water in abundance. We look for the cross.'

Then his tone changed to one of urgency. 'You may wonder why I am telling you this. I must go for help – enough help to overthrow Esar and restore the City. And to do this I must move quickly. I will have to leave you alone. You must stay here until I return, and keep watch. When I come back with our friends, you will be able to tell us of any changes. But if anything happens when I'm away and you don't know what to do, just follow the staves and look for that cross. The water has a way of leading you to where you are supposed to be. Remember that!'

'Why are you doing all this? Why would you save a stranger – my father?' Ruth asked, confused and amazed and overcome by it all.

'It isn't just about your father, although he's a part of it. There are more people down there who need the Order gone. They need this water – this is *living* water.'

Peter began to walk north at a quick pace. Ruth followed, running sideways next to him as he spoke to her.

'There is more to tell – much more, but now, I must go. I've not told you nearly enough. Your father is in terrible danger, if he is alive at all. I have a hope that he is. But there is no telling how many lives Esar has taken, or will take, if he is left unchallenged. Perhaps we can rescue your father. Only to do so, we must stop Esar and remove the Order, and we can't do that alone. That's why I'm going for help. I would prefer you to stay out of all of this – it is just too dangerous – but as you are here, you can at least keep a lookout over the City. Wait for my return. Stay up here, and keep out of sight. And remember – if you get in trouble, use the staves. They will guide you!'

'When will you be back?' Ruth cried, surprised by Peter's sudden need for departure.

'As soon I can,' he replied. 'Have you got anything to eat? No? Have this. My people aren't far away. Maybe I can reach them by midnight. I will come back with enough of them to take the City from the Order. Stay here and watch. We will need to know if anything is happening down there.'

He turned suddenly to Ruth and, again, she was taken by surprise. Peter clasped her hand, and pressed a small bundle of rough cloth into it.

'This is one more thing that you should see. Tomorrow when we meet, I'll explain it to you, but for now just have a look for yourself. Only,' and he stared so hard into Ruth's face that she could scarcely hold his gaze, 'whatever happens, keep safe. Keep out of danger.'

His eyes remained fixed on hers a moment longer. Then he nodded at her with a grin, and turned.

'It is time. Goodbye!'

The old man hobbled away at surprising speed, leaving Ruth to walk back to the little well and the sapling plants, clutching her pair of staves, the rough cloth and a chunk of unusual bread that he had given her.

When she reached the place, she sat down. She flopped onto her hands and knees and peered into the small hole. The little well was narrow and dark, so she couldn't see much except the occasional glint of reflected cloud on the small surface of the water. She was thirsty. Cupping her hand, she lowered it into the well. The water was very cold, but it was much deeper than she thought it would be; the small cavity in the sand was filling up slowly as the liquid seeped into it.

She withdrew her cupped hand and looked at its contents. The water was clear and fragrant and full of promise. She drank quickly, spilling most of it. Then she retrieved Naomi's clay cup from her bag and lowered it into the well. She could just about hold onto the rim and let it down without needing to widen the hole. When it was full, she brought it back up and drank again, relishing the now familiar but undimmed sensation of invigorating, fully satisfying water.

She leaned on her bag, cup in hand, and thought of the stale offering of the Jacobswells, and the vile, bitterness of Esar's Gift. If the Tribe and the Order were 'cousins', as Peter had said, there was no question to which side of the family Ruth wanted to belong. She anxiously wondered if she was good enough to be accepted. Peter himself had been into the City to invite people to join the Tribe. The idea was astonishing. Belonging to a tribe wasn't a matter of choice; you were born a Miller or a Herder, and then you knew who to hate. Ruth could not turn into a Herder, so did she really think she could become a Follower, one of Rain's people? Doubts blew up in her mind, a confusing sandstorm of ideas and wonderings. She cleared them with action, moving her things from the small well to the valley's edge where she could keep watch over the City.

While Ruth and Peter had talked, the afternoon had marched on quickly. The Millers were still in the fields, but oddly, the Herders had already returned with their flocks and were going back to their houses. Ruth lay on the sand to keep out of sight and watched the sun descend from above the blanket of cloud to light the western sky.

At length the Millers returned to their homes. All was quiet for some time, then, in ones and twos and small groups, the Cityfolk left their houses and went around the City on different errands. Ruth could not tell which was Herder and which was Miller. Some carried sacks, presumably of grass seed for grinding to flour. Others went to the edges of the City and began dismantling the derelict tents. Still others brought grass bundles for fuel. The settlement was a hive of activity. Ruth could see a general movement towards the west – to the other side – where these materials were being collected. Perhaps the evening party would take place on that side. And maybe at nightfall, under cover of darkness, she could sneak down unseen and scout it out. She might learn something to help Peter.

Ruth realised she was hungry. She did not have much to eat except for Peter's bread and some scraps of supplies she had taken when she left Boaz and Naomi. Put together, it seemed a small meal. The bread was the colour of the whitest sand and the size of her fist. It looked as if it would disintegrate into flakes at any moment, so she thought she'd better eat that first. She took a bite. A score of unknown flavours coursed through her mouth. There was an intense joy to the bread, and her tongue felt thick and sated with sweetness. The texture was fresh and light, and the dough pure and unmixed with ashen dust as Ruth had expected. She felt peaceful and stimulated, restful and invigorated, full even after a small amount. Once satisfied, she drank again, and replaced the cup in her bag.

Her hands brushed the coarse material of the cloth Peter had given her when he left. It was neatly folded and the back was alive with bristles of frayed thread-ends. She undid it carelessly, not seeing at first what it was. Then her hands paused in their hasty work.

Unfolding before her was a tapestry. It was a marvel. On the reverse side of the cloth, the dark tangle of thread-ends transformed into images of delicate, expressive beauty. Faces of men, women and children looked up at her from a land of vivid colours. Green, gold and rich red hills poured from the tapestry and into her wide eyes. She saw strange buildings, much larger than the City's squat houses; she saw animals unknown to her and men using wonderful devices to carve up the earth. There was life everywhere; there was no desert.

A man stood out. She recognised him – it was the Esar of the Order's tapestry. Or it was the man the Order claimed was Esar. This figure walked among the people and life followed him. There were clouds in the sky, and Ruth saw in the magnificent pictures before her the content of her visions: water moving in the world. It ran along the ground, and fell through the air, splitting into bright colours. She remembered Naomi's words that distant night with Salmon and Boaz; she remembered the earnest talk that spoke of only one person: Rain. Could this be him? Rain, the word on the whisper of the Third Tribe. He moved further through the tapestry, and seemed to leave the world in the care of his followers.

And then he was gone.

Ruth did not understand. There was no explanation.

Other men appeared in the images and with them came the dust. Greens paled to yellows and golden threads wore out. The men's faces were cruel and their clothes dark. The dust became ever stronger, and the men killed each other. Ruth could only guess at the meaning of the story unfolding before her, but there was war in the time of plenty. And the desert came on, bleaching the hillsides and filling the houses with the encroaching dust, while the water disappeared.

There was more to the tapestry, much more, only the day was fading fast. Ruth squinted at it, eager to see more of this strange story, but the light was too weak. She ran her fingers along the cloth's surface, desperate to understand. Their tips touched faces and hands and hillsides, but she could not tell what they signified.

The sun slipped lower and, the very moment it finally dropped behind the western dunes, the drums began.

Chapter Sixteen

THE DRUMS WERE HESITANT AT FIRST, as if the beaters were testing their skins. In a few moments the first confident throbs of a baleful rhythm echoed across the plain and around the valley.

Ruth needed to know what was going on. The light in the western sky was pale and fading fast. There was no movement on the eastern side of the City. She could enter it unseen and find out what was happening. Then she could go back to meet Peter.

She carefully folded the tapestry and put it, along with her worldly goods, into her skin bag. The staves she slipped into her robe and then picked up the spear, tucking the bag behind a solitary and ancient tussock that stood nearby. The cloud cover had brought on the dusk quicker than usual, so Ruth felt safe enough to slip down the side of the valley and race across the open plain. She would only find out what was going on, and then retreat back to the little well.

She entered the City exactly where she had done before, except that this time the surroundings had changed. Most of the tents on this side had been pulled down, leaving the crater remains of their sunken structures. All the materials that could be used for fire – the wood and cloth – had been taken. Those leftovers that would not burn were scattered in broken chaos across this side of the City.

Ruth moved quickly through this valley of dry bones towards the houses that were now the outer ring of the City's habitation. She ducked behind a low wall and listened. The drums were loud, and it was hard to hear if there was anybody about. She peeked around the wall's end. The light in the distant sky was almost completely gone, but she could see a little way down the dusty path that divided the houses. The way was clear. She moved quickly from dwelling to dwelling, always listening, always looking. Everybody was gone, presumably around the other side of the City to where the drums now beat a wild and primeval tempo. Horns sounded above the relentless rhythm, and light flared in the distance. In a few moments, a column of thin smoke rose above the houses and up towards the clouds. It took on a pink and orange glow from the fire below. Ruth moved on.

She wove quickly around the buildings and came out suddenly on the wide path that surrounded the holy mound. Still there was no sign of anyone. Standing on the path, she stared up at the tent, daring herself to climb the shadowy form of the Sanctuary hillock. She desperately wanted to, but now was not the time to draw back the curtain that divided the valley from the inner world of the Order. So she stepped off the path and continued north around the low hill, past houses like any other, until she came to the northernmost quarter of the City. Here, too, she could see on her right hand side that the tents had been dismantled and all the flammable materials harvested. The settlement had contracted. The drums beat on.

As Ruth made her way to the western quarter, the orange glow brightened. In the space on this side that had been the tented ring, she saw a tower of flame licking high into the night sky. A massive fire raged in the centre of a broad circle of cleared land. Small groups were clustered around it in tight knots. Men laughed. Women screamed. Closest to Ruth, there was a wide circle of onlookers who had linked arms and were shouting and jeering at each other.

As Ruth drew nearer, she saw that there were two figures inside the circle. This group of Cityfolk had made a rudimentary arena in which they were forcing two combatants onto each other. If one was not suitably aggressive to his opponent, he would be kicked from behind by the wall of sneering revellers. One of the two was badly beaten and wore a mask of blood.

Ruth circled around them as far as she could whilst remaining within the rows of houses. She lay behind one of the walls, her head just peeping around the corner so that she could watch and listen. Food was being passed around, as were skins of what was probably a brew of fermented grain, made primarily to change the water's foul taste. Yet it worked its side-effect powerfully.

Ruth saw a large number of drummers on the far side of the fire beating their instruments at a terrible pace, some with their hands and others with clubs. Dancers capered on the sand in the throes of dark euphoria. The little they wore was goatskin, with grass bunched around their knees and elbows, and their limbs flailed as they spun and leapt, to the amusement of the onlookers.

To one side, quite calmly, Esar was sitting observing the scene. He drank occasionally from a cup that shone red and silver in the firelight, and ate meat from a small platter of the same reflective material. Ruth did not doubt that he enjoyed the finest meat and the purest water. The dancing and fighting went on for some time and Esar oversaw it all, a proud and amused master of ceremonies amid the mad and the terrified. He was enthroned on carefully piled fuel that lay ready for the fire, and attended by a large contingent of his Order, their dusky robes hiding them well in the blackness. The darkness of night was barely kept away by the light of the huge fire. It swirled around the red flames, waiting for the weak fuel to run out as it surely would; it crept through the City where shadows danced with the flickering glow; it passed over Ruth as she lay mute and hidden.

The thumping heat and intentioned malevolence of the City was in full force, and Esar revelled in it.

The chill of the sunless hours crept into Ruth. She sat up behind the wall and rubbed the stiffness and cold from her limbs. Then she moved to the other end of the low house and lay in the same fashion there, well hidden but with a fair view of what was unfolding before her. She noticed immediately that Esar had stood up, and was now walking towards the fire and the dancers. The drummers played on until he raised his hand. Their beat petered out to nothing. The fighting revellers and their unwilling gladiators took a little longer to realise what was happening, but then they, too, turned their attention to the skinny figure wrapped in black that held such power over them.

'Friends,' Esar began with a smile, projecting his voice well above the intense crackling of the fire, 'I am so glad that you could all come this evening. It is good of you to be here on this historic occasion. For tonight is truly historic, because tomorrow is a new day that marks a new era. Life in our glorious City will change forever with the rising of the morning sun. Nature herself foresees it. What you see above you in the sky is a sign from the heavens that the Old Order is passing away – and the New Order is born!'

Esar paused as a wave of astonishment broke over the attending Cityfolk.

'You heard me!' he repeated. 'The Old Order is passing away and the New Order is begun!'

Raising his hand and nodding, he continued, 'I know what your concerns are. You are afraid that I will leave you and others will take over. Fear not, dear friends! There have for too long been unnatural divisions between the tribes of this City which exist for no good reason. Three tribes there are!'

There was another ripple of astonishment as Esar appeared to acknowledge the forbidden Third Tribe, but it quickly became clear that he had not. He raised his fist to count them off.

'One! The Herders; our favourite sons. Two! The Millers; our prodigal sons. Three! The Order; servants of everyone.'

Esar did not recognise Rain's people after all.

'These are the three separate tribes that co-exist within the peaceful harmony of the City. Yet there is no reason that there should be such division. The blood drinkers can sow seeds of division between us and rob us of our women and children. We will not let them! The Old Order is passing away and the New Order is born. This means that there will no longer be Herders and Millers and Ordermen. There will be one tribe for one City and *all* will be called members of the New Order.

'There will, of course, be Upper and Lower Orders, for administrative purposes, but one Order there shall be! We have begun to clear the tents and we shall complete this great task. We shall also take down some of the inner houses and use their bricks to construct an encircling wall, linking the outer houses to make a great defence. We will not be raided by the thieving wanderers!

'This is the night that marks the end of the world as you know it! Eat, drink and remember that I am the one who gave you all this, and tomorrow I will give you more!'

Ruth had heard enough. She crawled backwards behind the wall as the Herders raised raucous cheers above Esar's voice. The drums struck up again with renewed energy. The party, it seemed, would continue for some time yet.

She crept away through the houses, close to the outer edge, towards the northern quarter, then dashed silently from alley to alley across the paths and spaces between the low dwellings.

Suddenly, she brought herself up short, sure that she was being followed. She ducked into a house through a doorway that pointed out towards the plain, over the ruin of the tents. Staring at the opening, she held her spear at the ready. The drums were as loud as ever, but she swore she could hear somebody walking nearby, feet noisily cracking broken bones among the wreckage of dismantled shelters.

Through the doorway she saw a flicker of shadow. A man passed by. He was walking leisurely, as if in no hurry. Perhaps he had not been following her after all. This might be a sentry patrolling on the perimeter. Ruth waited a while to give him time to move on, and then crept out of the house and into the shadows to avoid the dwindling glow of the distant fire. A short way ahead, moving through the broken tents, was an Orderman, clad in black and hard to spot at any greater range. He was going east – her way towards the hills and the well.

Ruth panicked. She ducked back into the house to consider her options more safely. Could she follow him, and try to get past him? If she failed, the alarm would be raised and the Order would come for her. She could go due north right now, but if the sentry changed direction and returned this way, she would be seen in the firelight. Perhaps she could alter her route and find a different path out of the City. She might not meet other sentries, although that was unlikely. If there was one, there would be more. It was impossible that she could successfully hide for the rest of the night and all of tomorrow too, until Peter returned with help – if he returned at all, a voice whispered within her.

She reached into her robes and retrieved the staves. What did they really mean? They were just bits of wood. It was probably all made up – pure chance that Peter had found that well. She put down her spear and held one stave in each hand. Nothing. Told you so, the voice within her murmured.

Then one stick moved. A tiny twitch, the least of trembles, but it was there. Ruth saw it; she felt it.

She waited. Again, nothing. Then they both moved together.

She felt a strong impulse to stand and get out of the house. Leaping up, she tucked her spear under one arm, then left the low building and turned towards the centre of the City. It felt right. She ran between the houses, and that felt almost as right. She had to remind herself to hold the staves with open hands. In the glow, she saw them leaning in towards each other by a fraction. They were urging her on.

Ruth crossed a main path that bisected the northern quarter and approached the holy mound. Still the staves pushed her on. She reached the foot of the dune.

Something must be wrong, she thought. I'm not going up there, I've got to get out of here!

Nevertheless the staves pointed her forward, up the side of the mound to the tent. She checked and rechecked, holding them so loosely that she thought she might drop them. But every time the answer was clear enough to read in the darkness, and every time the impulsion within her grew. She stepped forward onto the foot of the holy mound.

Ruth began to climb up to one side of the summit, away from the tent itself, and more somewhere beyond. The staves were guiding her past the entrance, not towards it. To her great relief, there were no sentries at the top, and the glow from the fire was hugely dimmed.

She looked over to the party circle and saw that Esar's men were gathering fuel to replenish the flames. She had a few moments before they would light up the western side of the City once more. If she didn't get off the holy mound, she would be seen by any sentry who had it within his sight.

Still, the staves urged her onwards, away from the City into the hills, but something else was now beckoning. A dark impulse from the gaping maw of the tent's doorway summoned her. Contrary to her newly formed trust in Peter and Rain's people, Ruth began to listen to the seductive throb of curiosity. Her heartbeat pulsed through her mind as she fought with herself.

Out on the plain of destroyed tents, the first of Esar's servants approached the fire. Ruth made her choice; the blaze flared and a renewed glow lit up the City.

And she was inside the tent.

The interior was one room under a large patchwork of cloth

scraps. The light from the fire filtered through the sand-worn fabric and lit the tent's western side with a dull, orange haze. The material was supported by a series of long, wooden poles that ran away from Ruth in both directions around the centre of the tent, where the stone wall of the spike rose up out of the sand. The spike's wall dominated the room. It was very large, with strongly defined edges that cast sharp silhouettes into the gloom.

The room was full of things Ruth could not easily identify. There were strange and intriguing shapes in the darkness, and she reached out to feel them. She found there were heaps of bags made of skin or cloth, and her inquisitive fingers discovered the forms of grain or grass stalks or rolls of cloth. The space was full of precious supplies. There were great stacks of bricks and bundles of sticks, good building materials kept from the hands of the Cityfolk. She found piles and piles of straw torches, arranged near kindling and some flints. Jamming her staves into her robe, Ruth grabbed a torch and dared to light it. The orange tongue flared brightly in the tent.

She looked again at the face of the spike in the new light, and ran her hand across its rough surface. The wall was certainly not a natural formation. There were clear joins in the square-cut stones, as if someone had hewn them from a giant rock face and somehow fused them together. The slabs were even decorated, and the cornerstones appeared to be different colours from the greater part of the wall. Ruth walked around the spike and her fingers explored the changing texture of the different stones. Her hand bounced off an irregularity, and her torch caught the edges and marked them with black shadows: there was a gaping rent in the stonework and the darkness loomed from within.

Suddenly, she heard a noise – furtive steps from the other side of the tent by the entrance. Someone knew she was here! The spike stood between her and the newcomer, but which way he (or she) would come around it to catch her, Ruth didn't know.

She flourished her short spear in one hand, the torch clutched in the other. The steps came one way, and she turned to face them. Then they retreated and moved towards her from the other direction, and again Ruth twisted towards them. Her assailant knew he'd been heard so he charged. Ruth drew back the spear to strike and thrust the torch into his face. He threw his arms up to protect himself from the flames and Ruth lunged for his throat. The man slipped and fell backwards, and the spear point jabbed over his head, missing him. Quickly, Ruth pulled it back and stepped forward to finish the prone figure. His voice rang out.

'Don't! Ruth, it's me! Boaz!'

Sure enough it was. He lay on his back, arms raised in helpless defence. She saw that he'd dropped his millstones and his horn knife.

'Boaz!' she cried, surprised, delighted and annoyed. 'I could have killed you! What are you doing here?'

'I came to help,' he said pathetically. 'I followed you from where you left us. You could have been in danger. It wasn't hard to guess where you were heading, but it's taken me this long to find you.' His voice turned into a reproach. 'It was that torch that led me here. You can see it a mile off. Any one of the Order could come.'

'I thought that's who you were! Why didn't you say it was you?' she argued.

'Keep your voice down!' he hissed. 'I didn't say *anything* because I thought you were a prisoner. I found your bag in the hills. I thought you'd been captured, and it was as good a guess as any that you'd been brought here. I was coming to rescue you.'

Ruth softened then. 'Where's Naomi?'

'On her way to join the Third Tribe. She should have reached them yesterday.' Boaz shifted uncomfortably. 'Can we get out of here? Let's talk about all of this when we're safe. Why did you come in here anyway? This is the last place we should be.'

'If you knew where I was heading, you should have guessed why!

My father! I had a vision that day – the day of the avalanche; the day the clouds came. I saw him. He needs me.'

'We guessed it was because of your father,' Boaz admitted, 'but we thought … we thought you weren't yourself. We thought you had come here on purpose – to die.'

'No,' said Ruth in a hard voice. 'I came to rescue him. That's why I'm here … And that's why I'm going in there.'

She thrust her torch in the direction of the hole in the spike's wall. 'This is the way in.'

'What on earth is it?' Boaz gaped. In the dim light, he hadn't noticed it before.

'Peter says it's a well. But I think my father is down there.'

'Peter?' Boaz was becoming increasingly confused. 'Who is Peter?'

'Shut up, Boaz! Get some more torches. We'll need them.'

Ruth gave Boaz no time to object and marched to the threshold of the dark fissure. She leaned into it with the torch outstretched, balancing herself against the hole's frame. The rent in the spike's wall opened over a pit of nothing, a realm of absolute dark. Ruth leaned a little further, hoping to see something, anything that might help her find a way down. The torch flickered and struggled in the damp air that rotted slowly in the well's shaft, and she smelt the rank stench of old water turned to a foul soup by things long dead.

Yet it was down here that she must go – somehow. She saw that the shaft was largely square, with the same sorts of decoration in the stonework as on the outside.

Boaz returned with additional torches that he'd bundled up into a more manageable pack and slung over his back. He bent forward past Ruth, peering downwards, and whistled.

'This is unbelievable,' he said, awestruck.

'That's where we're going,' she replied, telling him by the tone of her voice more about her fears than she meant to.

'Let's get on with it, then,' Boaz shrugged matter-of-factly.

He glanced quickly round the inside wall of the well, and spotted what Ruth had missed: a frame of blackened rails that extended in two continuous lines up and down as far as either could see. The unbroken lines were bisected at regular intervals by a rung of the same black material. Boaz reached out and touched it. It was cold and hard – very hard. He leaned his weight on it. It was solid.

'I'm pretty sure I can climb onto that and get down. It will hold me, I think. Look, do you see how it's joined to the wall here and here? I bet this goes all the way to the bottom. Let me get on to it and then hand me a torch.'

Ruth nodded and moved aside to give him more room.

Boaz gripped the frame with both hands and tentatively placed one foot on a lower rung. It held him, so he pulled himself wholly onto it. He grinned at Ruth and held out his hand for the torch. She went to pass it to him, then quickly pulled it back.

'If I give it to you, you'll go down there and I'll be left in the dark up here,' she pointed out. 'Let me light another one first.'

Boaz hooked one arm around the climbing frame, pulled a torch from his supply, and leaned towards Ruth with the fresh one outstretched. She touched hers against his and, in a moment, the new one flared brightly in the dark column. Then he began to climb down into the well. He gripped his torch with two fingers of one hand so that he could still use both hands for climbing, pointing the flames to one side to avoid them. In their struggling light, Ruth saw details appearing. Thick ropes snaked up from the far wall towards the unknown ceiling above. Shapes of heavily patterned stone emerged from the darkness, like miniature doorways blockaded with scraps of wood.

Boaz looked up at her. 'I don't know how deep this goes, but if you're coming down, you may as well start climbing now,' he said. 'It's easy once you get the hang of it.'

Ruth steeled herself. The drop was immeasurable and the dark overwhelming. The black pit loomed beneath her and she swayed uneasily as she looked down. She closed her eyes and breathed, holding her torch like Boaz with a couple of fingers, and gripping the frame with the others. She did the same with the spear in her other hand.

The crosspieces were highly polished and slippery and Ruth did not like trusting them. She put one foot on a rung and stepped out fully. Her leading foot jerked sideways and banged painfully into the frame. In an instant, she lost her grip and grabbed at the rungs with snatching, fearful hands. Her torch and spear plummeted into nothing. The spear landed with a clatter a little distance below, and the torch roared after it as it fell, rushing past Boaz and down through the column of air, then bouncing in a breath of sparks next to it. They did not have far to climb.

The torch lay on what looked like a floor made of wood, cut to exact shapes like the stone and arranged with a skill unknown in these days. Ruth was not sure, but she thought she could see the shadows of two doorways leading away from it. Boaz was the first to reach the bottom.

'Unbelievable,' he whispered to himself, just loud enough for Ruth to hear.

She reached the platform after a few moments and picked up her fallen torch and spear. Then she crossed to stand by him, and saw what he could not describe.

They hadn't reached the bottom of the well at all. They were on a platform suspended above a chasm of perfect black. In front of them rose a panel of strange material. It was shattered and jagged in places, and there were many panes within it that were joined by a dark substance. The panes were encrusted with ancient dirt and damp, but when the two of them held their torches close, they could see through it where it was not too fouled. It gave them the sense that they were high up, overlooking something vast. They could not see what lay beyond the feeble glow of two little torches, but they sensed it. They smelt a massive cavern of air that hovered over an unseen expanse of rotten stone and damp wood. They knew the distance in the distant drip-drip of falling water. They felt it on their skin.

'He's here,' Ruth breathed with unshakable certainty.

Boaz did not need to question her.

'Which way?' he simply asked.

She looked around her and saw that there were two doorways, one to the left and one to the right. But which one? Before she found the answer Boaz spoke again.

'Look, here,' he said, pointing at the wall next to the right hand doorway.

A torch hung on a small, dark ring embedded in the stone. It was fairly dry, given the dampness that hung in the air. Boaz touched his own torch to it. With the aid of some breaths, it caught alight and spluttered into flame.

'I wonder if there are more?' he mused.

'May as well go this way,' Ruth said, unsure if it had been wise to light the torch. But they were carrying torches, too, so perhaps one more didn't matter.

Then she had a thought. If any Ordermen came down here, the two of them would be spotted easily; their torches would stand out in the dark, and extinguishing them wasn't an option. After all, the blackness would finish them more desperately than the Ordermen could. But if Boaz and Ruth lit all the torches they came across, and filled this hole with light, it wouldn't be so obvious where they were, or even where the Ordermen should start looking for them. That might give them the chance they needed.

'Good,' she said to herself, and to Boaz, 'Light any torches you see.'

Chapter Seventeen

RUTH STEPPED THROUGH THE DOORWAY on the right onto a spiral staircase. The darkness fled downwards. She held her spear in her right hand and the torch in her left, descending slowly and placing her feet carefully on the slippery steps. The spear's sharp point led the way. Nothing confronted her except the rising sensation of damp in the air and the darkness of unknown ages. She emerged onto a walkway that squelched underfoot. Black mud of old, wet sand and unknown foulness oozed between her toes and made walking uncertain. She edged slowly along, and whispered a warning to Boaz as he followed her out from the stairway behind her. She was pleased to see another torch, which she lit. The feeble light revealed in turn another not far away. She padded slowly towards it and lit that, too. She saw another, and another, and realised they ran the length of this floor. Boaz found a second stairwell, broader than the last, leading down to yet another floor.

Ruth lit more torches, and they fizzled and spat when the drips of moisture found them. She went further along, and discovered a strange structure of wood. Thick, wooden beams had been braced against the stone wall, holding a solid screen of planks in place. Just as in her vision, one vast trunk of wood, bigger than all the others, rose from the centre of the floor and pressed its strength into the wooden supports. The framework did not reach up to the ceiling, so Ruth supposed that it was not supporting anything. It was as if it was holding something back. She peered at the frame's edges where the wood met the stone wall. There was a change in the pattern, and she guessed that the wall became a doorway or window, but a window on to what? The unknown depths of the sand?

She moved on, lighting torches as she went. She saw that there were three such frameworks, all braced against the wall, apparently holding it back. She looked beyond as the torches grew in vigour and lit up the darkness, revealing more of the size and shape of the cavern.

Ruth and Boaz were on a long, narrow platform of stone, with the strange frames and high wall on one side and a low wall on the other. At the nearer end was the stairway up, and the second stairway down. At the far end was another door. Boaz was leaning over the low wall, looking down into the gloom.

'Look at this,' he said, and he stretched further over the edge with his torch extended.

Ruth joined him and peered over.

'Do you see?' he asked. 'Ripples in the blackness. There is water down there. Masses of it.'

Light danced on the surface of the still lake. Boaz waved his torch and Ruth saw the feeble glow shimmer on its dark skin. The water stretched into the unseen, beyond the reach of the small fire.

Suddenly, Boaz hissed angrily, his rage preventing him finding the words. He hauled himself upright and clawed the air as if he could strangle Esar.

'Thieving, lying, cheating …'

Then he spat violently into the darkness. Verbal insults could not do justice to his feelings.

He turned abruptly to Ruth to vent his fury on an agreeing ear. 'Esar's always told us water was scarce! He's taxed us to dust and sold it to us – a few mouthfuls for a Chief's ransom! All the while he had all the water in the world stored down here. He claims to send it to the fields but each year it seems less and less, and what we get tastes ever more bitter.'

Ruth nodded. 'You're right, Boaz, but now is not the time. We've got to find Father and get out of her,' she urged, but Boaz was unheeding.

'Ruth, people have died! Many people have died because of this,' Boaz appealed, his voice rising.

'Shhh ... yes, I know,' Ruth hissed, 'but we'll die, too, if we don't get out of here. Now, come on. Let's go down, find Father, and leave this place.'

Boaz opened his mouth to argue again, but Ruth talked over him.

'There's no time to explain. Esar will get what is coming to him. We will do something about this. Trust me. There's no time for this now.'

'All right,' Boaz agreed reluctantly, yet he couldn't help being intrigued by what she meant. 'Do you want to split up to search this place?'

'No,' Ruth replied, keen not to be alone in the dark. 'Let's just make sure we are quick. Can I have a fresh torch, please?'

She lit a new one with the dying remains of the last.

'Let's try here,' she said, making for the broad stairway down.

This time Boaz went first, holding his torch in front. Ruth waited at the top in the flickering light. In a moment, he reappeared.

'Can I borrow your stick?' he asked, and went back down the stairs with her spear.

Ruth peered into the dark stairway. Boaz was squatting on a step some way down, leaning forward with the spear. He gave a broad sweep with his arms, and she heard the sound of water gulping in the darkness. She saw him draw his arm back and thrust it forwards slowly. He stood and turned towards her.

'The water is deep here. It's very cold and I can't find the bottom of the stairs. I don't want to go in. We must try another way.' He added uncertainly, 'Do you really know your father is here?'

Ruth did not need to answer. A low moan quivered somewhere out in the darkness, the mere spectre of a human voice; the last plea of a dying man to a deaf, blind world.

'Father!' Ruth cried, and she dashed down the steps.

Boaz caught her before she plunged completely into the icy water, but they splashed down a few steps together before coming to a halt.

She listened for any sound that might tell her where Dan was in this black pit, but all she heard was the ripples recede around her feet and the constant drip of falling water.

'Father!' she cried again.

Still nothing.

She dashed upstairs onto the narrow balcony and raced across it to the far end. At the untried doorway, she stopped and gripped her spear tightly. Even with the added urgency of hearing her father's voice she must be careful.

The doorway led immediately to three downward steps and a small, square room. There was another low door in the far wall, and a very narrow stairwell that spiralled down away from Ruth. She began to descend, and had not gone far when she came across the intense dampness in the air, and the same chill that had preceded their meeting the icy water in the other direction. The top of the door was above the level of the water, but only just. She pushed her spear into the depths and tried to find the bottom. She could not, so she stepped into the water and down two steps. The cold wetness covered her knees and numbed her feet and calves. She leaned forwards and pressed down with her spear, holding only the very end of it. Her forearm disappeared into the murky depths before she was rewarded with the thump of wood on submerged stone. Stepping back out, she guessed how deep it was – and she was not sure if she could wade through that much water.

But perhaps Boaz could. She climbed the stairs again to where he waited.

'There's water down there, too,' she sighed. 'It must be one big bowl of it. It's too deep for me to get through, but I think you could. If you go down the steps and walk with your head held up you could keep it above the water. Then you could find out where my father is.'

Boaz did not look pleased, and frowned. 'Ruth, we've not tried all the ways yet. Let's go back up to where we came in and have a go the other side. There may be a way down there.'

Ruth did not argue. How could she? It wasn't Boaz asking her to plunge into the freezing, black water without any knowledge of what was in there.

'Come on, then,' she said, and turned back towards the platform.

They trod as quickly as they could across the slimy stones, and Ruth reached it first. She crossed quickly, with Boaz close behind, and descended. They moved as they had done before, lighting the torches, checking for doorways and passages, and looking out over the dark waters for any clue as to where Dan could be. He had not moaned again, audibly at least, since they had first heard him. But Ruth was sure he couldn't be far away.

They found the far platform to be the same as the other: there were torches and the strange wooden structures braced against the walls; there was an identical staircase leading straight down; and a small room with a spiral stairwell turning in on itself until it too met the water. They faced the same problem. The water was too high.

Ruth didn't know what to do, so she leaned on the low wall and looked out over the dank chasm. The newly lit torches lent their light to those burning mournfully on the other side. She gazed into the black world of stone and water and could see a little more.

The underground chamber was long and thin, running from the platform at one end across the slick of dark water to a far wall of stone and wood framework. Opposite, she could see that there were thick pillars of stone holding up the distant walkway, and the staircase in front of her dropped down below to where it plunged into the water. She looked up at the wooden platform and saw the torchlight glowing through the strange, translucent material encrusted with mould. She saw wooden beams extending from underneath the platform and disappearing into the stone. Also beneath the platform, some kind of machine of tarnished columns and a black, gaping mouth lurked. It was grand and mysterious, but it hung above the darkness like the shadow of a nightmare.

Ruth looked up, and saw for the first time a smooth, high ceiling, ribbed with beams of dark wood and decorated with elaborate carvings. Here and there were hints of once bright colours now faded in the grimness and the damp. Sections of the stone ceiling had cracked and fallen away in massive chunks leaving ugly scars and exposed stone. Ruth felt as though she was inside a buried corpse. The decay was everywhere.

Her eyes followed the ridges of the ceiling away to the end most shrouded in darkness. She looked down on to the surface of the water, staring, noticing more and more detail with each moment.

Just beyond the doors that led into the thin spiral staircases was a palisade of wood, highly decorated. Beyond that, through the intricately carved windows and the gashes where the wood had collapsed under the rot, Ruth could see a stone platform rise from the water. Steps climbed up out of the dark liquid and there on the island dais, she saw him – at least, she saw someone.

There was a body.

It could only be her father, Dan.

'Father!' she cried.

She went straight for the spiral staircase and made her way down. Boaz followed her. She gave him her spear and held her torch aloft. Then she stepped into the cold, biting water once more. She was far from accustomed to it. It was like being stabbed all over again, but this time through every inch of her feet and her legs. She winced in pain.

'Let me go. I'll get him,' Boaz urged, desperate not to see her suffer.

'He won't know you,' she said, determined. 'I've got to do it.'

'You won't be able to carry him back,' Boaz insisted firmly. 'I'm coming with you.'

He put his spare torches on the step and slid down next to her into the cold water. They descended together, Boaz holding his lit torch aloft. The needles of cold pierced them on all sides and Ruth was quickly out of her depth. She thrashed in the water, desperate to escape this unnatural environment that attacked her every nerve. She dropped her torch. It hissed in the water and was gone. Her head disappeared under the surface and she choked on the foul, black liquid … She was going to die.

Boaz caught her by the waist and pulled her upwards. She struck him in sheer panic with her flailing arms and legs, and it was all he could do to keep his torch above the water. When her head broke the surface, she spat out the filthy murk and screamed.

'I'll go alone,' Boaz insisted again, but Ruth quickly recovered herself.

'No! We'll go together. Just let me hold on to you.'

Boaz assented and gave her his torch.

'Hold it as high as you can,' he said.

Together they lowered themselves back into the water. Boaz could just about walk slowly through it, but Ruth found herself almost climbing up him to keep above the deathly liquid. She poured her fear into determination to keep the torch burning. They ducked under the low doorway and were soon moving out across the black floodwater.

They were immediately at the ruined palisade and, when they passed by it, they discovered some steps up. Ruth found she could walk here and keep her head above the surface. They sloshed on through the freezing fluid, and in a few stretched moments were climbing the steps out again.

Ruth ran up the last stairs to the top of the dais. She held the torch high and scanned the area. It was large and square with a stone block in the centre. The wall at the back was highly carved and decorated with strange images and symbols, including a four-pointed metal star – one of the signs of Esar's authority – which hung in the darkness, tarnished and dull. Mournfully, it reflected the torchlight, and Ruth saw that there was, on top of the stone block, rotten cloth scattered with dirty shapes and symbols. She stepped quickly towards it, and in a few moments recognised an ancient, ruined copy of Peter's tapestry. So the Order and the Third Tribe had been close in days gone by. They shared the same story. But as Ruth ran her eyes and fingers over this grimy copy, she saw that Esar or his Order had torn out three sections; the same 'holy fragments' which supposedly told the story of Esar saving the City. And here, in the dank and rot, lay the rejected threads of the rest of the tale. They seemed to tell a different story but she had no time to look now. There was only one reason she was here – her father.

She found him slumped on the floor behind the stone block, silent and still. But for his sickly arm, she barely recognised him. His skin was pale, like the dead. He had lost all his hair and his gaunt face was practically skeletal. Barely conscious, he murmured in a delirium.

Ruth grabbed his good hand and called to him. 'Father!'

There was no response, except for the slightest twitch at her touch.

'Father!' she called again, but to no avail. He was breathing, but it was shallow.

A light suddenly flared on the high wooden platform and they heard the indistinct echo of voices in the tower of the cavern's entrance. Boaz and Ruth looked at each other, terrified. They were trapped. Boaz threw his torch into the water, plunging them into darkness.

Ruth whispered to Dan, 'Come on, we're taking you away from this.'

As before, he did not respond, and the voices from above became more distinct. There were snatches of conversation about 'fetching the amusement' and sending something 'out to the fields'. At last, two men emerged onto the right hand balcony.

'Where is he?' one asked.

'At the front. Not in the antechamber this time. It's flooded,' said the other.

'How is he? Will I get any sense out of him?'

'Probably not. He didn't look too good last time I came down.'

'Ah, well. It won't last long for him now,' the first replied with a laugh.

'Yeah, but it won't end tonight,' continued his companion. 'The Minister only wants to play with him – you know, get him to beg for mercy. That sort of thing. But you wouldn't laugh if you were in his place. How would you fancy living down here?'

'It wouldn't be so bad. At least it's well lit,' remarked the more junior of the two.

'Yes … yes, it is,' the other man replied, slowly. He cast his eyes across the gloomy chasm. 'I wonder why …' and his voice trailed off thoughtfully.

'Some of the others must have come down,' the younger man shrugged. 'Anyway, you certainly wouldn't get thirsty down here!'

'Ha!' the older man exclaimed, and Ruth breathed a sigh of relief as he seemed to dismiss the torches she and Boaz had lit. 'I wouldn't drink out of there if you gave me all the food in the world. Here, hold this.'

He passed the other his torch and climbed up onto the balcony wall. Ruth heard a grunt followed by the long, continuous tinkling sound of a stream splashing into the deep water. It went on for a short while, until it lessened and stopped altogether. She guessed with a grimace what was happening. The man climbed down and retrieved his torch.

'You see?' he smirked. 'You don't want to drink that. That's the stuff we sell to the Cityfolk.'

'So where do we get ours? The good stuff?'

'In one of the other side chambers. One you've not seen yet. The water flows up out of a rock and we collect it. What we don't take flows down the stairs into there,' he gestured into the dark lake, 'and that's what we give them. I can't show you today, there's too much to do. I'll take you next time. Come on.'

They walked to the broad set of steps leading down to the water.

'Down you go,' said the man who appeared to be in charge.

'What? I'm not going down there!'

'Yes, you are. Do your duty. The Minister wants us to open the sluice gates to let some water out. There's too much in here. He says it's going to be a gift for tomorrow. The first gate's down there, around to the left. Go!'

The junior Orderman descended the steps and waded out into the murky reservoir. He turned away from Ruth's end of the cavern and pushed into the darkness of a side room.

Ruth and Boaz looked at each other, trying to guess what was going on. Then they heard the clank and groan of ancient metal on metal and the sound of ropes straining. This was followed by a foul sound of sucking, of water being pulled out of the underground lake, to where they did not know. The pool shuddered and gurgled around them. Boaz marvelled at it.

'So this is how they do it,' he whispered. 'They send the water out through gates and channels underground. Amazing! Who would have dreamed men could accomplish such things?'

At last, the sound of grinding metal began again and the noise of the suction stopped. Then they heard the younger Orderman wading through the water, as the voice of the older one echoed around the cavern.

'One more at this end, and then go down to the other.'

'Boaz, we've got to move,' Ruth whispered. 'He's going to come this way. Let's go now.'

She pulled herself up and peered over the stone block behind which they had been hiding. The Orderman in the water was wading across to a chamber opposite the one he had come out of. The older one up above was leaning over the low wall looking down into the water.

Boaz got to his feet and, taking hold of Dan's good arm, pulled him up over his shoulder. He carried him like that, across his shoulders and back, and held him secure by keeping a tight grip on one of Dan's legs.

'He's lighter than I thought he would be,' he remarked. 'I'm ready. Let's go.'

Ruth slipped silently into the water and found that the level had dropped. Boaz followed as quietly as he could. Moving too quickly would alert the Ordermen to their presence, but going too slowly could mean they would be caught anyway.

They were half-way between the raised platform and the palisade when they heard a similar clang of metal on metal. The sound of suction began again and a fierce current tugged at the backs of their legs. The increased noise meant that they could make more sound themselves, but moving in the surge of water was difficult. They hurried, sliding and slipping towards their goal.

Then Ruth misjudged the drop of the steps after the palisade and fell with a splash. She was able to stand, quickly regained her feet and dived for the stairwell – but it was too late. The Orderman on the balcony had seen her, with Boaz carrying Dan.

'Hey!' he shouted. 'What do you think you're doing here?'

He ran for the steps that led up to the wooden platform to cut them off. Boaz threw caution to the wind and charged through the deep water and up the stairwell Ruth had just entered. All three reached the balcony at the same time, Ruth and Boaz from one end, the Orderman from the other.

Ruth hefted her spear as Boaz laid Dan down against the wall. Then he straightened up and drew his knife, pulling his millstones out of a pocket with his other hand.

The Orderman held a fearsome-looking weapon. It had a long shaft with a crosspiece at the handle. Its foremost tip was broad and deep, and it looked to Ruth as if it was made from the same material as the frame they had climbed down, and the shining platter she had seen Esar eat from. The blade edge looked blunt, but that did not make it any less deadly. The Orderman twirled it as he advanced. The torches were dying, and it flashed in the gloom too quickly to follow. Their only hope was to edge past him and attack from two sides, but the narrow balcony would make that very difficult. Below them, the clanking noise began again as the junior Orderman closed the sluice gates. The rush and foam of the black water stopped and all was quiet. Ruth and Boaz had to get past their aggressor now.

'Help!' the Orderman shouted. 'Help me! Intruders in the Temple!'

The two of them rushed him together. He swung at Boaz who leapt back quickly. Ruth dodged sideways underneath the strange framework of wood, aiming to get past him on that side. The man whirled his weapon above his head and swung for a second time, this time at Ruth, who dived back underneath the wooden frame as Boaz came forward again. The blade bit deep into the rot-softened wood of the central beam and the whole frame creaked.

Boaz lunged for the man, who yanked the weapon free and punched the handle into Boaz's chest. As he fell, winded, Ruth took her chance. She jabbed the spear at the man's exposed side and caught him under his arm. The point drew blood and he howled. Boaz pulled himself to his feet and the injured man turned to strike at him, but Ruth lunged with the spear again as Boaz staggered back towards Dan. The Orderman spun sideways to block her thrust. In doing so, he caught the back of Ruth's hand with his weapon's haft. He swung again, as Ruth pulled her hand back with a yelp, but this time he missed. The blade connected with the underside of the frame's central support with a wet smack. It jammed fast; he yanked at it, twisting and turning to free it. Rotten wood scattered.

Ruth lunged again, this time hitting him under the ribs, in the same place where Haman had aimed to stab her. The Orderman screamed, the surge of pain enabling him to tear the blade from the disintegrating wood. He spun it wildly, scattering debris and rotten, woody chunks in all directions.

Ruth leapt back and, as she did so, the wood panelling on the wall caved in. The framework crashed to the floor and fragmented. The panel itself hovered upright for a moment, then slammed forward onto the injured man, knocking him down.

For the merest instant, in the failing light of the dying torches, Ruth saw what lay behind.

She glimpsed a picture of another world.

Dark, metallic lines enmeshed shapes like coloured stones that glistened in the torchlight. The separate pieces were fitted together by some ancient craft to form an image that now leapt out of the dark incarceration of uncounted years and into the light.

She saw the outline of a man leading a flock of strange, goat-like animals. The beasts were alike to the flocks Ruth knew, except that they were hornless and had great shaggy coats, very like the tapestries. The man was seemingly unremarkable, but he stood under a bright blue sky gently brushed by high, white clouds. Ruth felt sure it was Rain. There were mountains behind him – many mountains – and he walked by running water. The land he travelled on was green. It was a perfect place; the place of Peter's dream.

A place without sand.

The next moment, broad cracks appeared all over the image. Dust ran between them, and then the picture imploded in a flood of sand. The Orderman beneath the broken panelling disappeared

under the deadly torrent, his muffled screams obliterated by the hard
weight that thundered down upon him.

Ruth waved her arm at Boaz across the overpowering noise.
Shouting was useless and she was on the other side of the falling sand.
Boaz guessed her meaning and ran back to Dan. But just as Ruth
turned towards the broad stairs, the junior Orderman bounded up
them. She wheeled the spear around her like a club and caught him
across the back of the head. It was enough to send him sprawling
forward. He crashed into the wall opposite and lay still.

She plunged down the stairs and into the dark lake below. The
water level had dropped considerably now and she could wade
through easily. The torches on the far side were flickering and dying.
Boaz emerged from the other staircase and she pushed through the
murky liquid to help him with Dan. Together they climbed back up
the broad steps, over the prone form of the younger Orderman, and
up the flight that lead to the high platform. When they reached it,
they saw that the Ordermen had replenished the torch which was
burning merrily.

Ruth looked up at the hole, high in the shaft, through which
they must escape. It seemed a long way to climb with the added
weight of Dan.

'Can you do it?' she asked Boaz, gravely.

'I must,' he said, 'though it would be better if we could carry him
together.'

His eyes fell on the ropes that ran the height of the well. They
were gathered by a piece of woven straw which Boaz cut easily. There
were four ropes that he could use. He drew one over to the ladder,
climbed a little way and sawed at the fibres with his knife. With some
effort, they gave way, and Boaz returned to the platform with a good
length of rope. He tied a loop under Dan's arms, making the knot
tight, then held out the other end to Ruth.

'Take this,' he said. 'You go first and do what you can. I'll lift him from underneath. If you need a rest, say so. I'll do the same. I'll take your spear if you like.'

Ruth did as he said and together they climbed, Ruth lifting from above and Boaz pushing up from below. It was hard, but each could take the weight to help the other. Slowly they made the ascent. Nobody disturbed them.

Ruth reached the top, climbed out of the hole onto the floor of the Sanctuary tent and braced herself, one foot on the sand and the other on the wall. She heaved and Boaz pushed. Dan appeared first, still murmuring and drifting in and out of consciousness. Then Boaz emerged and they caught their breath, but only for a moment.

There was movement below. The young Orderman was climbing up to raise the alarm.

'We have to stop him,' Boaz hissed. 'If he makes a noise, he'll bring the whole Order down on us. We've got to kill him, and do it quietly. Get out of sight!'

Ruth ducked to one side and dragged Dan with her. He was much lighter than she remembered. Boaz pinned himself to the wall next to the hole and glanced down. The Orderman was nearly at the top, his speed of ascent impeded by the torch he had picked up from the platform ring. His head appeared, then his shoulders. Just as he bent forward, Boaz leapt in front of him and brought his foot up in a vicious, outward kick. The Orderman was thrown backwards, and he disappeared in a cloud of sparks back down into the well.

Boaz smiled at Ruth in sheer relief … Then suddenly, they both slammed their hands to their ears and fell to the floor.

A single sound, louder than any they had ever known, shook the well. The tent and the floor beneath their feet quaked with a deafening chime. In his rapid descent, the Orderman had grabbed at the ropes Boaz had left hanging loose. He had become entangled in them, and his weight caused a vast machine hidden in the darkness of the space above to peal. The mechanism concealed overhead turned over, and the world was riven by vibration and noise. As the body of the Orderman jerked on the rope, the excruciating ringing continued.

All of a sudden, an ominous creak sounded from above, followed by a violent crack. A rush of air blasted from the hole and a dark shape flashed by.

The machine had fallen.

There was one moment of near silence – then it obliterated the wooden platform in a thunderous crash.

A deep and disturbing boom rolled up the well and out across the City as the enormous bell smashed into water below.

CHAPTER EIGHTEEN

NEITHER RUTH NOR BOAZ COULD HEAR very well in the aftermath of the bell's clamorous descent. It did not matter, however, as there was only one course of action: to get off the holy mound and out of the City as quickly as possible.

Ruth grabbed her spear from Boaz, who then had hands free enough to heave Dan onto his shoulders. Half-deaf and dizzy, they staggered out of the tent and into the starless night. Down the side of the mound they went, torchless, and without thought as to where they were heading. They only knew they had to get away, where they could hide and rest. Ruth needed to think, but there was no time. She pulled Boaz on as fast as she dared, and they raced into the narrow alleys between the tiny, crumbling houses. Her head was beginning to clear a little, and she was dully aware of shouting to the west by the fire. The Cityfolk were running as quickly as they could to discover the cause of the unearthly din. Ruth was sure they would be armed or, if not, they would find weapons quickly.

They stumbled almost to the southern edge of the City. The Order was spreading out to comb the area immediately around the holy mound. Ruth dived in through a doorway and Boaz followed. She had to think! Where could they go? Her supplies were in the eastern hills.

Peter would be coming from the north. Her enemies were approaching right now from the west. But there was nothing to the south. Was there any way of guessing what the Ordermen would do?

She dropped her spear and gripped her head in her hands. She had to think.

'Ruth …' croaked Dan, weakly in his delirium. 'Ruth …'

'Yes, father!' she cried, going quickly to where Boaz had laid him. But Dan did not seem aware of where he was or what was happening.

'Ruth! Bring her to me!' he slurred, his head rolling limply from side to side. 'I want to see my daughter! I won't talk without her!'

He raged at the monsters of his imagination and tried feebly to shake his wasted fist at them. 'I'll kill you!' he shouted suddenly.

'Shh! I'm here, Father,' Ruth whispered. 'You're safe.'

'Not yet, he isn't,' Boaz remarked darkly. 'We've got to go. Now.'

Ruth felt anger rise in her, but she knew he was right. Her anger wasn't really for Boaz anyway. It was aimed at the City, and the malignancy that lay rotting at its core: the Order. The Order that had taken and ruined her father, that had condemned and killed countless people.

And now they were coming for her.

She felt so foolish. It had been rash to enter the holy tent tonight. She had promised Peter that she would wait for him to return with the Third Tribe before attempting a rescue. She had only meant to sneak into the City to see what Esar was doing. It had never been her plan to attempt a rescue. One more day, and Rain's people would have come. Maybe even Rain himself.

But these thoughts were not helpful; she must work out their way to safety.

Ruth paced up and down the floor of the small house, patting her sides with her hands as if by doing so she could stimulate thought. Her elbow hit something hard tucked into the robe above her belt.

She reached into the folds and pulled out the staves Peter had given her when he had taken hers. Could they help? It was completely absurd, but there was nothing else. She didn't know what more to do, so she cast all her hope on the sticks.

'Pick him up,' she said to Boaz, indicating Dan, 'and take the spear if you can.'

Then she closed her eyes. Doing so did not leave her at any great disadvantage – the City was dark, the starlight and moonlight kept out by the swirling, black cloud-blanket, and most of the fuel and torches had been taken to the west side. She held her hands up and slightly forwards, touching the staves as lightly as she could. Then she took a deep breath.

The sharpness seemed to return to her hearing, and she was aware of the Cityfolk milling about in confusion far in the west. To the north, by the holy mound, there was a disturbing sound of rock grinding on sand, and the suction of quicksand. Men were shouting. She followed the twitching and angles of the staves, and stepped out into the night. She could smell fear in the air, the rude smoke of straw half-burned, and death.

The staves guided her due east, and Ruth walked on with Boaz carrying Dan behind. They went as fast as they could manage, but Boaz was tired. Ruth had the sudden urge to stop when the staves crossed. She kept her eyes closed in concentration. Feet thundered past, just across their path, going north.

'That was close,' Boaz said. 'Sentries returning from out there, in the fields. But I hardly heard them. Did you?'

Ruth ignored the question and focused her mind on the staves. They uncrossed and she moved on, finding their way through the houses to the eastern side. She could hear men in the northern and southern quarters shouting to each other. The search was heading their way.

'Let's go, come on!' urged Boaz, ready to go out onto the plain and into the eastern dunes.

It was the obvious thing to do; the Ordermen were coming this way and Ruth thought they could not possibly hope to get through them if they went west, north or south.

She turned to go east; the staves did not. Yet the only thing that made sense was to head east: her bag was there with food and millstones; the well was there; Peter might go there to find her. But she had to force the staves around to point that way. Something was wrong; they were indicating due west, back to the holy mound; back into the jaws of the Order.

Boaz waited no longer. He forced himself into a jog and went east out onto the plain. Ruth felt he gave her no choice, so she followed. She stuffed the staves back into her robe and took the spear. Boaz shifted Dan's weight and surged forward. They crossed the ground quickly, and under the cover of shadow-filled darkness. Lights twinkled in the City behind them as men with torches arrived at the eastern side, but the feeble glow did not reach them.

Ruth and Boaz climbed the dune and when they made the top, a shout rang out across the plain. They looked at each other. They were lit up under the moonlight. Fear flashed upon both their faces and they ran east again. Ruth kept an eye out for the little dip in which Peter had dug the well, where she had hidden her bag. At last she saw it, brushed with silver by the moon.

She scrambled past the well, trampling the young plants underfoot. They crunched, and the sand felt dry. The water source that had led Peter here had moved on. Ruth pushed this from her mind and grabbed her bag from the desiccated tussock where she had only half hidden it. Boaz had carried on walking, heading further east, and was pressing out into the desert to get as far away from the City as possible. Here the stars were as bright as ever and the moon was high. The desert glistened, a sea of pearl and silver under the familiar, profound black of the night sky. There was nowhere to hide; they urged themselves on, with nowhere to go.

For what seemed like hours they pushed on further and further, before Boaz, exhausted from carrying Dan, could continue no more, and Ruth buckled beside him on the ground. As she faded into unconsciousness, her only hope was that their pursuers would not dare follow this far into the desert.

Ruth awoke to discover with horror that someone was tying her wrists behind her back. She struggled and shouted, but doubled up where she lay when somebody kicked her hard in the stomach. She moaned. It was still dark but for the moon and starlight. She did not know how long she had been asleep. Boaz was next to her, still unconscious, with his hands tied behind him. Only Dan was not bound, but he too was motionless and silent.

Ruth turned her head towards her captor. The one tying her hands finished his knots and stood, and with him she saw four other men, some armed with clubs. She guessed the others were armed too, probably with unseen knives. One was going through her bag. Another held her spear and was picking idly at the blood that encrusted its splintered point.

'Get up,' one of the men ordered, and kicked her in the back. She cried aloud, rolled onto her front and pulled herself to her knees.

'I'd drag you back,' he grunted, 'but I can't be bothered. Maybe I'll drag you the last bit, over all those broken bones. How would you like that?'

Ruth didn't say a word. So this was it. She had failed. They would be hauled back and burned. Or worse.

One of the men stamped on Boaz's leg and woke him. Then he pulled him upright. Two of the others carried Dan. They complained about it to the one who seemed to be the leader, but he told them just to get on with it.

'The Minister wants them all brought back. None shall escape justice.'

To Ruth, it seemed he was repeating his orders as if he didn't understand what he was saying.

'Anyway, the more of them there are, the more fun for the rest of us! If you don't carry that one,' he added, 'I'll make sure you don't get a turn with her,' and he slapped Ruth on the shoulder.

Again she cried out, and Dan murmured in his dream world. Boaz glared into the night, silently fuming and trying to work his fingers into the knots that held them. He achieved nothing, and received a sharp beating for his trouble.

The distance dragged out on all sides, and the desert became enormous in Ruth's mind, but not large enough to separate her from the City. It was drawing her back to itself. Each step was pain, and the men around her told stories of the 'fun' they'd had with the 'lawbreakers, outlaws and offenders' they had caught.

At length, Ruth and Boaz were again under the shadow of the thick clouds. From a distance, the top edges were silvered by the moon, but walking beneath they seemed as black as the night itself. No light penetrated the dense layer of turning, tumbling layers. There was a marked difference from when they had left the City in their futile escape attempt. The air was heavier. Every step was an ordeal. Ruth felt the weight of the atmosphere and beyond bearing down upon her and on the City. It crushed her, and made her want to lie flat beneath its growing rage. There wasn't the slightest tremor of wind. Even the City's constant dull roar that usually oppressed Ruth's mind seemed cowed.

Their captors dragged them down the eastern dunes and barely stopped for them to get to their feet before pulling them out onto the plain. They were soon crossing the ruins and remains of tents and passing through the houses. Ordermen were on every corner, armed and waiting. Some had torches. More torches were brought for their colleagues. Ruth saw faces in doorways staring out at them. The Cityfolk were in their homes, probably under a curfew, awaiting the morning. But Ruth did not know if she would see another dawn.

They reached the path that encircled the holy mound, and in the Ordermen's torchlight, Ruth saw that a great pit had opened up to the south-east of the hill and its spike. A vast quantity of sand had subsided into the lower depths of the world. This surprised their captors, who took them back in amongst the houses, and finally they came to the last dwelling at the foot of the holy mound, below the tent's entrance. The men forced them into it, dropping Dan down, and pushed the others to the floor. Their feet were bound, and their mouths gagged. One of the Ordermen leaned close to Ruth and whispered, but loud enough for Boaz to hear.

'I'll just be outside, my sweet. If you get scared of the dark, you let me know and I'll come in and keep you company. I'll bring my friends, too. Sleep well. See you in the morning.'

With that he stood up and was gone.

Ruth wept silently. Bound as he was, Boaz pulled himself around and lay on the sand next to Ruth. In the thin torchlight that filtered into their prison, she saw a fierce spark burning in the depths of his eyes. It was not of anger or resentment or blame, but of unconquerable bravery. Wordlessly, through the sheer force of his intention, Ruth knew what Boaz wanted to say.

'Courage,' she read in his eyes. 'Do not fear what is coming.'

The night passed in a mist of tears and misery. Boaz was silent and even Dan's incoherent ramblings ceased for a time. At last, a pale light crept into the far eastern sky. It was barely perceptible at first, but as the moments passed, it crept over the distant dunes and pressed against the brooding clouds. The morning began in earnest and for a short, glorious stretch, the rising sun cut a broad beam of gold between the hills and the low clouded ceiling. Then it was gone. Darkness returned as the heavy blanket reclaimed the daylight and blocked it out. The curfew had not yet been lifted; the City was quiet.

In Ruth's mind, the atmosphere seemed to swell and twitch. Her head throbbed, and her body ached all over. The sensation of ever-increasing pressure from above returned. The ground felt different beneath her, as if it were unsure of itself.

Something was coming; something was going to make itself known.

Ruth remembered the pit of sand that had opened up in the night. She hoped the same would happen under her so that she could escape into a quick death beneath the dust in the silent depths.

Somewhere nearby, she heard a torch crackle into life. There were voices, and the Ordermen posted outside the house stirred and stretched. Feet approached. Ruth listened as the guards talked about ordinary things: about food, something to drink, about how cold the night was. She was thirsty, but that now seemed the least of her worries. She struggled against her bindings but to no avail, and the noise of her exertion only drew the attention of the Ordermen outside.

'Not long now, love,' one called.

Another sniggered.

And it wasn't long; all too soon Ruth and Boaz heard voices in the City shouting, 'Gather! Gather!'

The Cityfolk emerged from the curfew and made their way to the foot of the holy mound. Esar's voice came, indistinct at this distance, shouting over the City. From his tone, they knew he was berating the Cityfolk, at once swearing at them, cursing them, begging them, and soothing them. Then he was exciting them and enraging them, whipping them into a murderous ecstasy of blame and retribution. It could mean only one thing.

Some kind of signal must have been given, because three black-clad Ordermen strode into the house, took hold of Ruth, Boaz and Dan, cut the ropes that bound their feet and hauled them upright. Then they were forced into the open.

It was still very dark – a twilight in mid-morning – and the clouds were like the living hands of night, opening and closing and grasping above them. A breeze touched Ruth's cheek, and she shivered. The Ordermen leading Ruth and Boaz felt it, too, and looked at each other. There was something more to the wind today.

The captives were dragged, driven and carried up the mound, past the Cityfolk who were congregating a little way around the base. When they saw the three figures, many of them roared and spat and cried for blood. Others slunk backwards in between the houses and crept to the western plain. Ruth thought they sensed a storm in the air.

Esar turned on them like a madman. He was foaming anger and his skinny frame shook with unbridled rage.

'There is no question of your guilt!' he screamed. 'You have defiled the holy tent and tried to destroy its life-giving secrets! But you have failed! You have no defence. The only question is,' and he turned to face the crowd, though he still addressed Ruth, Boaz, and the staggering form of Dan, 'will you beg for mercy from these people whom you have so terribly wronged?'

He did not expect an answer, nor did he get one. Ruth glared as defiantly as she could, and Boaz stood like a man ready and waiting for his death. The crowd roared.

'Stake them, stake them!' they cried. Some whistled. Others threw scraps of broken bone that fell far from the three, carried sideways by the gathering gusts.

The corner of the tent's door curtain flickered restlessly. Ruth felt the wind caress her face, and she breathed the cool, calming air. Esar seemed suddenly far away, and the sound of his ranting dulled. She looked up at the blackening heavens and the world appeared to fall quiet.

Something small caught her eye, high above. It turned as it fell in the darkness, catching what thin light there was and spreading it. Soon others like it were falling, sweeping across the sky in a downward charge.

The first plummeted between Ruth and Esar.

Thud.

The second landed on Esar's bald head and splashed onto his neck. His speech was cut short as it touched him, and his words died in the rushing air.

Soon the drops were everywhere, thudding into the sand and hammering on the houses. The Cityfolk looked upwards in one movement of awe and confusion.

Seizing the moment, Esar yelled above the deluge, 'See! Even nature itself demands a sacrifice! Turn back to me and together we will ...'

But his words were obliterated by the universal roar and rumble of thunder from above. Louder than the falling bell, more terrible, primal and omnipresent than anything Ruth had known in her life, the sky spoke and rage poured out across the City. The people dived to the ground, and covered their ears. Those that had crept away from the trial fled en masse south and west out through the houses, onto the plain and towards the dunes.

As the echo resounded around the valley, the falling water renewed itself and poured down in a flood not seen in any living memory.

Soon the remaining Cityfolk who lay prone beneath the mound were on their feet, pushing and fighting to get out and into the hills beyond. A second barrage sounded from above, and now only Dan stayed standing, laughing into the storm. Everyone else cowered. The tumult unlocked his voice and he shouted, but the sound was lost against the onslaught. His eyes flashed in the thunder.

Only the Order remained. Some of their members had fled, but the core of Esar's power lingered on the hillside. The water crashed down upon them, and the dirt of decades darkened into the fresh liquid and ran down their beards. Their upturned faces changed. Esar screamed at them but very few among them heard. Most were overawed.

Esar stepped to one side and bent over. He straightened up and held in his hands a short spear. Its tip was dark with blood. He flourished it, and came towards Ruth.

'You killed my men with this,' he snarled. 'Even though the fools won't see it, I will ensure justice is served.'

He drew the haft back behind him with one hand and grasped the tip with the other. Ruth stepped away as he came closer, slipping out of the grip of the storm-struck Orderman holding her. She stumbled backwards, thinking only of escaping the sharp stake that now snaked towards her. Then she fell and sprawled painfully on her still bound hands. Shrieking in fear, she thrashed sideways, but still Esar came on. Boaz yelled her name and fought against the Orderman holding him, but he was quickly overcome when the guard with Dan went to help in the struggle.

A moment more, and Esar stood over Ruth menacingly.

He was about to speak when suddenly his head whipped round. Dan had unexpectedly broken from his mumbling and charged, driving his right shoulder with all his might into the small man's back. Esar was sent tumbling down the holy mound, and landed with a thump at the bottom. The spear fell next to him.

The Orderman who had been guarding Ruth grabbed Dan's weak arm, bound as it was behind his back. Dan howled, whipped round and head butted him savagely, dropping him to his knees. The man's face became a vision of blood which quickly ran in the falling water. Ruth leapt up and kicked him in the back of the head, then he too rolled down the mound. He fell further than Esar, and landed hard on the edge of the sunken pathway. The sand moved beneath him while the thunder pealed above, and the water hammered all around. And the Orderman began to sink!

Esar crawled away back towards the safety of the mound, ignoring the pleas of the terrified man, and took the spear with him. Another of the Ordermen slipped and slid down the side of the hillock to help his master.

Strong hands suddenly gripped the sinking man's robe and he was wrenched bodily from the collapsing sand. His rescuer laid him by the doorway of one of the houses and turned to face the holy mound.

As the newcomer raised his head, water shone on his brow and ran in rivers down his cheeks. It glimmered in his beard and soaked into his robe. Ruth recognised the fine cut of the battle-scarred coat, and saw in the man an ancient, primal dignity that matched his attire. Her heart leapt. She knew Esar's time was over because, into the deluge of the storm, the figure from the magnificent tapestries had marched – Rain had come!

But where was Peter? Where was the rest of the Third Tribe?

She cast her eyes around the nearby houses, excitedly searching, expecting to see Rain's tribesmen running to their Chief's aid – but there was no one. Where were they?

'You!' hissed Esar, his rage returning after the indignity of his fall. 'I have no words for you. Seize him!'

The few remaining Ordermen leapt to obey their Minister. Soon Rain was surrounded, but the pack of circling men would not pounce. When they tried, a vast barrage of thunder exploded above and they instinctively fell back.

'Take him!' Esar screamed.

At last, three of the larger Ordermen took hold of him, one on each arm, and the third by the neck. They dragged him roughly up to where their master had climbed, in front of the entrance to the Sanctuary tent.

Boaz, unattended by Esar's henchmen, had found a fragment of bone and was sawing at the cord around his wrist. After a moment, it frayed apart, and he dashed to Ruth to free her too.

Without losing a second, Ruth charged towards the cluster of Ordermen who held Rain, not knowing how she could help him but desperate to try. Esar twirled Ruth's spear in his hands. The young girl's soul howled in her body as she threw herself across the void between them.

Esar addressed his men.

'Hold him up,' he said, evenly, and his black-robed followers lifted the man high off the ground, two supporting an arm each and the third hugging his ankles. Why did Rain not resist?

'How many times do I have to kill you, Rain?' Esar spat, as Ruth raced towards them. He did not see her coming.

'You'll never know,' Rain said.

Just for a moment, Ruth thought she saw him catch her eye.

Esar drew back the spear.

Ruth sprinted.

But then he struck. He drove the spear deep under Rain's ribs and up into his chest.

Rain threw back his head and roared his pain into the storm. The thunder broke again overhead and the men holding him staggered. Esar twisted the spear and ripped it out. Red flowed with the water. He plunged the stake into Rain again, harder, deeper, and Ruth's world exploded.

She fell in a vision of blinding terror. She was aware of vivid light, and a fist of darkness, lunging and straining at the brightness. The fist transformed into a savage claw, and Ruth was aware of conflict, great suffering, of pain and of despair. The light grew still more brilliant, and it swirled above an ocean of water, active and vibrant. Yet the darkness was not aware of the foaming sea below. It extended its claw and where the fingers touched the light, they disintegrated in pain.

Then everything was white and grey, and suddenly Ruth was lying on a sandy hillside under a storm of falling water. She sat up. Esar stood a little to one side of her, screeching in triumph into the gale. The thunder rose to a new volume and the wind whipped to hurricane force. The men holding Rain threw him down the slope. His patchwork coat turned dark red around two new tears as he tumbled down and lay prone in the path that divided the City from the holy mound.

It was then that the ground moved.

For a moment, Ruth thought it was another peal of thunder. The

Ordermen threw each other looks of great alarm. Esar stopped his cheering and stared at the mound, puzzled.

Boaz threw an arm around Dan and hurried him off the hillock, shouting for Ruth to follow.

Then the sand heaved, as if something beneath was awakening.

Ruth looked to Boaz and ran straight down the side of the hill. She could not see Rain anywhere. The ground shuddered again, and the houses around began to crumble and shift. Boaz dragged Dan onto the path that ran around the mound and raced along it, weaving his way north, half-carrying the older man. Ruth followed, throwing glances this way and that in the hope of seeing where Rain's body had gone. They passed the collapsing houses as the sand gave another almighty heave. The Sanctuary tent disintegrated in one sudden, downward plunge, and the Ordermen scattered. Esar stumbled backwards down the slope and stood speechless at the bottom, watching his world collapse.

Boaz ran on with Dan into the plain, but Ruth slowed and looked back to the City. The holy mound writhed and the spike shuddered. For a brief moment, the hill subsided, demolishing nearby houses as some great, unseen body thrashed about underground, before the entire mound exploded upwards.

The spike rose high into the air, and became a tower as the outside wall of the well was exposed. Higher it rose into the thunderstorm, soaring above the crumbling City like a spear raised in bloody triumph. Dust poured from newly exposed windows and the faces of strange, stone creatures once more glared over the City for the first time in unknown ages. The rumble of the ground rose to meet the thunder of the sky and, in one vast eruption, the east end of the City burst upwards.

To Ruth, it looked as though the well tower was the first extended finger that punctured the sand, and now the rest of the hand followed in a fist. The eastern quarter was obliterated by an emerging ridge that tore a gash in the ground's surface. The gash widened, and out of it rose a sloping roof, and walls with huge windows that yawned into the daylight and the storm. After these came attending chambers, sand pouring from every surface, until at last the vast monument had emerged. The structure swayed and shook as the earth lurched beneath it, and the remnants of the ruined houses slid from its roof onto the fractured dust below.

Ruth saw Esar walking backwards in awe of what was unfolding before him. He gaped up at the vast structure with open-mouthed wonderment. Raising his arms, he laughed, he crowed, and over the sound of earthquake and thunder, she heard him shout, 'The Temple! The Temple! Glory! Glory!' before cackling like a madman. He danced and capered, and she knew in her mind that he was building the story of how he, Esar, had accomplished such a wonder.

Suddenly, she was aware of someone else.

So was Esar.

He paused in his adulation and looked terrified. He shouted for his men and scrabbled around in search of a weapon.

Ruth ran back towards the City and the newly-risen Temple, holding her arm across her face against the swirling sand thrown up by the building's eruption. She hurtled into the eye of the storm and saw a figure – was it Rain? – advancing upon Esar. The smaller man fell back afraid.

The figure spoke – it *was* Rain!

He did not shout, yet Ruth heard him over the distance; over the noise of her racing heart and her pounding feet; over the collapsing City; over the heaving sands pouring down.

He said,

'What little you had shall be taken from you.'

Esar squirmed and cowered. He shouted out. On some level he

seemed to comprehend, horrified, what was about to happen.

'No! It will not be! I forbid it!'

The inexorable voice of Rain spoke again.

'And it shall be given to others!'

Rain raised his arms above his head, clapped his hands together and, in that moment, there was a final peal of thunder and the tower cracked. The top of the spike split, and much of it slid sideways, tumbling with a tremendous crash down to the sand below. The upper sections of the core structure imploded and the roof crumbled downwards, but the lower walls burst outward, releasing a vast body of water that flowed in all directions.

As the floodwaters rose, they swept down over the remnants of the City. They covered the houses, and ran out into the ruined tents, swallowing whatever remained.

Ruth turned and ran, following the distant dots of Dan and Boaz into the far north hills. Up ahead, shapes appeared on the skyline; moving; walking.

The Third Tribe was here! They had come!

But why were they late? Why had they not come with Rain? Why had he faced the Order alone?

Behind her, she heard the final crashes as walls collapsed into the floodwaters, and the noise pushed her questions aside. She was still not out of danger.

She pressed on, eager to catch up with her father and Boaz. Perhaps Naomi would be there too, with Peter. She found new energy in those thoughts, and quickened her pace. Leaving the spreading flood behind, she neared the northern dunes.

The Third Tribe was descending.

Peter had come too late. He had kept his word; he had brought help, but he was late. Still, it didn't matter. Rain had come, and even though Ruth didn't really know if he was dead or alive, he had crushed the Order. And the Third Tribe, Rain's people, were here now.

'Ruth!' Naomi shouted from the northern ridge.

Ruth slowed to a jog and looked up to see her friend sliding down the sandy slope, then running across the gap between them. Naomi crashed joyfully into her and gathered her up in a hug.

'Ruth, I'm so glad you're safe! I've been so worried! I'm sorry – I'm so sorry we didn't get here on time. I …'

Ruth burst into tears, prompting more apologies from the older woman, and the girl began to laugh through her weeping.

'It's all right, Naomi, it's all right!' she sobbed.

Naomi wept and laughed too, and together they climbed the dunes.

Ruth sat on the hillside overlooking the valley. The sky was clearing and the sun was breaking through. Someone brought her some food, but she wasn't hungry. She pointed to her father and Boaz and sent the food to them.

What clouds remained were shrinking rapidly to tufts of delicate white, and the sun glistened onto the spreading lake. The water was finding its way south, flowing in rivulets that thickened in the slight undulations of the plain at the far end of the valley. The thirsty ground drank the moisture, yet more kept rising from the wreck of the holy mound and the once-sunken cavern.

Naomi put her arm around the tired girl. She looked at her and smiled.

'What?' Ruth asked, suddenly self-conscious. 'What is it?'

Naomi didn't say anything; she didn't need to. She smiled again, and looked back over the valley and the emerging river. Ruth sensed the Cityfolk in the western hills watching their world transform.

And it shall be given to others, she thought.

Yes, it shall.

EPILOGUE

The water was black and murky at first, but the more that came, the cleaner it was. The old filth of the Order was being washed away by the storm and the flood. The valley changed, turning from brown to green in the days after the storm. It was not long before the spreading waters found their level and the new river established its course, running south into the desert.

The Cityfolk returned and picked over the ruined City. Joined by the Third Tribe, they rebuilt their houses, not from the broad, crumbling bricks of sand, but from the Temple's stones that had been cleansed by the fierce churning of the flood. The dark stain left by the Order was removed, leaving only rubble and a bright spring bubbling in the sunshine.

Some of the surviving Ordermen joined the reborn settlement and pleaded to be allowed to live to make reparation for their cruelties. Others returned, intent on reasserting their power, but the abundance of water and food made their plans impossible. Those who could not make their peace were driven away.

Nobody knew what had become of Esar; it was widely assumed his frail body had been crushed when the Temple fell.

Ruth's story of Rain appearing in the midst of the storm became an oft-repeated wonder, and the Tribesfolk added it to their stories. They were all amazed that she'd come so close to him, that she'd seen him and heard him speak. It made them all the more eager to follow his way in the desert.

Clouds were now common, and the distant rumble of approaching thunder became a sound to enjoy, not to fear, as the Tribesfolk eagerly anticipated the refreshing deluge and the resurgence of life. New plants grew in the fields, bearing fruits that were largely unfamiliar to Ruth's eyes, but some she recognised. She knew the small, red berries that Naomi had once given her, as they ripened and swelled in the rain and shine, and they tasted sweeter than she would ever have believed. They were no longer the shrivelled, bitter fruits of Esar's day.

The sun was still fierce at its highest, but the abundance of grasses and newly-grown wood to dry for the fires meant that the nights were no longer cold. Ruth became accustomed to the Tribe's songs and dances, and she added the best of her own to their tradition.

At length, some among the Third Tribe became restless, longing once again for the changing desert sandscape and the whisper of water running in new places. Peter and the tribal elders decided to move on, to follow the moving waters. Some wished to stay with the Cityfolk, and to continue rebuilding and teaching the people their ways. To this, the elders gave their blessing.

Ruth and Boaz decided that when the time came, they would follow. Naomi and Dan would stay behind. Naomi said she could only feel at home in the City, and now that the water had broken free she would not want for anything. The desert held no promise for her that the City did not already provide. And there was much to do; she was needed.

Dan was a different man. Quiet and sometimes withdrawn, he had been injured within by the ordeal of his underground imprisonment. Each day he would sit on a bend in the river and watch the Cityfolk in the fields. He spent his time quietly, enjoying being near the flowing water as it chilled his feet, letting it heal him a little bit at a time. Before she left, he became better friends with Ruth and they shared their meals on most days. He appeared at peace, just glad to be in the open air.

The valley seemed a paradise. Yet something pulled at Ruth to come away. She and Boaz had learned to follow the twitch and tremble of the staves, and how to look for the cross of wood in desert places. The staves seemed to point south into the hills and away.

One evening, Peter and some of the friends announced that they would depart before the next moon. Ruth's decision was made. When the time came, she said her farewells tearfully and kissed Naomi and Dan. Then she turned to the dunes with Boaz, and together they followed along where the water led downstream.

They followed the Third Tribe.